POLAR

Fears and Dr

POLARIS

Fears and Dreams

A Novel by

JOHN WINTON

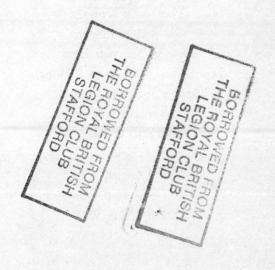

MICHAEL JOSEPH
London

MICHAEL JOSEPH LTD

Published by the Penguin Group
27 Wrights Lane, London W8 5TZ, England
Viking Penguin Inc., 40 West 23rd Street, New York, New York 10010, USA
Penguin Books Australia Ltd, Ringwood, Victoria, Australia
Penguin Books Canada Ltd, 2801 John Street, Markham, Ontario, Canada L3R 1B4
Penguin Books (NZ) Ltd, 182–190 Wairau Road, Auckland 10, New Zealand

Penguin Books Ltd, Registered Offices: Harmondsworth, Middlesex, England

First published 1989

Typeset in Linotron 11/13pt Plantin by Wilmaset, Birkenhead, Wirral
Printed and bound in Great Britain by
Richard Clay Ltd, Bungay, Suffolk

A CIP catalogue record for this book is available from the British Library

ISBN 0 7181 2929 6

CHAPTER 1

'THERE SEEM TO BE MANY more of them today. I wonder why?'

'Those women, you mean?'

It was odd how all the naval wives always referred to them as 'those women', never as 'the peace women' or 'the protesters' or 'nuclear disarmers', or any of the names the women themselves, judging by their press and TV interviews, would have preferred. It was always '*those* women', with an inflection of the voice, not so much actual contempt as incomprehension mixed with impatience. In any case, there were normally as many men protesters as women, perhaps even more. But they were still always called 'those women'.

'They just seem to congregate at certain times. No rhyme or reason to it. And *don't* say it – it is *not* the time of the month.'

'I wasn't going to say any such thing.'

'No, but you were thinking it. One of your Captain's dafter jokes, and probably the most boring of them all. He must be the original male chauvinist pig. And a captain of a Polaris submarine to boot.'

'Now, now. Mustn't be disloyal.'

'I'm not. Trouble is, I find myself agreeing with a lot of what he says.'

In fact, he had not been thinking of the Captain's joke. But it was curious how 'those women' did appear, quite unpredictably, at certain times which seemed to have nothing at all to do with the seasons, or the moon, or the weather, or anything else.

1

One would have thought that maybe the end of the school holidays, or weekends, or fine weather, or a burst of publicity in the press might have brought them out. But it didn't, not necessarily. Sometimes the protesters were there, a great crowd of them, in a black freezing frost, while on a lovely summer's day – not that there were many lovely summer's days in these parts – their camp site would appear to be completely deserted and many of their ramshackle-looking vehicles, the buses and lorries and battered caravans, painted in garish colours with strange devices and slogans, would be driven away. Then, after weeks or even months of calm, for no apparent reason, one day they would just appear again, 'like mushrooms', as somebody in the chief's mess once put it. You never knew when they were going to turn up.

But they never entirely deserted their camp, which was sited just opposite the submarine base approach road. They always maintained a presence there. There were always a few vehicles left, with one very large blue caravan, with a kind of shelter or verandah in front of it, which never moved. Perhaps it had no wheels. Probably it was their base, or meeting place, or it might even be their temple of some sort.

They had been there so long, some years in fact, that there were quite mature trees growing round some of the caravans. They now had a permanent address, 'The Peace Camp'. He had been told they even had a postcode, and a telephone and a number in the book. You could ring them up, if you wanted.

This was one of their noisy days, which was unusual. Normally they were as quiet as mice. But once they started, they seemed to be tireless. They could, and did, keep it up for hours. The noise could be heard from some way down the road from the town.

One thing was certain: very few of them were locals. There had been locals there originally, to start the whole thing off, but they had nearly all gone. These were from outside, from England and even from America, he had been told, although there were still some Scots accents among the shouts and the catcalls and the renderings of 'We Shall Overcome'. The Scots were a canny race. A job was a job was a job, and anything that brought seven thousand good jobs to the west of Scotland, as Polaris had, could not be all bad. Most people round here had long ago learned how to stop worrying and love the bomb – or at least to tolerate it.

Some of the protesters were clearly well educated. One of them, in one of their court appearances after some disturbance or other, had said he had a degree, from Durham University. And they were brilliant at courting publicity. They could run rings round the naval Public Relations Department's so-called public relations officers. Those men were basically just Ministry of Defence bureaucrats and those women made them look like idiots – not that that, in the general opinion of the submarine base, was ever very difficult to do.

The submarine base staff had also learned, long ago, to treat those women with caution, to avoid any comment, or anything at all which might lead to controversy. Even the local police had discovered the need for circumspection; over the years they had evolved a curious *modus vivendi* with the protesters, live and let live, so that everybody could have as quiet a life as possible. Those women were expert at manipulating publicity to suit themselves. As the Captain often said, if the Polaris base ever needed a motto, it would have to be 'No Comment'.

That motto had needed some living up to the previous Christmas, when those women had delivered a Christmas card to the base main gate, at the same time sending a copy to the local and national press. The actual 'card' was nine feet high by six feet wide and portrayed an unmistakably phallic missile, with the text: 'Wishing you all a Merry Prixmas'. The Christmas before, he had heard, three protesters dressed as Santa Claus had crossed the wire fence, penetrated the security area and actually reached the casing of a Bomber before they were arrested. That had made the MoD PloD even more bloody-minded than usual.

'They've got some new placards today. Sam . . . you don't think they somehow get to know when your sailing dates are, do you?' There was real concern now in her voice. If those women did have such information, it would be a direct threat to their family.

'It's something we've discussed. I don't know what the official view is, but I do know that if I really wanted to make out a schedule of Polaris sailings all I would have to do would be to set up a watch-keeping roster down at the narrows there, twenty-four hours about, and just keep my eyes and ears open. Come to that, you don't even have to go down there. Anywhere along the main road would do. I gather they do keep a watch on us and log us all in and out, although God knows what they do with the information. Send it to the Kremlin, most likely.'

'They might at least try and dress a bit better.' That, Sam thought, was a typically Janet remark. With her, appearance was everything, or almost everything. You should turn up to your own execution 'at least looking as if you had made the effort'. But she did have a point. Several of those women looked as though they had no figures at all to speak of. All wrapped in swaddling clothes, as the saying went. It was probably the weather that made them dress like that. Certainly this was no climate for topless bikinis.

The car was slowing down now, approaching the main gate. As always, it was a hive of activity, except that most of these were not bees but drones. As always, there seemed to be dozens of the Ministry of Defence police, the MoD PloD as they were always called, on every shift. Someone was saying the other day that the numbers of MoD PloD in the district had risen lately to nearly a thousand officers. They were all of a certain type: intellectually dense and utterly without personal initiative, but suspicious of what they perceived to be intelligence in others and eternally on their guard against anything which they fancied might be a joke at their expense. 'The combination of Calvinism and concrete skulls,' as the Captain said, 'was undefeatable.'

Janet stopped the car, obediently, and put on the hand-brake, as she had been taught. Sam held his base pass up and out of the car window. The nearest MoD PloD looked at it without saying anything. The silence lengthened and still the

4

man said nothing. Sam looked at him. He had his eyes fixed on something on the other side of the road and he waved them onwards, without looking down. It could have been a loaded revolver Sam was holding out. Sam thought of Leading Seaman Basing's celebrated *recitatif*. ' . . . *MoD PloD eye-test* . . . We don't test 'em, we only count 'em . . . *MoD PloD IQ test* . . . If you're warm, you're in . . . *What's the difference between a MoD PloD Land Rover and a hedgehog?* A hedgehog has all the pricks on the outside . . .'

'Will you be home tonight? Do you want me to come and collect you?'

He shrugged. 'I'll have to give you a ring, if I can. On crew. Coming up to Day One . . .' He shrugged again. 'You know how it is. Life gets more and *more* fraught.'

Janet looked resigned. This had happened many, many times over. He was already starting to wear that preoccupied expression, already beginning to show that quick temper, that exasperated impatience whenever she tried to mention anything outside the submarine, which was always a sure sign that another patrol was coming up.

She knew the routine now, just as all the Polaris wives did. Every Polaris submarine in commission, all the 'Bombers' as they were called, had two crews, Port and Starboard, who took it in turns. One crew, the Starboard Crew, say, would support and prepare the boat for its next deterrent patrol, and then carry out the patrol, after which the Port, stand-by, Crew would take over. Port and Starboard Crews each had their own Captain, their own officers and complete ship's companies, mirror images of each other in every way. It was Sam's Port Crew who were now in their final days of hectic preparation before they sailed for a week's 'Index' of independent exercises, just to get their hands in again after a long lay-off, before they actually sailed for the deterrent patrol proper. Janet knew that sailing day for the Index was known, for some reason, as Day One. Sailing day for the actual patrol had, for some reason, never been given a permanent nickname, although some people did sometimes call it 'Der Tag'.

Janet had to wait to allow a stream of cars to pass, before she could turn their car. The whole establishment seemed to be governed by tidal flows, just like the loch, and beyond that the sea itself. At times the cars flowed in, at others they all flowed out. Most of the officers drove themselves in and parked their cars in the base. Janet had heard of some who left their cars parked in the base for the whole sixty days of the deterrent patrol. But Sam preferred her to drop him off at the Gate on the last few days before Day One. It was a clumsy and rather inconvenient way of doing things but Sam liked it.

Sam walked through successive gates, which gave admittance, according to one's security clearance, into various sectors of the base. The sectors had colours allotted to them. Sam could never remember which colour zone was supposed to be more secure than the rest. Red, probably, for the Kremlin, as someone once said. The whole place was security mad, with passes and gates and a platoon of armed Marines waiting somewhere out of sight, ready to charge out and, literally, gun down anybody who looked as though they were committing an act of terrorism. They might even do it to someone who only had the wrong coloured pass.

Then there was the wire, the barbed wire. Every week, and certainly every month, there were more and more yards of higher and higher and fiercer and fiercer-looking wire fences. Now thrive the barbed wire manufacturers. The countryside for miles around was beginning to look like a prison, keeping the people who lived there either in or out, nobody could be sure. It was Colditz on a colossal, country-wide scale. The latest barbed wire, he had been told, was scientifically designed and manufactured so as to have the maximum holding power on the human skin. If you ever let it snag you, so Sam had heard, you had to go to hospital to have the wire surgically cut out of your flesh.

Yet, judging by that MoD PloD's indifference at the gate, the security was only superficial – skin-deep, you could say. Sam had no doubt that anybody who cared to forge a likely-looking pass would be able to get in and out with nobody laying a finger on him. That could be one of the ways in which the MoD PloD's treatment of the sailors could yet be counter-productive. There must be many a sailor who would love there to be a serious security breach, if only to see all those red MoD PloD faces.

The thunderous noise of pneumatic drills arose from the office block wall nearest the loch and the submarines. That was another thing. They were always tearing the place down and putting new buildings up, bigger offices . . . bigger bases . . . bigger bombs. Well, not bigger bombs, not yet, not until Trident came along. Heaven knows what those women would do when *that* arrived. It would drive them into even greater frenzies, no doubt.

The stairs and corridors of the office block were hung with ceremonial nameboards. There were quite elaborate boards, made of smart-looking wood, possibly mahogany, with names neatly inscribed in gold leaf, every name with its rank, and its initials and, where applicable, its decorations. There were the names of admirals, the names of commodores, the names of captains of the submarine squadrons, the names of anybody who was anybody who had served there over the years. Sam had heard that even the office block cleaning ladies had their own board, with their names on it, going back to the first Polaris cleaning lady, down in the basement where they kept their mops and buckets.

Chief Bluntstone was in the office, with that expression on his face.

'It's the MoD PloD, sir. And Basing.'

'Don't tell me he's gone and thumped one of them?'

'No, sir, though he might have done. They breathalysed him last night, sir.'

'Oh my God.'

'He had his girlfriend in last night for a couple of jars in the Club. They got him when he was taking her home. Or rather, when he came back. They may be dumb but they're not stupid, sir.'

'What do you mean? I don't follow.'

'Well, sir, if they'd breathalysed him on the way out of the base, they'd have had his girlfriend on their hands, she would have been a problem for them, got to get her home. So they let *him* take her home and then got him on the way back.'

A prolonged burst of drilling rose up from outside the window, so that neither of them could speak for some time.

'God dammit!' Sam clenched his fists. 'Must they do that, right under the bloody window. I'll see Basing later, before I go in and tell the Captain. That's the sort of thing he always wants to know. Anything else?'

'Oh yes, sir.'

Of course there was. There always was. Chief Bluntstone had a list, of inspections, and tests to be done today, and stores due to arrive, and people who were expected to arrive, and other people who were due to go, and gear that had to be dispatched, and gear that had to be accounted for. Some of the workload did seem to be left over by the Starboard Crew. Sometimes, the two crews accused each other of shifting the load unfairly, of making life difficult for each other by leaving undone those things that ought to have been done and doing those things that ought not to have been done. But in fact, as everybody admitted, to themselves though not to the other crew, when they were being honest, it was six of one and half a dozen of the other.

There was a pounding on Sam's office door.

'Knock knock!'

'Who's there?' Sam forced a smile, knowing what was coming.

'Sam and Janet!'

Sam gritted his teeth. 'Sam and Janet who?'

'Sam and Janet evening . . . You may meet a stranger . . Across a crowded room . . .'

It was Joe, the Polaris Systems Officer, the Chief 'Polaroid' himself. Joe did not know many jokes, but he knew this one, and having once two years ago achieved a laugh with it in the wardroom at Sam's expense, he had been trying ever since to repeat the great *coup*. The joke was not even original. Joe must have heard it on some radio or TV show. But it had now, by long usage, become part of the daily morning ritual of greeting, at sea and in harbour, summer and winter, rain or shine, till death us do part.

'Seen the Captain yet this morning?'

'No?' Sam mentally went to action stations at some note of warning in Joe's voice. 'Why?'

Joe shrugged. 'Nothing. Just got a funny feeling he's in a funny mood this morning.'

What's new, Sam thought. 'No, but why do you say that?'

Joe shrugged again. 'That Doomsday look.'

Everybody in the boat knew what that meant. They had all learned, the hard way, to study the Captain's daily appearance. Sam had a dim memory from prep school of some poem, by somebody or other, all about somebody or something learning to trace, the day's disasters in his morning face, or something like that. That could apply just as well to this boat.

There was another furious banging on Joe's office door. 'Captain would like to see you, sir!'

So, there it was. No more time to get prepared, no time to see Leading Seaman Basing and hear all about it, not even any indication of what the Captain might want. Sam got up from his deck and straightened his tie, using his reflection in the glass of the picture of his last submarine which hung on the bulkhead to the right of the office door. Ah, happy days those were . . . His own boat . . . A nice little diesel-electric . . . God's own sort of submarine . . . If God had wanted us to go nuclear surely he would have given us all lead heads . . . And if he had wanted us to serve in a Polaris Bomber he would have issued us all with Smarties to put in the warheads . . . Now he was talking like Leading Seaman Basing again . . .

The Captain's office was almost next door but Sam went the long way, round the whole building, almost in a square, along three corridors and most of the fourth, so as to arrive back at the Captain's door, from the wrong direction, but having had just a little more time to think.

There was no doubt but that their Captain was a very funny fellow. Funny peculiar. Certainly not funny ha-ha. Rumour had it that the Captain had only just passed his Perisher by a miracle. Maybe that had given him a sense of insecurity which made him edgy. Sam thought it unlikely. But then, he himself had also only just scraped by in his Perisher and had become a submarine captain *mirabile dictu*, or whatever the hell the expression was, rather than *cum laude*. On second thoughts, he himself *did* suffer from a sense of insecurity. It seemed that in recent years all the Teachers had been descended from Dracula, needing a constant supply of fresh, raw human blood. They seemed to set out looking for failures.

Oddly enough, Sam had been pretty confident during his Perisher. It was Janet who had first rumbled that he might have a problem. If was Janet who had warned him, one weekend in the middle of the Perisher when he had managed to get home for a few days, that if he didn't watch out, Teacher would fail him. Sam wondered if the Captain's wife had similarly warned *him*. But that would have had to have been before the divorce, of course.

'Come in, Sam! Don't hang about. Sorry to disturb you, I thought you were in your office.'

'That's quite all right, sir. Good morning, sir.' So the Captain must have noticed the direction he had come from.

The Captain was sitting in his office chair, with his great uniformed forearms bulging out over the armrests, looking like Henry VIII, or Charles Laughton, or even King Kong, depending upon one's point of view. He was scowling and then frowning, and then wiping his face clear of expression with a downward movement of one hand, as though he did not wish to be observed showing any emotion.

Their Captain had the largest, reddest, most grossly fat face Sam had ever seen on any human being. His cheeks hung in great folds of mottled purple flesh on either side of his huge mouth, where the corners of the two bulbous shining wet red lips came together. His eyes were bright blue, and tiny by comparison with the rest of him. His hair was sandy, thinning on top, but growing bushily in giant 'buggers grips' in front of his gigantic jug-handle ears. He was a grotesque man. He must weigh eighteen stones at least. He had once stepped on Sam's hand when they were both coming down the ladder from the bridge in a hurry. That weight, in a sea-boot, was like having one's hand put under a drop-forge. The Navy periodically had bouts of concern about physical fitness and published exhortations and warnings about overweight officers. Sometimes there were even threats, which never came to anything, that promotion might actually be prejudiced by obesity. But the Captain never took an iota of notice nor lost a sliver of weight. Some of the more maliciously minded in the squadron said that one of the reasons Rosemary had divorced him was that she simply could not stand the weight.

The Captain's desk was completely bare of everything except a blotter, a calendar and one of those ornaments with ball-bearings on wires which had once had a vogue as businessmen's toys. That was another of his idiosyncrasies, that he abhorred what he called a 'load of bloody clutter'. At sea, he had been known suddenly to sweep everything off the chart-table, including the chart they were actually using, in a spasm of irritation at 'all this load of bloody clutter'.

'What's this I hear about Basing and the fuzz?'

Sam actually smiled before he could prevent himself. The Captain never read a book, or a newspaper, or anything at all except the bare minimum of correspondence demanded by the Navy of a submarine captain in command. He never gossiped, he had no small talk and could not make polite conversation. Yet he somehow knew things, almost as though he felt them through the soles of his enormous feet on his way in each morning.

'I don't think it's as funny as you do, Sam. These MoD PloDs are just getting a bit too much. I suppose Basing asked for it?'

'Not exactly, sir, as I understand it. I haven't actually had a chance to see Basing yet, but briefly, sir . . .' Sam told the elements of the story, just as he had heard it from Chief

Bluntstone. Not for the first time when speaking to the Captain about the boat's affairs, Sam had the suspicion that the Captain already knew, through his own mysterious sources, much more about the matter than he did himself.

'I'll have to decide whether to have another showdown with the Chief Inspector.' The Captain's last 'showdown' with the GoD PloD Himself, as he was known, had been a memorable battle. It had arisen after the MoD PloD had searched their whole crew as they went through the gate after coming off a deterrent patrol. Two of their sailors had actually been strip-searched. According to the Captain, GoD PloD, 'who was even thicker than the rest of his flock', could not or would not take the point that their ship's company had been at sea for sixty solid days and could not possibly have been involved in drug or any other kind of smuggling. Legend had it that GoD PloD had very nearly arrested the Captain himself.

Sam stared at the bulkheads of the Captain's office. Those, too, were bare except for the large boards with the photographs of all the officers and ship's company. The Captain spent a lot of time glaring at them, memorising names and faces. It worked, too, for the Captain. He almost never got a name wrong, and never more than once. Sam had found himself lost for a name or two just recently, even people he actually knew quite well. That was a bad sign. But he had this weariness which overcame him, at any hour of the day, or day of the week. He just could not summon up that old flare and interest. Maybe it was the seven-year itch. That was the length of time he had been in submarines. Janet had noticed it. She was always quick to notice Sam's moods. Just as she had realised his problems with Teacher on the Perisher, now she was telling him that if he did not brace up he would be having more problems with this Captain.

'. . . So I can leave that to you, can I? Can fix?'

'Oh yes, sir.' The Captain had been speaking and had just asked him to do something. But Sam had not the faintest recollection of what it was. He knew he should say something, or at least ask, but dared not and instead found himself shuffling towards the door. He was glad to go. At least, Doomsday seemed to have been postponed for a little while.

'Ask Chief to come in and see me, as you pass his office would you?'

'Yes, sir.' Submarine engineer officers, in the days when each submarine only had one, were known as 'Chief' from time immemorial and the Captain always used the old nickname for the Senior Technical Officer, just as he used old nicknames for many of the submarine ratings. It was a fad, which some of the more senior submarine officers indulged, to show how long they had been in boats. But it was not a pose with their Captain, although he had been in boats as long as anybody serving now. He called 'Chief', 'Chief', because that was what he had always done. In fact, there were four or five technical officers in each crew now, and usually at least one extra as a supernumerary under training, going along for the ride as a 'makee-learn', before relieving somebody on board. In fact, many of the ratings on board also had their shadows, about to take over their jobs. In a way, it was like an extra cast of understudies in a stage play. But it did make the accommodation on board even more crowded than it should be, especially in the Chiefs' Mess.

When Sam got back to his own office, going the short way round, he found that it was, in fact, the problem of the Chiefs' Mess that Chief Bluntstone was waiting to talk to him about. Sam remembered, too late, he had had some points to make which he had written down on a sheet of paper. But it was still at home, or still in the car, maybe. It was one more thing he had forgotten to do.

'I'm going down the boat now, Chief, if anyone wants me, that's where I'll be for the next hour at least.' Sam could no longer ignore the exasperated look on Chief Bluntstone's face. The man was deliberately standing directly between Sam and the office door. 'I haven't forgotten the Chiefs' Mess, I'll come back to you on that.'

'Are you all right, sir?'

'Of course I'm all right!' Bloody impudence of the man. Just

13

in time, just as the retort was coming to his lips, Sam remembered that Chief Bluntstone was a good man, one of the best. They all had reason to be grateful to him. In those last weeks towards the end of a patrol, the very dregs of time, when it seemed their sentence would never end, when they had all forgotten what a normal existence was like, with sunshine, and rain, and the smells of earth and smoke, when they sometimes felt they themselves would never be normal people again, then it was always Chief Bluntstone who cheered things up, who put a crude but apt cartoon on the control room noticeboard, or began to sing a ridiculous song, who did something, *anything*, to remind them all of the world outside the steel circle of the boat.

'Of course I am, quite all right, Chief.'

But outside, in the sunshine, as he picked his way between the holes in the ground and the bare-chested workmen with their deafening pneumatic drills, Sam remembered that he had forgotten to pass the Captain's message to the STO. He wondered whether to go back, or telephone from the boat, or what he should do. His legs decided for him, by taking him onwards, down to the jetty.

Sam looked down at the submarine with a critical eye. The gangway was in a shocking state, with oily stains and slack guardrails. But that was the base's responsibility, not theirs, although he could have the guardrails tightened. The ensign and jack and both their staffs were clean and they were hoisted the right way up – that might seem elementary but it was something one could not always take for granted and it was one of the things that made the Captain most mad.

It was always difficult to keep a Bomber looking really smart. Something about the shape of the hull defeated everybody's efforts, as though the boat itself were shrugging off such irrelevancies. The dull black hull looked smooth enough, but from close up there were irregularities and apertures and roughnesses, where plates joined or overlapped, or some fitting or equipment emerged from, or was welded into, the hull. It was actually like the thick skin of an animal, perhaps a quarrelsome and anti-social whale, with all the scars and wounds and cicatrices of its various arguments and disagreements showing.

The trot sentry stood at the salute as Sam walked down the gangway. It was Able Seaman Draper, looking uncommonly smart. Draper had been giving a little trouble recently. He wanted to buy himself out of the Navy, having taken unto himself a wife who did not like the Navy; even more to the point, Draper now had a mother-in-law who wanted her daughter close at hand. They might, Sam thought, have thought of that before the marriage took place. But Draper and the Navy were now having a difference of opinion as to how much his training was worth, now that he wished to discharge himself before the Navy considered it had had its money's worth.

Sam thought it would be better, that it would save time and trouble in the end, to let the man go, without all this argument. In the end, the Navy could never win in such cases. Besides, it might make everybody else more responsible if they knew that an application to leave the Service would be acted upon, and almost certainly granted, at once. They were supposed to be adults. They ought to be treated as adults, who knew the consequences of their own actions. But the Navy persisted in treating them as though they were bluejackets of the nineteenth century.

Sam noted the wires and cables going through the forward hatchway, down into the submarine. Those always made Sam nervous. He was always uneasy until they were unrigged. A submarine that could not shut its hatches was vulnerable. Unable to dive, it was no longer a submarine. There ought to be many more shore connections, so that a submarine could take all it needed from shore, without having to keep hatches open.

Down below, the boat was in Sam's least favourite state, neither one thing nor another. There was somebody trying to clean up the passageway with a mop, and somebody else was trying to get past him with a box of stores of some kind, and in so doing was stepping on the place he had just cleaned.

15

Meanwhile they were both being hampered by somebody else, who had his backside stuck out into the passageway as he looked at an electrical access panel which he had opened for repair or inspection, or something. He had pulled out all the leads, so that they were spilling down the bulkhead like a spray of multi-coloured entrails.

In the wardroom, the mail had arrived and was lying in a heap on the table. Sam looked through it: nothing but bills for himself. His days for that sort of mail, what you might call *proper* mail, had long gone, although, he had to concede, he hardly ever wrote a proper letter himself. As the sailors always said, you had to write one to get one.

There were piles of official mail for Chief and the Polaroids. And there was one giant *billet doux* from the Navigating Officer's paramour. Pilot had a big thing going with a Wren Third Officer down in the MoD. He wrote to her once a week and got down there by car every weekend he could. She replied to him at least once a day and sometimes, or so it seemed, once an hour. She used Pusser's paper, reams of it, and Pusser's envelopes, big brown ones. Her missives in the mail were as unmistakable, and about as frequent, as the chart corrections from Droggy or the bills from Gieves. Sam knew that the sailors' view of the *affaire* was that she was not serious; she was merely getting in some practical experience before becoming a romantic novelist.

Sam settled down to work. The Petty Officer Steward had the coffee ready. That, too, was Pussers, both instant, and instantly recognisable, from no species of bean known to botanical science. There was a certain rhythm about a fore-noon's work down the boat, a kind of tidal ebb and flow, of minor crisis and temporary solution, of voices raised and others replying. Somebody had not turned up where they should have done. Somebody else would never turn up because he had gone on draft and the paperwork was not yet complete. Somebody else had left undone those things he ought to have done, and had done those things he ought not to have done, and there was no health in the health physics department.

16

Absorbed in what he was doing, Sam overheard snatches of conversation, about hydraulic leaks, and a defect on a gas-steam generator, of official forms which were missing, or incomplete, or incomprehensible. The wonder, Sam thought, was that any submarine ever got to sea. But a Bomber had to go to sea on time, to make the deterrent credible, or so they always said. That was Rule One, Line One, and the second was like unto it, that one must love the Bomb with all one's heart and all one's soul and all one's strength, and, forsaking all others, exert oneself so that the Bomber always went to sea. The Bomber must go on.

In his preoccupation, Sam became conscious of another, harder, more insistent voice. It was Chief, his black beard bristling. Very few submariners had beards these days, although the piratical image did linger on. The rest of the wardroom used to say, kindly, that Chief must have been frightened by an Errol Flynn film at the age of two.

'Thank you very much *indeed*, Sam, for nothing at all,' Chief was saying. It was not like Chief to be sarcastic. Indeed, sarcasm was the eighth deadly sin in the Navy. Some would even say it was the first, whether from officer to man, or from officer to officer.

'You might have told me the Boss wanted to see me, Sam.'

Sam held his head in unaffected dismay. He had become so wrapped up in the cares and daily decisions of the morning on board that Chief's summons to see the Captain had completely slipped his mind.

'. . . There was I, just walking past his office, not suspecting anything, not a care in the world, when he summoned me in and chewed me into little pieces. It was only later I found by putting two and two together that he'd asked you to tell me to come and see him. You might have slipped me the word. Don't you think?'

So it seemed that Chief had concealed Sam's lapse from the Captain. That was exceedingly good of him.

'It's very good of you . . .'

'Enough's enough, Sam.'

'What is that supposed to mean, exactly?' Sam's gratitude evaporated as swiftly as it had been aroused.

'Well, you seem to be on another planet these days, Sam. Can't get through to you at all. I've got a list of things as long as my arm I have to talk to you about.'

'Well, talk to me then. I'm here.'

'Yes, you're here, in body. But not in mind, half the time.'

'Oh, balls to it all.'

'My sentiments exactly, Sam. But unfortunately, not everybody agrees with us.'

It was on the tip of Sam's tongue to say 'and balls to you, too', but the wardroom was filling up. More officers were coming in, looking forward to their stand-easy cup of coffee and gossip. This was no time to pursue a pointless and rather childish argument with Chief. In fact, they should not be having any such argument at any time. They ought to be working together, not fighting each other. Sam knew that very well, but there was something in Chief's personality which jarred him, especially when the Captain was looming in the background, always ready to arbitrate in a way which left neither party satisfied. He remembered that Janet did not like Chief's wife, whatever her name was. Sam could not recall it. That, too, was on the tip of his tongue. Big, busty woman, with a Devon accent. *Pauline*. That was it. That was the name. They had three children. But there was precious little hope of him ever remembering *their* names. Janet would know them, though. That was the sort of thing Janet nearly always knew.

Sam looked round the faces in the wardroom. He knew them all so well. The Port Crew was going through a period of unusual stability just at the moment. They did not have a single understudying officer. Everybody had been on board for at least three months, and most had been in the boat much longer than that. It was the most trumpeted inducement to join the Polaris programme: stability in your family life. Join the Polaris programme and avoid appointing turbulence. Or, as the sailors said, don't be buggered about. It was true: your leave periods, your sailing dates, your refits, were sacrosanct. You could plan a wedding six months ahead and expect to keep the date. Not many people in the Navy could count on that. Such an unusual lack of disruption in one's personal and family lives did appeal to a certain kind of man, and to certain families. There were senior ratings in this very boat who had joined the Polaris programme as able seamen. They had done many deterrent patrols, some of them as many as a couple of dozen patrols, as they were advanced through the rates in their particular branch, from able seaman, to leading seaman, to petty officer and to chief petty officer. Chief Bluntstone was a good example of just that. Some of the youngest and most newly-joined sailors amused themselves by asking rhetorical questions, though not of Chief Bluntstone himself, about what Nelson had said to him on the very first Polaris patrol.

It could even happen to officers. Danny Bennett, the Assistant Polaroid, and Joe's right-hand man, did several Polaris patrols as a young artificer before he was commissioned. Now, he had two stripes on his sleeve and, below the submariners' gold double dolphin badge on his jacket, the ribbon of an MBE, for his part in putting out a machinery compartment fire in another submarine a year ago. He also had a young wife and a small baby, who lived down in the south. They had a flat in Gosport, and his wife refused to move up north. She said she hated Scotland and the Scots. Sam had only met her once, at the party on board after the commissioning service. She was a strikingly good-looking girl, but she had that flat, unattractive Portsmouth/Southampton accent. Sam could hear her now, saying she was 'not going up there and live amongst all them sheep and porridge eaters'. So Danny Bennett was another of their officers who commuted down south whenever and as fast as he could.

Sam watched Danny Bennett pouring himself a cup of coffee. He was a good lad, Danny, and was going to go a long way in the Service, though he did, as Sam noticed, and not for the first time, have dirty fingernails.

'Have we got the football pitch list yet, Sam?' Danny had the coffee cup held to his lips, with his little finger, his 'pinkie' as they called it up here, sticking out incongruously. 'Two more matches to go in our knock-out tournament. I'd like to fix them before Day One, if I can fit them in.'

'Up in my office, Danny.' That was another thing he could have brought down to the boat, if only he had thought of it. He knew Danny wanted the list.

'I'll get it,' Danny put his cup down. 'In fact, I'll do it *now*.'

That was typical of Danny. Action man. Do it *now*. He was the Captain's blue-eyed boy. Sam could remember a time when he himself had had such energy. Nothing had been too much trouble then, no hours too long, no difficulties too great. But now, every day left him tired at the end of it. Some of those watches at sea, which he used to keep without strain, now seemed interminable.

Looking back later, Sam could remember little about that particular day except that it left him especially tired, almost exhausted. The Captain had come down to the boat later in the forenoon, had stumped up and down the control room criticising and complaining about everything he could see, refused to sign the papers which Scratch had specially taken down to the boat hoping he would sign, had a long gossip with the Coxswain instead, drank two extremely large gins and tonic, and then went inboard for lunch and, presumably, to get his head down for the afternoon. One thing one could say for the Captain: he did observe, most faithfully, the old Submarine Service custom that Captains should hardly ever come down to the boat in harbour during the daytime. Unfortunately, having no wife living locally, he did tend to come down more often than usual in the evenings.

That evening, Sam felt he could not face the Captain, should he appear, could not bear to hear any more of his jokes, or his political views, or his plans for the future, or his grievances about his divorce. He knew that it was an essential part of his job to humour the Captain, to provide a sounding board and a foil for him. He knew that he would be doing the ship's company a considerable favour by keeping the Captain in a good temper. He knew, too, that if he was not there in the wardroom that evening, then the burden would fall upon the unfortunate Sonar Officer, who had the duty.

Sam wanted to go home, but was too tired even to telephone Janet. He did not know how long he would have sat in the wardroom, leaning his head against the bulkhead, had Danny Bennett not come to his rescue.

'You look absolutely knackered, Sam. Are you going home? Can I give you a lift?'

Sam would rather Danny stayed on board to handle the Captain, which he always did so superbly well. But the offer was too good to refuse, although Danny lived in the mess and did not need to go ashore that evening.

'I thought I'd go ashore and have a couple of pints at the sailing club. I'll drop you off, if you like.'

Even the sailing club was not strictly on the way to Sam's home. Danny would still be going some distance out of his way.

'You look absolutely bushed, Sam. I think you ought to ask Hamish to have a look at you before Day One. Certainly before the next patrol. You don't mind me saying this?'

Sam shook his head. 'Not at all. And there's nothing wrong with me, so I won't be bothering our good doctor. But I would like a lift, thank you very much.'

When they reached the casing, it was raining.

'What a bloody awful climate. No wonder the Scots emigrate all over the world. They can't stand Scotland. Like my wife. She can't stand it either.'

Danny's car was long past its prime. The bottoms of the doors were marked with rust. Part of the body had rusted right through. One wing was dented, and the paintwork scraped, as though somebody had driven the car into a lamp post or a garage door. There was something wrong with the lock on the door on the passenger's side so that Danny had to fiddle with it before Sam could open it and get in. It was, altogether, not the sort of car Sam would have expected Danny to run.

Danny had caught the look on Sam's face. 'This is what is euphemistically known as our second car. Neither of us think it

21

matters a damn what sort of car we have up here. I'm going to junk it after the next patrol.'

The MoD PloD on the gate waved them through. Sam looked to see if it was the same officer as had been on the gate that morning. But, like Chinamen, they all looked the same. 'Why is it that they always succeed in setting your teeth on edge? Fancy being a rozzer in this part of the world. What a life.'

'Oh I don't know.' Danny was gunning the engine as he drove along the approach road, almost as though he were afraid the engine was about to stop. 'It depends what your expectations are. Did you hear that local councillor on the radio the other day? Justifying the presence of Polaris here, and what it was doing for the region? It means *our* children can be civil servants, too, he said. Good God, what an ambition, on the face of it. And yet, if you come from these parts, you can see what he means.'

Danny reached the end of the approach road to the base. As he drew out into the main road, level with the caravans of the peace camp, the car seemed to lurch, swung into the side of the road, and stopped.

'Oh bugger it. That's all we needed. Puncture.' Danny expelled his breath in a long sigh of exasperation. 'We've got a spare tyre, but no jack. I happen to know. Right in front of the bloody peace camp, too. They'll be no use. I don't suppose they'll even know what a jack is and even if they did they're hardly likely to help us, the Anti-Christ. It'll be quicker to walk back to the main gate and get somebody from the base. Ring up, or something. Hold on, I'll go back and see what I can do.'

Sam was content to sit where he was, happy that nothing, no effort and, above all, no decision, seemed to be required of him.

But they had been noticed from the peace camp. A man and a woman were already standing by the roadside. The man was tall, with blond hair sticking out from under a blue forage cap. With that cap, with his camouflage jacket all studded about with metal badges, and camouflage trousers, tucked into black rubber boots, he had an oddly military-looking appearance, for

22

a protester. And, for such a man, he had a curious air of command about him. Sam thought it possible he was the head protester of this camp. He had plainly not shaved for some days. He was smiling, so that Sam could see that he had a large gap between his two front teeth.

'Trouble? Spot of bother?' The man had a high-pitched Cockney voice, with a cheeky inflection. Sam braced himself for what he was sure would come: some witticism, about Polaris submarines breaking down on the Queen's highway, or some such thing.

The man was looking down at their tyre. 'Not surprised it's flat. It's bloody nearly *bald*. I'm surprised you ever got through your MoT with *that*.'

The contempt in the voice was so marked, Sam expected Danny to bristle. But, on the contrary, Danny seemed to recognise a fellow technical expert, and merely shrugged. 'Have you got a jack?'

'Yes. Hydraulic jack, set of tools, the lot. Only thing I haven't got is an inspection pit. I used to run me own garage once. Gave it up to come here.'

Neither Sam nor Danny could think of any comment to make on that surprising statement. But in any case the man had already turned on his heel and was walking towards a large yellow van, which had been driven well off the road and parked amongst some mature birch trees. Clearly the place had been used for parking for months, if not years. Now that Sam looked more closely, he could see nearby a small plot of cultivated garden, with some plants which looked like herbs growing there. The whole site had an atmosphere of permanence about it.

The van, like the caravans around it, had been decorated with symbols and slogans in what approached very nearly a genuine form of pop art. There were hearts, and sunflowers, and human silhouettes, and the sign of the Campaign for Nuclear Disarmament, all outlined or picked out in different colours. The word 'Peace' was repeated several times in differing scripts. There was a 'Nuclear Free' poster on the side of one caravan and the appeal 'Gay Whales Independent Liberation Front'. There was an inscription, painted in excellent, almost professional, lettering along the side of the yellow van. 'O let them be left, wildness and wet,' Sam read, with astonishment. 'Long live the weeds and the wilderness yet.' Yet, on reflection, Gerard Manley Hopkins would probably have approved whole-heartedly.

The man was coming back, pushing in front of him with one hand a big wheeled jack, of the type used in garages. In the other hand he carried a large metal tool box.

Danny was looking at the man and his equipment with admiration. 'Are you in charge here?'

The man shook his head. 'There's nobody in charge here. We don't *have* people in charge. That's one thing we don't have. My name's Terry.'

'El Tel. He's El Tel.'

While the man laughed as he slid the jack under the rear of the car, Sam and Danny looked at the woman in surprise. This, the first time she had spoken, was apparently gibberish. Or else her marked Scottish accent was making her impossible to understand. It sometimes happened.

'It's his nickname. His name's Terry. We call him El Tel.' The woman appeared to think no other explanation was necessary.

Sam braced himself to get out of the car while El Tel, if that was what he was called, jacked up the car.

'And what is your name?'

'Mary Carmichael.'

As though on cue, Mary Carmichael and El Tel, who was bending down by the back of the car, began to recite together. 'Yestreen the Queen had four Marys, the night she'll hae but three. There was Mary Seaton and Mary Beaton, and Mary Carmichael, and me.'

Once again, neither Sam nor Danny felt able to contribute to this surrealist conversation.

Mary Carmichael was wearing a blue anorak several sizes too large for her, with the hood half turned up, jeans, and leather sandals with no socks or stockings. She had hunched her shoulders and had driven both hands deep into her pockets. Sam found it hard to guess at her figure, under the huge shapeless anorak. The jeans hid her legs. But she was very young – a girl rather than a woman, as he had first thought her. She had an attractive face, pleasant rather than beautiful, with red hair, faint freckles over her nose and blue eyes. It was a face from the country, not from the town. She was probably from Lomond side, or possibly further up, from Argyll. Wasn't that another song, something about Mary of Argyll?

'You're looking fair exhausted.' She was looking at and talking to Sam. 'You should take more care of yourself. We don't want you Johnnies cracking up.'

Sam could detect no trace of irony in her voice or her expression. 'Actually, my name's Sam. And this is Danny. I must admit, I am fairly tired tonight.'

'You been slaving all day over a hot missile?' El Tel's voice seemed to come from underneath the car. 'Sam, Sam, the nuclear man. And his friend, Dangerous Dan Deterrent.'

'I thought the *other* one was bald!' El Tel was exclaiming at the spare tyre, and holding it up in the air, while he pinched it with expert fingers, testing its pressure. 'But just look at this! And it's pretty well flat, too.'

They all watched him go back to his van and bring from it a foot pump. He placed the pump on the ground, fixed its short length of tube to the tyre valve, and began methodically to pump up the spare tyre. His black rubber boot rose and fell on the pump pedal with almost hypnotic regularity. He had such a neat and economical way of moving, so obviously the master of whatever he was doing, that they were all content to go on watching him.

El Tel looked severely at Danny. 'This car is nothing more than an accident waiting to happen. Strikes me you blokes are much more dangerous on the roads at home than you are at sea, with all your missiles.'

Sam and Danny exchanged glances. It was a fair comment, in the circumstances.

25

'Would either of you like a cup of coffee?' Mary Carmichael gestured towards the largest blue caravan, which was probably their communal vehicle. 'Won't take hardly a minute.'

Once again, Sam and Danny looked at each other. Sam suddenly found himself intensely curious to see inside their caravan, to get some inkling of how these people lived together. But he found himself inexplicably shaking his head.

'No thank you. It's very kind.'

'Och, please yourself. It's up to you.'

'There you are. Service with a smile.' El Tel was standing up, wiping his hands on a piece of rag, and he was indeed smiling. He began to collect his gear. 'But if I were you I'd seriously get some new covers right away. This lot are right dangerous. In fact, you really should get a complete set for all four wheels and the spare.' He kicked the tyre nearest to him. 'But that would probably cost you more than the whole car's worth. It depends on how badly you want to go on living. But I suppose, with the things you do to earn your living, you don't mind about such things.'

It was the first direct reference to their profession and it struck the first jarring note of discord in what had so far been a very pleasant and civilised acquaintance. Sam discovered that he was sincerely sorry the subject had ever been raised.

'How did you know we were in a Bomber?'

'I didn't. I only knew you came from the base, and I class everybody from there alike. *Are* you *in* a Bomber?' El Tel seemed to be mimicking Sam's pronunciation and accent. 'You know, I never met anybody before who actually lives in one of those things. What does it feel like?'

'Hellish dark and smells of cheese.'

Sam knew, as soon as he had said it, he had made a mistake to be so flippant. El Tel scowled and kicked the wheel nearest him again.

'I'm surprised *patriots* like you would have a *foreign* car.'

The friendly atmosphere had gone completely. Sam remembered something else. 'Do we . . . ? Should we pay you for your time? . . . You've saved us a lot of trouble . . .'

26

'Forget it. I'll send the Ministry of Defence the bill.'

'I just thought you might . . .' What Sam wanted to say, but could not, was that the people in the peace camp might be short of money.

El Tel seemed to read his mind. 'We get money from the DHSS. Anything extra we spend on campaigning. People send us money all the time. But it would *never* do for your Polaris money to go to *us*, would it? You'd probably get drummed out of the Brownies!' El Tel laughed, evidently in a good humour again. He was still grinning as they got back into their car and drove off.

Danny kept one hand on the steering wheel, while he scratched his chin with the other. '*There's* a very funny fellow, don't you think? Fancy coming across a skilled mechanic in that place. Just when you needed him most. He was good, too. I must say they were nothing like I imagined them. You felt you could almost have a proper debate with them.'

'Yes, I suppose so.' Sam, too, was still thinking over their encounter. 'Drop me at the end of our road. I'll walk.'

'You sure? You were looking bushed, just as that woman said.'

'No, I'm fine.' It was, astonishingly, true. Sam was surprised to find that his tiredness had indeed vanished. He felt mysteriously invigorated, as though he had drunk from some refreshing draught without knowing it.

Danny dropped him at the bottom of their road, and Sam began to walk briskly up. By luck or possibly even by design, most of these roads, including theirs, ran slightly uphill and at right angles to the river. Sam wasted little time on the view, but one could turn and look back, if one wished, and survey the whole panoramic sweep of the river itself, and the backdrop of cranes and buildings and the coastal hills of Renfrewshire beyond, on the other side. The trouble was that where the eyes could see the winds could blow. In winter time the bitterly cold winds seemed to come straight off the Polar ice-cap and their house was the first solid object they struck with their full force.

Sam had not wanted to buy a house because he feared it

would lock them ever more securely into Scotland and make it that much harder to leave when the time came. But Janet, though she came from the South, actually liked Scotland, unlike most of the naval wives who, whether they admitted it or not, yearned for the South. Also, Janet was always unwilling to live on Married Quarters patches and avoided them whenever she could.

Even Sam had to concede that theirs was a nice little bungalow. It was somewhat cramped, with only one bathroom, when the children were at home, but it had been a very good investment, much more profitable than renting, and one did not have to submit to the petty interference of the Ministry's bureaucrats, who themselves lived permanently in the choicest married quarters, over furniture, and inventories and break-ages, and all the rest of the wretched paraphernalia of Married Quarter bureaucracy.

The road had trees, quite pleasant ones, growing at intervals in the grass between pavement and road. Sam was not in the least interested in trees or gardening. He did not know, neither did he care, what kind of trees they were but he did notice their blossom when it appeared. It was one of the penalties of existence in a Bomber, that each deterrent patrol amputated a portion of one's life, so that one could sail when trees were flowering and return when the fruit was ripening. One could miss a whole season, be it strawberries, cricket or Christmas, just as if it had never existed.

The gardens on either side were all well kept. Sam had little idea of who their neighbours were or what they did. He knew the Sonar Officer of the Starboard Crew had a house in the next road but the rest were more or less a mystery: Glasgow bookies, he had heard, and a man who managed a pop group, and a bank manager, and many civil servants, of course, of many different grades and departments, all up here for the nuclear submarine deterrent planning and building programme.

The newcomers had brought added prosperity, of a kind, although judging by the local newspapers the locals were not sure whether to be pleased or not. The Captain, a noted

Hibernophobe, in the word he himself had coined, often said that the Scots hated the English but wanted their money. 'What they really want us to do is to stay in England but keep on sending them a whacking great cheque every month.' Certainly, Sam could not but agree when the Captain was holding forth on what he thought were some of the least attractive aspects of the Scottish way of life: the rain, the high rates for domestic housing, the greed in low places, and the intensely insular outlook. It was a Scottish newspaper, the Captain always claimed, which had reported the loss of the *Titanic* under the headline: 'Kirkintilloch Man Lost At Sea.'

Sam was not sure even whether their next door neighbour, who was outside in his front garden, was a bank manager or a bureaucrat, or even a bookie. His name was Smith. As Sam wished him good evening, he was glad to see Janet also working in their front garden, snipping at their front hedge with clippers.

Janet was wearing jeans and a bulky blue sweater and sandals. With these, and her fair hair, she had a disconcerting resemblance to Mary Carmichael.

'. . . Thought you were going to ring me if you were coming home?'

'I was. I was going to sleep on board but suddenly I just felt I *must* get out of the boat, willy-nilly. Danny offered me a lift into town so I just came. We had a puncture or we would have been here earlier.' For some reason, Sam found himself suddenly unwilling to mention Mary Carmichael.

But Janet, with her almost uncanny sensitivity, had already noticed. 'You're looking brighter. Has something happened? Have you met somebody?'

CHAPTER 2

ELL, I HAVE MET somebody actually.' There was no
harm, Sam decided, in admitting it. After all, it was all
perfectly innocent. 'We had to stop at that peace camp because
of the puncture.'

'Don't tell me those women mended your puncture for you?'

'No, not the women. But one of the men changed the wheel
for us. Danny hadn't got a jack. This chap had everything.'

'They can't be as bad as they're painted, then.'

'I don't think anybody ever said they were all bad. I found
them very interesting to talk to. They're entitled to their
opinions, just as we are. They can camp there if they want to.
It's a free country.'

'Have you had supper?'

'No. I just made up my mind I had to go and left.'

'That Captain of yours been on your back again?'

'No. As a matter of fact I've hardly seen him at all today.'

'I'll just finish this hedge and then I'll make you an omelette
or something.' Janet was rarely surprised when he came home
earlier or later than she had expected. She took everything in
her stride, like a true naval wife. So she should, with her family
background. In a way, it was bred into her.

'Anything happened today?' He watched her methodically
snipping at the hedge. In a curious way, her movements
reminded him of El Tel. She was as competent and as
economical of effort.

'No. Shopping in town. Letters from the boys. Took next door's cat to the vet and left her there to have that thing taken off her eyelid . . .'

'Next door' was the widow on the other side, who hated vets and could not bear to take her pets to them.

'. . . Renewed the TV licence.'

That was the main quality expected of Polaris wives – the ability to keep the home fires burning. Indeed, some of them were so good at it, they became accustomed to making all the household decisions, large and small. Sometimes, they actually resented their lord and master, when he came home and began to criticise the brand of Corn Flakes the children were eating for breakfast, and the way the lawn-mower had been repaired, and the colour of the new lampshades in the dining-room.

'Mother rang to say she'd probably come up this time.'

'This time' meant this, next patrol. Some of the Polaris wives packed up and went south, like swallows for the winter, when their husbands left on patrol. But Janet nearly always stayed in their house. Sometimes her mother came to stay with her, but more often it was friends, from her schooldays, or from London before she was married. Janet had a lot of friends and was always delighted to see them, and entertain them, and hear their gossip. But she was a remarkably self-sufficient person. She did not mind being alone and was quite happy, for weeks on end, working in her garden, writing letters, taking the dog out, doing her needlework or something for charity. Sometimes she drove out to see one of the other officer's wives, or they came to see her. She almost never went to any of the functions or parties at the base while Sam was away, not even at Christmas time. 'I don't need that,' she always said. She was a sensual woman, and needed a man, but Sam had never for one moment had any reason to suspect her fidelity. She never complained of Sam's absences, or, as had happened in the past before he joined the Polaris programme, when his ship visited a port abroad without her. Now, of course, Polaris submarines never visited ports, except for one trip across to America for the test missile firings on the range off Florida. Otherwise, they

31

went on patrols to nowhere and they came back, weeks later, having not been anywhere. Janet took the sailings, as she took the returns, philosophically. Sam expected and trusted her to be still there when he came back, and so she was. She was the heart and core of their family. As Simon, their eldest son, had once remarked, 'Mummy, you're a brick.'

'Are things going all right?'

'Yes. Why?'

'Well, it's just that you've seemed a little bit . . . I don't know how to put it . . . *down* lately. But now, to look at you, you're actually quite chirpy. Not at all like you usually are just before a patrol. Sometimes I think you hardly know I exist. Or else you bite my head off.'

'I'm sorry. It *is* a tricky time. There's a hell of a lot to do and we're all under a lot of pressure.'

Janet shrugged, as though to say, Pressure my foot. Sam recognised the gesture. It was one she always told the boys off for using, although they had probably learned it from her.

'You going to have a bath?'

'Yes. Unwind a bit.'

'You sound like a clockwork toy.'

He remembered that remark as he was lying in the bath. Their bathroom was tiny and seemed almost to have been added to the back of the bungalow as an after-thought. It had three outside walls and a lean-to roof and was always very cold. The one small window always steamed up furiously.

Sam could see, on a shelf above the bath, a row of the children's bathtime toys. The boys and Alice were growing out of them now, so that, in their own way, those toys were relics of childhood, the visible and tangible symbols of the stages of growing-up. There were museums, Sam had heard, which collected such things.

Amongst them was Johnny's yellow plastic submarine. It did not dive of its own accord. You had to hold it down and when released it always bobbed up to the surface – a very essential attribute in any submarine, Sam said.

Johnny always said he was going to join the Navy and be a

submariner when he grew up. Sam did not doubt it. Johnny was a very determined boy and he had been fascinated by anything to do with submarines since he was very small. Sam had once given Johnny for Christmas a much more elaborate submarine, a light green hollow one, made of metal, with a clockwork motor inside it which drove a propellor aft. It was called *Nautilus*, after Jules Verne's *Twenty Thousand Leagues Under the Sea*. It had foreplanes fixed in the 'dive' position, and after planes fixed in the 'rise' position, and when wound up it literally drove itself under water. It had a rudder which could be adjusted so that the submarine went round in a circle.

They tried *Nautilus* on a pond on Boxing Day. Janet had said that they were being very silly, they ought only to sail it in the bath. But they had tried it in the bath on Christmas Day and had soon been bored with it. As Johnny said, a pond was much more like the real thing. But after only two or three dives in the pond, the submarine itself seemed to weary of the game and sank. Sam had had to wade in and feel about on the muddy bottom in the freezing cold water until he found *Nautilus*. It was not only Sam who had thought this very depressing. Johnny never played with the toy again. It was still there, gathering a little rust now, on the shelf.

Janet came into the bathroom with a towel to dry him. Sam stood up. This was something she had done for him, every night he was home, since the first night of their honeymoon, indeed since their first night together, soon after that Fort Blockhouse summer ball. He took a Third Officer WRNS as his partner. Another submariner had taken Janet, who was also a Third Officer WRNS. They had exchanged partners almost from their first glance that evening and then went on, everybody agreed, to behave very badly indeed.

'Cor, it's *freezing* in here.'

'Can't help that.' Janet was rubbing so vigorously it stung his skin. The towel was very large and rough and was still warm from the airing cupboard. She kissed him on the hollow of his shoulder, above the collar-bone. He lifted her sweater and kissed her between the breasts. As always, the heat of the bath, the rough massage from the towel, the sight of her body, worked their excitement.

Janet looked down at him. 'Not now. It's my time . . . I can't do it now. Here.' She put the towel round his shoulders. 'You can finish yourself off.'

It was what she said to the children after their baths. 'That's what you say to the children.'

'And that's what I say to you. I'll have supper in a minute so don't be too long admiring yourself in the mirror.'

'It's all steamed up.'

'Oh dear dear . . . *Superman*.'

He could not complain of Janet's time of the month. That was one cycle which even the inexorable routine of the Polaris deterrent patrols could not affect, except occasionally, Sam had heard, when a boat was due to return. Some Polaris wives, Sam had been told, menstruated prematurely in sheer anticipation and had to go to the doctor to get pills for it. How true that was, he did not know.

He wrapped the towel round his middle and put on his dressing gown. On his way to their bedroom he stopped outside the smallest bedroom, where Alice was sleeping, and opened the door. With only three bedrooms they had to chop and change about whenever the boys came home from school. Really the children ought to have their own rooms, and there should also be a spare room, when someone came to stay. In fact, they needed a bigger house. But that was financially impossible at the moment.

'You going away again, Daddy?' Alice was not asleep. He could see her eyes wide open, in the light from the door. Luckily, Alice was not afraid of the dark. None of their children ever had been. He had heard of other couple's children yelling and shouting, especially when their father was away in his submarine.

'Yes, in a few days. But I'll soon be back.'

'Oh good. We *like* you.'

'Oh good. That's nice to know.' He bent down to kiss her goodnight. 'School tomorrow.'

34

'Oh I know. Morag and me are learning a poem.'

'Oh? What's it called?'

'I don't know. It's about a battle against the English.'

Morag was Alice's special friend. Sam could not remember what Morag's father did. He had been told but he had forgotten. The little girl herself had red hair and a brace on her front teeth and spoke with the broadest Scots accent. Sam remembered she had come to tea at their house one day and spilled all her orange juice down her dress and swore like a Greenock shipyard worker.

Alice, too, had a Scots accent, which she could put on and off at will, learned from her local day school. She was a bright child, and enjoyed school, and the schools here were very good, although Sam sometimes wondered what the teachers thought of the Navy. He could still remember an incident when he and Janet had taken Alice to her first day at the school, when he had overheard another mother, a local, also bringing her first-day daughter, loudly impressing on the child 'Remember and tell the teacher yer *no* Navy.'

It was typical, Sam thought, that Alice was learning a poem about a battle against the English. In some ways, the Polaris community lived a beleaguered existence up here. There was a Roman legion in Britain once, Sam had read somewhere, who marched north, and simply disappeared. They were cut to pieces or captured, every one of them, by barbarians. The Ninth Legion. In some ways, they were a modern Ninth Legion. The Ninth Submarine Squadron.

'Me and Morag are going on a picnic. We'll take a piece.' Alice had slipped into her Scots accent. 'We'll have our own baps, and we'll buy chips.'

'Should be good. Now, good night. You go to sleep now.'

'Good night, Daddy.'

Sam shut the bedroom door. Someday soon they would have to face the problem of boarding school, or not, for Alice. They already had two boys at boarding school which, technically, should not be possible on a lieutenant-commander's pay, even with submarine pay. But, with the Navy's Boarding School

35

Allowance, and grandparents' covenants, and some cutting and saving, they managed. Janet's father had had some family money, until he reached the rank of Captain, when he had spent it all, he always used to say, entertaining Her Majesty's guests. His last appointment before retiring had been Commodore of the Barracks, when his entertainment allowance went nowhere near covering his expenses. Even the children's parties there, for which his in-laws were famous, had cost money. But Janet's mother still had some money left and was generous with it.

Sam's own people had no money. His father had worked in a bank. Ironically, his father had spent all his working life looking after other people's money and never made a penny for himself. He had never even been manager of his own branch. Always the best man, never the groom. Always the First Lieutenant, never the Captain.

When the time came, Sam was sure Janet would press fiercely for Alice's education. Janet herself had gone to a girls' boarding school, and then to finishing school in Switzerland, and could have gone to university if she had wished. Instead she took a secretarial course and then a course in cordon bleu cooking. 'Educate a girl and you educate a whole family,' Janet said, echoing her mother's words. He could hear his mother-in-law saying it. It was a cliché, but true. Maybe he would have made Commander by then. That would help.

Janet was laying the table for supper in the dining-room. That was another point about this bungalow: the dining-room and the table were hardly big enough when the boys were at home. They needed more space.

'Anything in the mail?'

'Bills. And bills. Oh, and letters from the boys.'

Sam had not gone to boarding school himself, but he knew, by proxy, so to speak, the boarding school routine for letter-writing. There was a strict Sunday morning ritual for 'Writing Home'. Certain conventions had to be observed. Every boy had to write at least one letter home very week. Nobody had ever heard of any boy who wrote home more than once a week. *The* letter had to be more than one page long. The writing on the second page had to consist of at least one sentence and occupy more than one line. It was not enough merely to write 'Love and kisses from Willy' on the second page.

To assist the letter-writers in their composition, the house master wrote various subjects of topical interest, such as school events and doings of the previous week, up on the blackboard. It was curious how the boys chose different subjects. Simon wrote about the weather and the food and sometimes of the book he was reading, Johnny always about cricket or football in season, and his own feats therein.

'Seem to be getting on all right. No moans and groans.' He remembered the other mail. 'What about the bills? Anything serious?'

Like many Polaris wives, Janet usually dealt with the household bills, using their joint bank account. She had to deal with them anyway when Sam was away and somehow it had come about that she carried on even when he was at home. In Polaris families, under the sign of the Bomber, it was the woman who became the arbiters of the family finances. It was an almost continental practice, as in French restaurants, where Madame sat in a cubicle by the door and took your money as you left.

'No, nothing serious. We seem to be doing okay, for a change. And we do seem to spend a lot less when you're away. I don't know why.'

Sam could guess. When he was away on patrol, it was as though they were not a complete family. It was as though their life as a family was put into temporary suspension until he returned. Janet would never take on any serious financial commitment, would not even buy herself any new clothes, while he was away. She spent less on food, less on heating, less on everything, while he was away.

'Supper's up. Scrambled eggs.'

Janet's scrambled eggs were always special. Like all Janet's cooking, Sam thought. They were always made with just the right amount of milk, and they were always cooked just long

37

enough, and they had herbs or some suspicion of an added flavour, to give them 'a certain flair', as Simon had once said of his mother's cooking.

Sam ate in silence, just as his sons did when they were at home. They were made to make polite conversation at meals at school, he had been told. They had to talk about the weather or the news, and they had to ask their neighbour for the salt and pepper or bread to be passed to them, and they could not start eating until the monitor at their table had been served and had started to eat. From the boys' descriptions, mealtime at their school was like the court of Versailles in the bad old days before the Revolution. But Janet's cooking was too good for anybody to waste time or attention on talking while one was eating it. The boys' manners at home, Sam thought, must be a big disappointment to their housemaster.

After supper, Sam was at a loose end. He had brought no work with him, and he did not feel like doing any jobs around the house. It was often like this: when he had an unexpected evening at home, he could find nothing to do.

Janet had taken up her tapestry. That was another of her talents. She worked at her tapestry when he was away – cushion covers and pyjama cases, and even occasionally something really ambitious, like a small carpet, for a passageway or a hearth. The house was full of Janet's tapestries. Sometimes, she bought an old music stool at a junk shop, cleaned it up, and then worked a tapestry cover for the top. They made very acceptable wedding presents, with the names or initials of the bride and groom, and the year of the marriage, worked into the design. Lately, Janet had tired of bought patterns and had begun to design her own, with flowers, and clouds, and ships, and bright, bold blocks of colour. Many of her best were impromptu designs, done just to use up the spare wool she had left over. Many people had commented on them already. They were just as good as the shop ones, Sam thought: better, in fact.

Sam switched on the television set. There was the end of the main evening's news. The headlines. Trouble in the Middle East. As usual. There was always trouble in the Middle East.

There had been trouble in the Middle East, on and off, ever since Sam had joined the Navy. The Captain had a story of how years ago, when he was Fourth Hand in his first boat, they had gone straight from the middle of a NATO exercise into four weeks' extra patrol in the Arctic, all because of a flare-up in Iraq or somewhere. It seemed odd, to send submarines to the Arctic, because of trouble in Iraq. But the main point of the Captain's story was that because of the unexpected time at sea they had nearly run out of food and, what would have been infinitely worse, rum.

There was a local programme to follow. Some discussion. Sam recognised the face of one of their local councillors. That chap was always on the box. There was always some controversy, and it was always to do with Polaris. The coming of Polaris had polarised – that was the right word, certainly – the whole neighbourhood. Those who made their livings from tourism objected to it. But there were as many who were employed by it. The whole countryside was split down the middle. It was a current affairs television producer's dream. Every scheme had its proposers and its objectors. For every one in favour, there was somebody against. For every opponent, there was a supporter.

This programme was about some road or other they were going to build through some obscure glen up in the hills. The idea was to relieve the existing main road of most of the heavy construction lorry traffic which was going along it. Those who lived on the main road, of course, wanted the new road. They said the heavy traffic was shaking their houses to pieces, and their dogs and cats were being run over, and the children couldn't get to sleep at night, and the local vicar said that anybody getting married or christened or buried at his church couldn't park outside without going in peril of their lives – even those who were being buried? said the interviewer.

But those who had shops and pubs along the main road said that the new road was bound to affect their trade. The chap and his wife from Birmingham who ran a craft shop in the summertime said it would ruin them. The two shepherds and their dog who actually lived up in the glen, and the fellow who owned the moor just above it, and the bird watchers, and the nature conservancy freaks, and the wild flower enthusiasts, and the people who looked for prehistoric Celtic graves up there – they were all against the new road.

They seemed to have got a cross-section of the community, for and against, although some of the arguments were beginning to sound a little thread-bare locally.

Suddenly Sam sat up. There was El Tel and, behind him, Mary Carmichael and some of the other peace protesters.

'There's the chap who mended our puncture! Fancy seeing him on the telly!'

Janet put aside her tapestry to watch.

El Tel was being interviewed standing on the other side of the road to the camp site, with the wire fence of the submarine base stretching into the distance behind him.

' . . . Of course, we oppose the new road, and all new construction up here.' His cockney voice was quite distinctive in its timbre. 'We think this place is already too big, too dangerous, and should be removed. The more roads are built, the more capital investment is made in the infrastructure here, the sheer number of buildings and construction, the more difficult it will be to get rid of this place. The more money this government puts into it, the harder it is going to be to shift them. Look at this . . .' El Tel gestured over his shoulder at the barbed wire. 'This is new, this wire. Heaven knows how much it costs. Did you know that if you get stuck on that, if it catches you, you have to go to hospital to get those barbs cut out of your skin? *Surgically* cut out. Imagine it. Literally cut out!'

The camera followed the line of the wire up to the brow of the hill, before returning to El Tel, and then fading.

'He's very persuasive, isn't he?'

'He certainly is.'

'Were those some of his followers, those women in the background? They're obviously protesters with him. Those women, I mean.'

40

'I don't know about *followers*.' For some reason, Sam objected to that word. Surely one could not describe Mary Carmichael as El Tel's *follower*? Sam had been hoping that she would be interviewed. He would have liked to have heard her voice. But after one last glimpse of her and the others, the cameras had left.

'Why, do you know them?' Janet had taken up her tapestry again.

'I knew one of them, yes. She was there while he was mending our puncture.'

'Oh, I wish I'd known. You should have mentioned it. It's always nice to see somebody you know, or know of, on the television. Which one was it?'

'Oh, I don't know. She was wearing a blue anorak thing.'

'I didn't notice her.'

'There's no reason why you should.'

'Oh Lord, football now. I always think it's football every other programme while you're away.'

Sam thought of their conversation again, as he lay in bed watching Janet undress. It was a nightly ritual, when he was at home. He loved to see her undress and she knew he did. He recalled overhearing a remark at a party years ago, down some boat or other. Somebody had said of Janet, 'She's one of the few naval wives who actually enjoys making love to her husband.' He did not know how the speaker knew but it was one of the remarks which had given Sam most pleasure in his whole life. Even now, he remembered it with glee.

Janet was blushing slightly. 'It's that stare of yours.'

'I love to see some bare bottom.'

'Don't be so crude.'

'Not got the summer nightie on yet?'

'No. It's not summer yet.'

Janet turned off the lights, drew back the curtains, and jumped into bed, as she always did, with a most unladylike leap.

'*Gor*. What an elephant!'

41

'Me and the elephant, we still remember you.'

Sam lay looking at the glow of somebody's headlights passing across the bedroom ceiling. It was their next-door neighbour's car, just driving away from his house. Sam remembered now what he did. He worked in the hospital. Some sort of shift work, or perhaps he was on call for something or other.

'Do you ever wake up early in the morning, afraid of something, you don't know quite what? Just a vague feeling of something to be worried about?'

'That's supposed to be one of the symptoms of alcoholism.'

'*Is* it? How do you know that?'

'Don't know. Must have seen it on some television programme, I expect.'

Sam had a familiar twinge of guilt. It did seem hard on the wives, being left all the time. 'I know you have to watch a lot of TV when I'm away and the children are at school.'

'It's not too bad. Long as it's not football.'

'It must be lonely for you. I know I've asked you before, but couldn't you go to some of these things they organise?'

'You know what my answer is to that.'

'Balls. I know.'

'I'm not alone, you know, darling. A lot of wives don't like being organised. All this counselling, and caring, and organising things for lonely wives, they object to all that. They think it's patronising. Rosemary used to try and organise things, when she was up here.'

'Very much the Captain's lady.'

'Oh no, not at all. She did her best.'

'Those words. Like an epitaph. She did her *best*. She died with her boots on.'

'She tried to do things for the sailors' wives.'

'. . . Officers' wives get pudding and pies, sailors' wives get skilly . . .'

'Oh don't be silly. It's a thankless business anyway. I don't think the sailors' wives really welcomed it all that much, you know. They don't know how to react when you call, or when

42

you just . . . when you just meet somewhere at some do. I don't
mean that snobbishly, well I suppose it is snobbish really, but
they go to such extremes! They just can't be natural. Either
they go way over the top and take far too much trouble, a
ridiculous amount, and polish everything and put on their best
as though the Queen were coming to tea or they go exaggera-
tedly the other way, don't bother, don't care, as if to show you
they don't care who you are, and they're more sort of offhand
than they would be if their own friends were coming. It's a sort
of reverse snobbery.'

There were more headlights on the ceiling. It could not be
their neighbour back so soon. People did use this road as a
short cut up from the river front to the hinterland of the town at
the back. Sam could hear a siren, or a fog-horn, from the river.
It was so far away, and barely audible, yet one could hear the
sadness in it. Somebody leaving, somebody trying to find their
way. He thought of all the naval wives living in the area, in
their own houses and in the married patch, in Moon City, and
some of them as far away as Arrochar, at the top of Loch Long.
They were all coming to terms in their own way with their
husbands' absences. Every patrol brought its crop of domestic
dramas. Last time, the Starboard Crew had come back to find
that their Petty Officer Steward's wife had gone off to live with
a MoD PloD. Leading Seaman Basing had had a field day with
that. He had composed almost a complete sod's opera around
it, with theme and variations.

'I was just thinking of those peace protesters.'

'Oh? They seem to have had quite an effect on you.'

'I was thinking of their freedom. They can come and go.
They can come and live in that camp, for a few weeks, or a few
months, or a few years even, and then they're free to go, off
they go . . .'

'. . . Like the raggle-taggle gypsies, oh . . .'

'Yes. Like that. But meanwhile we're locked into a routine,
in fact it's the Polaris routine that seems to appeal to a lot of
people, this sort of *inexorable* routine, grinding round and
round.'

'*They're* probably envying *us*, our stability, and knowing just where we stand.'

'Each side looking for what they think the other side has got.'

'*Very* profound, for this time of night.'

'Yes please, hold me.'

With his thoughts of the peace women dissolving into dreams, and Janet holding him, Sam fell asleep.

Janet was always a slow starter in the mornings. She tended to be grumpy and snap at everybody as they had their breakfasts. Sam had learned, just as Alice and the boys had learned, to keep a low profile over his Corn Flakes. When they first came to Scotland, Janet had made them all porridge, but even her legendary touch could not make it acceptable. After just one morning, porridge was never mentioned in their family again.

Janet was to take him into the submarine base again that morning. Local geography and timing meant that Alice had to get ready and come in the car too, and be delivered to her school after Sam had been dropped at the base.

They had to wait some time before the traffic would let them out on to the river road. It certainly was getting worse and worse. The local people had justifiable cause for complaint; twice a day, cars full of Ministry of Defence bureaucrats flowed to and fro, going up to their offices in the base in the mornings and back again in the evenings. The only free days were at weekends. MoD bureaucrats never, ever, worked on Saturdays or Sundays.

On the way Alice delivered a running commentary, an unopposed monologue, about Morag, and what she and Morag, jointly and individually, were going to do that day, and what Morag had said, and what Miss Farquhar, their form teacher, had said, about her and about Morag. Sam found it strangely refreshing, to listen to his daughter and know that no response of any kind was required of him.

As they turned into the road leading to the base, Sam looked across at the peace camp. There was nobody about. Perhaps

44

there was a smudge of smoke from the chimney of their cooking van, but otherwise there was no sign of life. He looked to the front, at the base gates coming larger and nearer, and knew that Janet had noticed his glance at the camp.

He kissed Janet, and said goodbye to her, with that same, almost fatalistic, feeling he always had, and could never entirely repress; he knew it was absurd, but he could not help himself feeling that this might, just might, be the last day he ever did it.

Otherwise, the base was the same as the day before, and the day before that. Sam had once read a medieval description of hell, where there was endless, pointless noise, and people running aimlessly about all the time. Maybe it was the original definition of Pandemonium. But the base seemed to be just like that.

Sam stood for a few moments on the pavement, while the roar of engines and the hooting of horns and the crowd of pedestrians surged past him. He had physically to brace himself, as though he were about to withstand the shock of a plunge into freezing water, before he could bring himself to go down to the boat.

The Captain was sitting at the wardroom table, as usual spreading himself over about three seats' width. He had brought a *Times* with him and was reading it. His presence and *The Times* were in themselves very bad signs: the Captain normally never read newspapers and never came on board until much later in the forenoon. The fact that he had got on board before Sam was ominous.

'Good morning, sir.'

The Captain put *The Times* down. 'Middle East again. Did I ever tell you about the time we went up the Arctic during one of these Middle East dos . . .'

'Yes, sir, you have.' Sam was conscious that he spoke for the whole wardroom.

'I was looking for you last night, Sam. What happened to you?'

Sam remembered that, strictly speaking, he should have told

45

the Captain before he went ashore. 'Ah, I thought I'd go home for a bit, sir. For a bit of a break.'

'A bit of a *break*!' The Captain's voice was incredulous.

'Yes, sir.'

Sam was pleased and relieved to see that he had, at least for the moment, rendered the Captain speechless. But it was only temporary.

The Captain held up a large brown official envelope. 'I just came on board to pick this up.'

Sam thought that, on the contrary, the Captain had for some reason known only to himself come down to the boat unusually early and was only sitting in the wardroom now just to show that he had indeed arrived before Sam. 'I heard on the grapevine they'd sent it down.'

'Leading Seaman Basing's case, sir?'

'Yes.'

'Was he over the limit?'

'Yes he was. I'm going to go inboard now and see if I can possibly sort something out with the MoD PloD. Though I'm not very optimistic, with the sort of Incredible Hulks they employ these days.'

'I'll come up and see you over the gangway, sir.' It was no more than Sam's duty, in any case, and should not have needed saying. But the Captain always made Sam nervous, making him blurt out more than he meant to or should do.

Up on the casing, the Captain looked about him, with a savage grimace on his face. There was nothing ostentatiously amiss, so far as Sam could see. The trot sentry was properly dressed with webbing gaiters and belt, as he should be, and he was standing where he ought to be, by the gangway, ready to salute. Two sailors were working at the forward end of the casing, as they should be, on a working forenoon. Some more sailors were bringing stores on board, in the normal manner, to be expected just before a Bomber went to sea.

Nevertheless, the Captain clapped his arms, fists clenched, against his sides, in a gesture of anger and frustration. 'It's a *shambles*. A bloody *shambles*.'

46

'Aye, aye, sir.' The sailors on deck stood at attention, and Sam and the sentry, and Jimmy the Sonar Officer, who was officer of the day, stood at attention and at the salute, as the Captain went ashore.

But it seemed only minutes before the Captain was back, wearing the same savage expression and muttering about 'a shambles'. And there was something else.

'No joy about Leading Seaman Basing, sir?'

'I might just as well have saved my breath.' The Captain sipped at the coffee which Murdoch the Petty Officer Steward had known, by the very sound of the Captain's heels on the deck, was going to be very necessary. 'It was like talking to some hard-of-hearing aborigine somewhere, who has to have everything repeated to him in his own barbaric dialect several times over before he can grasp enough of what you've been saying to be able to completely misunderstand it.'

'So what can we do, sir?'

'Not much. Next thing we know, they'll come down the boat and demand that Basing be taken off the patrol and put ashore, in case his case comes up while we're away. After all, it would never do to put the MoD PloD to any inconvenience. Little things like the country's nuclear deterrent have to come second to them.'

The rest of the wardroom made no comment. They knew that such things had happened before, in other boats.

'I might be able to sort something out with Captain S/M. His Secretary is pretty good at this sort of thing. Barrister, and all that. I'll go and see if I can have a word with him.'

Once again, Sam took his cap and followed the Captain up on to the casing. The scene there was much as it had been earlier in the forenoon, but this time there were no histrionic exclamations about 'a shambles'. Maybe, Sam reflected, a real problem stopped the Captain inventing imaginary ones.

Sam stood at the salute, with Jimmy the Sonar Officer beside him, both observing a thoughtful silence, as they jointly watched the Captain mount the gangway with swift furious strides and disappear behind some dockside buildings.

Jimmy the Sonar Officer let his hand drop from the salute. 'Dear Rosemary. Come back. All is forgiven.'

'Amen.'

Together they began to walk back to the hatchway. 'You okay in your department, Jimmy? All parts taking an even strain?'

'Yep. Just about ready to go for Day One. All the kit's ready. Very few new chums this trip. So everybody should know what they're doing. All the Big Ears flapping.'

Jimmy always used this fragmented, somewhat elliptical form of speech whenever he talked about his department. It was often difficult for a layman to follow his idiosyncratic phrasing. The rest of the wardroom put it down to a trip he had once made as liaison officer in an American Polaris Bomber. But Sam knew that Jimmy was another very able officer, although he had not been a volunteer, either for submarines in general or for the Polaris programme. He was what was known as 'a pressed man'. But he had taken to submarine life, and had settled down and, as so often happened, now enjoyed it more than many a volunteer. He was another who might go far. That is, if he wanted to.

When Sam reached the wardroom again Hamish the doctor had just begun what everybody had come to know as Hamish's tale of the day. This one was about his opposite number, the doctor in the Starboard Crew. ' . . . A few days ago, he was telling me, he was driving out of town towards the base and he saw one of these peace protesters hitch-hiking. So he stopped and gave him a lift, with all his haversacks, and his God knows what in the way of gear. When the chap said he wanted to go to the peace camp he said "Hop in". But, instead of dropping him at the camp, he took him way right round to the north end of the base, to the gate there, which, as you know, is miles from the camp. When the chap looked at him, he said, "This *is* the peace camp, mate, *here* on the submarine base. This is the *peace* camp. Yours is the *protest* camp!" '

As the others laughed, Sam wondered if the hitch hiker had been El Tel and, if it had, what answer he would have made. El

48

Tel could have been counted on to have a ready reply. Mary Carmichael, too, for that matter. Sam wondered whether he ought to report his encounter with them. Strictly speaking, the MoD security boys wanted to know of all such contacts. Sam guessed that MoD security made more, and more intrusive, researches into people's lives than people knew. It could well be that El Tel and his friends were quite right to be suspicious, to suspect quite unwarranted breaches of personal privacy, all perpetrated in the name of security. It certainly was a sign of the times in the modern Navy, how naval officers now submitted to the most extraordinary intrusions by policemen. Imagine Jackie Fisher being breathalysed by a MoD PloD.

'I always say "Good morning campers" whenever I drive by.'

'Have you brushed your teeth this morning?'

'I imagine they must pong a bit. Campers of the world unite, you have nothing to lose but your drains!'

It was curious, Sam thought, how often the wardroom indulged themselves in this sort of mindless badinage. He found himself resenting the accusation that the peace campers smelled. They did not. But maybe, in some curious way, the very fact that so many jokes were made at the peace protesters' expense showed that everybody was aware that they were there. They had no actual effect upon the submarine base, which proceeded about its everyday normal business just as though the protesters did not exist. Nevertheless, they were still there, at the back of everybody's mind. Maybe, this continuing passive physical presence would have more effect, in the long run, than the most violent and newsworthy action.

But as Day One came nearer, even the peace protesters faded from Sam's mind. It was his portion, as the Captain's right-hand man and the boat's second-in-command, to be interested in everything, concerned with everything. All departments, all aspects of the boat and its life, were his concern. Although the Captain was officially the final arbiter, in practice disputes always fell to Sam to resolve.

Sam found himself enjoying it again. He was good at it. He

was good at his work. He had always known of his own ability, in an almost arrogant way, ever since he joined the boat. He acknowledged he had recently been through a roughish patch, when everything had seemed to gang up on him, and everything had always seemed too difficult. But now it was all coming good again. He felt the wardroom and the boat responding, as they always did to proper leadership. Even the Captain had started to come down the boat later and later in the forenoons, which was always a very good sign.

As the few days left unrolled towards Day One, with patrol Der Tag always looming behind it, every defect, every missing spare part, every snag, every hitch, no matter how seemingly small or insignificant, assumed a fresh importance. The big question always was: would it, whatever it was, affect the Bomber's ability to go to sea on Der Tag? Bomber sailings were sacrosanct. Der Tag was the day beyond which nothing could be put off, on which everything simply had to be ready. The Buck, as they said, stopped at 0800 on Der Tag.

Day One was upon them almost before Sam was aware of it. He telephoned Janet from the boat on the night before sailing, using the shore telephone connected to the control room. It was hardly private, with people passing by all the time, and somebody actually working on a display panel only a few feet away. The control room itself was like a sounding box. It occurred to Sam that maybe somebody had even designed it that way; maybe there really was some little boffin in Bath whose sole purpose in life was submarine internal acoustics, so that even whispered orders could be heard clearly yards away.

'Hello, darling. How are you?' Sam paused. He had almost said 'All parts taking an even strain?' It was odd, standing in this control room which he knew so well, with every gauge and light and instrument familiar, and speaking to a voice from another world, which he knew just as intimately. There was a clock on the control room bulkhead. There was another clock, very similar to it, which he himself had bought from a mail order advertisement in one of the Sunday newspapers, on their living-room wall.

Janet was audibly glad to have the telephone call. But, as usual, it was an anticlimax. After all, there seemed nothing of moment worth saying. She had finished cutting the hedge. The first bulbs were showing up well. She was well. The boys were well. Alice was well. Morag was well and Miss Farquhar was very well. Johnny had scored a goal. She was watching the television.

'Not football, is it?'

'No, thank God. You know me better than that. It's all about the Middle East. When are you off tomorrow, darling?'

Sam wondered whether he should give such information over the telephone, even to his own wife. Maybe the MoD PloD were listening in, and would descend upon their little bungalow, with detector vans and dogs and loud-hailers, as soon as the boat had sailed.

'Tomorrow evening. I can't tell you the time.'

'Of course not. But I'll think of you. I might even come down to the narrows to wave goodbye . . .'

'Oh no, don't do that! Please! That would make it worse. You do understand?'

'Yes, of course.'

There really did seem nothing else to say, not over the telephone anyway.

'Bye, love . . .'

'Goodbye, darling, I love you . . .'

They sailed just before dusk on Day One, when the first lights were coming on in the houses along the shore. Cars were showing the first headlights on the coast road. From the bridge, Sam could see the lights winking and glowing, more and more of them, as the daylight failed. Above the hills to the east, a half moon was rising, a mottled yellow behind streaks of thin cloud. A Bomber's moon. Ahead of them, and keeping station on them, but leading the way, was a tiny pinprick of light – the stern light of the police launch. This was the MoD PloD's great moment of glory. The local bye-laws and regulations gave them the power to clear the loch of all other traffic when a Bomber was on the move. It was just as though they

51

were frightening all the lesser fry from the waters, before the approach of some great predatory fish. Sam had often seen Bombers from the shore and he had to admit they did look like huge prehistoric monsters. Even those who had never seen a Bomber in their lives before, once they had caught sight of one moving across the surface of a Scottish loch, would know instinctively that that black shape could be up to no good.

As they neared the narrows, a sudden brilliant and quite unexpected shaft of sunlight from the west shone over their shoulders as they stood on the bridge and lit up the rocks and the sandy point with its iron beacon. Sam could see figures standing there. By some trick of the light they all appeared to be dressed in white, like priests or druids. It was impossible to see whether they were protesters or not. But not one of them waved.

The light went as quickly as it had come, and it was hard to see anybody standing there at all. As the light faded, Sam had a recurrence of a scene in his mind's eye which he had not had for years, since, in fact, he first joined the Polaris programme. It was the typically melodramatic imaginings of a newcomer. Probably everybody new to a Bomber had such thoughts: what would it be like if, on one patrol, they actually fired? The Polaris base was an obvious target for retaliation. Might they return, if they ever did, to find a charred and blackened countryside, with no lights, and no people, and no houses, and no cars, nothing, for ever and ever more? It did not bear thinking about, and as the total of deterrent patrols one had done mounted up, so such thoughts were rarer and rarer. Contrary to St Augustine, or whatever, it was perfectly possible to live with the unthinkable. One simply did not think about it. In any case, not to worry; as the sailors said, everybody knew those long tubes were all full of Smarties.

CHAPTER 3

S AM LEFT THE BRIDGE as the submarine rounded the tip of land to the north, at the end of the loch, and headed down the main river. The Chief Stoker was waiting for him at the bottom of the ladder. His proper title was Chief ME, but submarine Chief Stokers were always called Chief Stoker whatever new designation they might officially have been given.

'Trim's on, sir.'

'Thank you, Chief Stoker. No problems?'

'No, sir.'

It was a constant source of wonder and amazement to non-submariners – how did a submarine dive? Sam wished he had a pound for every time he had tried to answer that question. The answer was that it did, and it was Sam's duty to make it as easy as possible. The aim to be achieved was a blessed state of neutral buoyancy, in which the dived submarine tried neither to rise nor to sink, because the weight of the submarine, and the men, machinery, weapons, stores and fluids inside it, equalled as near as possible the weight of the water the submarine displaced when dived. Archimedes had the gist of it: the downthrust of the submarine's weight was counter-balanced by the upthrust of the water it displaced.

Calculating and then adjusting the amount of water in the various internal tanks, to compensate properly for any changes in the submarine's bodily weight – more or less men, more or less stores, fuel consumed, torpedoes embarked – and so to achieve this state of neutral buoyancy, was a skilled business, verging upon an art form. It was called, and had been since time immemorial, 'putting on the trim'. Sam worked out the trim, and gave the figures to the Chief Stoker, who saw to it that the amounts of water were in the tanks just as Sam had calculated. It was virtually impossible to make the calculation exactly, but one could be near enough. How near would be shown as soon as the submarine dived.

Sam hung his cap on a peg outside the wardroom.

'Open up for diving, please, sir?'

The Outside Wrecker was waiting, wheel spanner in hand, looking almost like a big labrador hoping to be taken for a walk. This was the second great pre-diving ritual – 'Opening Up For Diving'. No matter how big or modern a submarine, no matter that it carried the instruments of Armageddon on board, certain things had to be done, certain precautions taken, valves and openings checked, fittings and indicators in the right order and sequence, before the submarine could dive safely. Although many more things were checked shut than open, the process was traditionally known as 'opening up for diving'. Again, it was Sam's duty to open up for diving, accompanied on his rounds through the submarine by the Outside Wrecker – the artificer, so nicknamed, who was generally responsible for the upkeep of machinery outside the main propulsion systems. Although the Outside Wrecker's duties were less clearly defined now than they had been in the old days of diesel-electric submarines, the nickname survived.

They began, as always, up forward. Here were the sonar cabinets and some of the displays for the boat's main listening gear. These were the realms of Noddy and Big Ears, as the sailors called them, where one could listen to underwater sounds and furies, many miles away. Below was the Tube Space, with the torpedo tubes, and the forward escape tower, with the spare torpedoes in their racks, and the loading and ramming gear. Below that, was the Torpedo Flat.

This part of the submarine used to be called in the old days the fore ends, where most of the sailors used to live. Now, so

Sam had heard, there was a battle going on in Bath and the MoD. Some ignorant MoD bureaucrat, who had probably never been to sea in a submarine himself and knew nothing of the life, wanted to enforce a regulation whereby any space in a submarine that held torpedoes was officially classified as a magazine, and therefore could not be used for accommodation as long as the torpedoes were there. If that had been enforced in the old days, submarine ship's companies would have had to spend most of their patrols standing up because there would have been no room to do anything else. But, as always, it looked as though the bureaucrats were going to win. Did the other services, Sam wondered, did the pongos and the crabfats have the same trouble with their bureaucrats, or was there a special breed of bloody-minded bureaucrat for the Navy?

It seemed odd to see torpedo tubes in a Bomber, anyway. A submarine's object in the old days had always been to gain contact and then close its target to attack. The Bomber's task was exactly the opposite: to shun any contact gained, to evade and, like Brer Rabbit's Tarbaby, lie low and say 'nuffin'. Only when all the missiles had been fired, or if so ordered at any time, would a Bomber revert to a hunter-killer submarine's role.

'All right, sir?' The Outside Wrecker had checked everything in this section, had seen that Sam had watched him check, and was now waiting to move on. It was a matter of checking that certain things, such as hatches, were shut, and others, such as the valves that admitted high pressure air to blow water out of the main ballast tanks, were open. It might seem obvious to check that the hatches were all shut before diving a submarine, but some strange things had happened in the past.

'Yes, please, Dawson, let's get on.'

The Outside Wrecker nodded. He was not known for his conversation or his sense of humour. He was a dour, taciturn man from Derbyshire, the son of a coal miner and with that peculiar arrogance such men sometimes had he was always impressing his family background upon everybody. He was heavily built, and black-jowelled, as though some of the family coal dust had embedded itself permanently in his complexion.

In the next main section were the wireless office, the galley, the main dining hall, the senior rates' lounge, and there was a laundry, run by two stokers. It was a dark noisome compartment with a warning notice outside, detailing charges, times of opening, and the admonishment 'No Nix or Sox'. Below, were the bunk spaces, and some storerooms – Jack Dusty's Castle.

Some of these compartments, the dining hall and the senior rates' lounge especially, were huge by traditional submarine standards. But they were still not nearly big enough – and they were beginning to show the submarine's age. They looked clean enough and fresh enough, but anybody who looked more closely would see the scratches on the table top surfaces, the paintwork scuffed and chipped, the floor coverings worn, all signs of the pressure from the sheer numbers of bods on board. Once again, the malign influence of MoD bureaucrats could be seen at work. Any new equipment brought on board was always fitted at the expense of the ship's company's living space.

In the galley, there were the same signs of wear; cracked tiles on the deck, and scratches on the metalwork, telltale evidence of hard usage, on the coppers and the ovens. The potato-peeler, one of the most vital items of machinery on board, was growing temperamental. They had tried to get more spare parts than the allowance, or better still, a brand-new machine, but had only received a knife, carefully wrapped and labelled 'Knife, Peeling, Potato, Admiralty Pattern' from a naval stores officer with a misplaced sense of humour.

There was now a special stores computer, which could order up spares more quickly than Ariel could throw a girdle round the earth, and could even communicate, eyeball to computer eyeball, or byte to byte or whatever, with other stores computers around the United Kingdom and even, so Sam had heard, across the Atlantic with an American computer in Charleston, South Carolina. Sam imagined the computers conversing with each other. It was grotesque.

The PO Chef and his team were already preparing to dish up supper as soon as everybody fell out from special sea dutymen. In the old days, the Coxswain did the food, under the general aegis of the First Lieutenant. Submarine food had had a certain spectacular unpredictability, depending upon the Coxswain's arithmetic and the Chef's love life. Even Sam could remember early submarine days when the food had an unusual, some would even say unearthly, flavour about it. Now, it was all processed and frozen and dehydrated. It was all technologically stunned and then brought hurriedly on board before it recovered. They did not cook it so much as revive it. Now, they even had a Supply Officer on board who worked out the menus beforehand, to the last green pea, and could say exactly what they would be having on a Tuesday dinnertime in the middle of next month.

The galley staff had their own fantasy world, as well. They gave themselves nicknames, such as the Pecos Kid, and the Main Man, and Boxcar Wilfred. They spoke a special argot amongst themselves and kept the galley clock hands showing what they called 'Rocky Mountain Rhythm Time', six hours ahead of the rest of the boat.

They all seemed in good humour in the galley, as did everybody in the boat. Sam always enjoyed opening up for diving. It gave him a chance to go through the boat from end to end and gauge the temper of everything and everyone. One could tell a great deal about a ship's company from an expression on a face, or a certain look in an eye, or a remark, made accidentally-on-purpose loud enough to be overheard. Today, there was a pleasant air of expectancy in the boat. This was the first trip to sea, the first dive, for some time, and they seemed to be looking forward to it.

Sam followed the Outside Wrecker's broad back through the boat, watching him try a valve here, put his weight on a handle there, and then look back to check Sam's reaction. This was a routine they both knew by heart. But it still had to be done thoroughly each time. Familiarity could so easily lead to contempt and then to an accident.

57

He was surprised, as he always was on the first day at sea, by the number of faces he had not seen, now he came to think of it, for some time. It was extraordinary how many sailors managed simply to disappear in harbour. As the Coxswain said, 'Some of them just pop up out of the woodwork – and pop back in again, if you don't keep an eye on them.'

Sam climbed through the circular door into the Missile Compartment and paused for a moment on the grating inside. He had read somewhere that Polaris sailors called this 'Sherwood Forest', but he had never heard that description in this boat. Their sailors called it the 'rocket shop', if they called it anything at all. This space had long since lost its novelty in Sam's eyes, but it was still an astonishing compartment for a submarine. There was even an element of Jules Verne about it. The lines of missile tubes seemed to stretch right away into the distance. They were all numbered, the numbers painted in striking black on the circular access hatches half-way up the tubes, odd numbers – 1 to 15 – to starboard, even numbers – 2 to 16 – to port, according to the custom of the Service. They were so big and so wide and there were so many of them, they should have achieved a sort of collective dignity, like columns in a great cathedral. But they merely succeeded in making the whole huge compartment appear bleakly functional, and almost overcrowded. Maybe the proportions were wrong, or the spacing, or the paint was too staringly white, or the light was too glaringly bright.

It always seemed to Sam ironic that the missiles inside the tubes were cosseted, their daily well-beings anxiously checked, their temperatures carefully taken and recorded, as though they were the most fragile and precious of invalids. But, as the sailors always said, 'Mustn't let the Smarties melt.'

Sam could never pass through the tunnel over the reactor compartment without at least a *frisson* of anxiety. He knew very well that he would get more radiation from cosmic rays if he stood on the casing in the open air than he was ever likely to get inside the boat. Nevertheless, he always passed by as quickly as he could and he had a lot of sympathy with the sailors' fantasies – that they had once seen a gigantic fly with six heads in there, or a cockroach with huge human hands, and green hair on its back.

The air temperature rose noticeably as they went through the door leading to the machinery compartments aft. These were the realms of the engineers and the electricians, the lands where the Clankies and the Greenies lived. Sam always felt sorry for anybody who had to work and keep watches back here. The compartments seemed no better designed or laid out, and were certainly no easier to work in or to keep clean, than the machinery spaces of small surface ships designed a quarter of a century before. The Health and Safety at Work bureaucrats ashore would have a fit if they ever saw the working conditions the stokers and the electricians had to endure back aft in a Bomber. Unlike the American Bombers, there was a permanent shortfall of air-conditioning capacity. Something in the British temperament believed that to be comfortable was equivalent to being sinful, and these spaces aft were always hot and steamy and very cramped. Furthermore, the whole propulsion unit had been designed on what Sam had once heard some wag describe as the 'Olympic system' of ship-building. The fastest dockyard matey won. If the electrician happened to be quickest on his feet he could lay his eighth of an inch of electric cable in position and then watch the slower boilermaker bend his eight-inch diameter special steel pipe around it.

They were just passing Manoeuvring, which was the centre of the boat's technical world, apart from the missiles. The main and auxiliary machinery was all watched over and controlled from here. Here, the Outside Wrecker was among his peers, and subjected to the traditional jibes.

'You found it yet, Derby?' It was always popularly supposed that the Outside Wrecker was going through the boat looking for something, as though searching for some private holy grail.

'It's not here, Derby.'

As always, the Outside Wrecker made no comment.

Manoeuvring was not a separate compartment, nor just a cubicle. It was a section of the boat whose limits were marked out by walls of instruments and controls and gauges. No doubt, at some time in the past, it had been specially designed and laid out so as to present its information, and readings and figures and letters, in the most striking and easily visible form. But, over the years, there had been alterations and accretions and afterthoughts and now, like every other instrument panel in the Navy, Manoeuvring was a mess. There were unsightly human additions: the teacup stains on a ledge, somebody's newspaper tucked into a crevice, somebody's jacket hanging on a valve hand-wheel. Chief was not scrupulous enough, in Sam's opinion, about his department's tidiness. Apart from which, gash sculling around could be dangerous if ever there was a fire or a flood.

Sam nodded to Chief, and then had to grasp a rail near him for support, as the deck heeled sharply. He had been aware of the slow movement underfoot as he walked through the boat. This must mean they were clearing the lee of the land and heading out into the open sea. They would be diving very soon. Some Captains liked to leave diving until as late as possible. Some liked to dive as soon as they could. This one was what you could call a precocious diver.

There was more confirmation of that. Chief was mouthing some message from the broadcast, which Sam had not heard.

'Did you get that, Sam? From the Captain, have you opened up for diving yet?'

Sam gestured aft, to indicate the amount of the boat still to do. Chief nodded, and Sam saw him speaking into the Manoeuvring main broadcast microphone.

Sam pursed his lips. The Captain knew very well how long it took to open up for diving. He also knew very well that Sam would do it as quickly as he could. There was therefore no reason for the request, except to annoy Sam.

They finished right aft, with the steering gear. Sam and the Outside Wrecker exchanged nods. The boat was opened up for diving. Sam thanked the Outside Wrecker, as he always did.

'Thank you, sir.' As always, those were virtually the only words the Outside Wrecker had spoken since they met.

60

'Pass the message, boat opened up for diving.'

Soon, they could all hear the Captain's voice on the broadcast. 'D'you hear there, the boat will be diving in five minutes' time.'

In what seemed to Sam only a few moments, there was the sound of the diving klaxon, the officer of the watch and the look-out were down from the bridge and shaking rain off their oilskins, there were thuds from above as the hatches were shut and clipped and reported shut and clipped, the control room was full of men at their diving stations, and the Captain was at the periscope. Sam had done this and practised this, and had even dreamed this, so many times, that in a peculiar way it did almost seem like a dream, which was all happening in front of his eyes.

The Captain rapidly took periscope bearings of lights, so as to fix their diving position exactly.

'Keep me up, Sam! I can see fuck all, Sam! Number *One*, do you *hear* me, I can see sweet fuck all!'

'Aye aye sir.' They did not seem to be heavy. In fact Sam had just been mentally congratulating himself on catching a trim at once.

'We're heavy! Heavy heavy *heavy!*' The Captain's voice was rising to a roar. 'What the hell do you think you're doing, Sam?'

'Aye, aye, sir.' Sam studied the movement of the inclinometer bubble closely. It was steady enough, considering. So, too, was the depth gauge. The Coxswain did not seem to be having any problems with the boat's depth or attitude. But the Captain had fully launched upon his *recitatif* and *aria*.

'Pump, pump, pump . . . Blow blow blow blow blow . . .'

'Blow main *ballast*, sir?'

This time, the note of startled concern ran right round the control room.

'No, no, I didn't mean that.' For the first time, the Captain's voice held a touch of apology. Ambiguous orders, given in jest, could be dangerous, even terminal, in a submarine. 'I meant, for God's sake, isn't it time you caught a trim?'

The Coxswain looked round in his seat and caught Sam's eye. But the Coxswain's face was expressionless. Sam was the Captain's accredited butt.

Sam looked at the bubble again, and at the back of the Coxswain's neck. Both were at peace. The boat *might* be a little heavy, perhaps. Maybe they could do with just a *little* less forward. But only a purist would carp at a trim like this.

'Could we stop and put the planes amidships, sir?'

That was the sure and certain way of checking the trim. Just stop, put rudder and planes amidships, and then watch the depth gauge and the bubble. If they were bodily heavy, they would sink. If they were bodily light, they would rise. If they were light forward or heavy aft, the bows would rise and the bubble would run forward. Likewise, if they were heavy forward or light aft, the stern would rise and the bubble would run aft. Clever chaps, these submariners. Mind you, with a boat this size, it took time for any of these effects to show themselves. The planes and the propellors between them could hide a trim which was many tons heavy or light.

'No, no, no. We haven't time for that. Must get on with the programme.'

As Sam was well aware, the last thing the Captain wanted was a demonstration of Sam's trim. It was the old 'don't confuse me with the truth' syndrome.

Whenever they went to sea for an Index, the ship's company always wondered which performance the Captain was going to give. From the first dive, it became clear that this time the Captain was rendering his well-known impersonation of the Roaring Boy. He roared when he was at the periscope, and he roared when he was on the bridge. He roared when they were deep, and he roared when they were on the surface. He was roaring when they surfaced and was still roaring when they dived again.

He roared constantly in the control room, especially when they were changing depth, claiming that they were not going deep, or coming up from deep, fast enough. Here, Sam thought, the Captain really was being particularly unreasonable. This was a big boat. She took her time about changing depth. She was never built for violent World War Two patrol manoeuvrings. She was somewhat ungainly, and rather elderly, and anyone who listened could actually hear her complaints about this treatment, with all her hull plating twanging and clanking under the changes of pressure, as though she were actually protesting audibly at being made to undergo this *adagio* performance at her age. Sam had a sudden thought of a somewhat rheumatic old bitch being made to chase around a field.

But the Captain continued to roar at Chief and his team when they exercised their reactor scrams and other emergency drills. He roared at Joe and the Polaroids, when they exercised missile launches. He roared at the divers, when they exercised leaving and re-entering the boat through the escape towers; a Bomber could never surface whilst on patrol, and any inspection or repair of the hull or its external fittings would have to be performed by divers. He roared at Hamish, when he and his Medical Assistant laid out their emergency operating theatre in the senior rates' mess; the premature return of a Bomber from patrol would be a matter for the Secretary of State, and ultimately the Cabinet, to decide. It certainly would not be approved because of any personal medical emergency amongst the officers or the ship's company. It would be up to Hamish to carry out an operation, such as an appendectomy, or to try and suppress the infection with drugs.

Most of all, the Captain roared at Sam, whatever he did. Sam tried to take it all in good part, as usual, although he could detect an extra edge of venom in the Captain's onslaught. Maybe this was related to Sam's own performance, which he knew himself had been below par recently, in which case this was all largely his own fault, for laying himself open to such an attack. The Captain was critical enough in any circumstances. To give any hostages to fortune was simply asking for trouble, where the Captain was concerned.

But Sam and the rest of the officers and the ship's company endured the Captain's complaints and oaths and tongue-lashings because, deep down, they shared his concern. During in Index, any defect in machinery or drill could be critical. Every hour brought the boat nearer her patrol sailing deadline and every snag had a wider significance: the question always loomed behind every occurrence, will this affect our sailing? It was always possible to carry out major repairs right up to the moment of sailing, but nobody liked that. It meant that the technical staff started the patrol tired and touchy.

The climax came during an exercise missile launch, which was always the most sensitive of their drills. It followed a dramatic script which they all knew now by heart. But although they knew it so well, it always caused the slightest flutter of heartbeats.

It was a procedure designed, as everybody on board knew, to prevent any unauthorised person or persons interrupting or interfering with the process of carrying out an authenticated signal to launch the missiles. It was also designed, though this was not stressed to the same extent, to prevent any person who, for any reason, failed to play his proper role and thus attempted to obstruct or delay a duly authorised launch.

At first it all went according to procedure. The ship's company closed up at diving stations. The submarine was in Condition One SQ for launching, and was hovering, using an automatic system of trimming, so that the submarine remained absolutely motionless in the water and at a steady, accurate depth. The signal was received in the Wireless Office. Sam and Joe were summoned to authenticate it. The necessary combinations were set, the inner and outer safes were opened, the signal to launch had been authenticated by both Sam and Joe. Joe had opened his own safe in the Missile Control Centre and had taken from it an inoffensive-looking handle with a thumb-grip, which was actually the missile firing trigger. All the lights on Joe's panel were changing to the correct colours. The Captain had inserted his key, turned it in the lock and was about, so everybody thought, to give permission to fire when there was an interruption.

Launching missiles required the direct, active co-operation

64

of some two dozen men involved in the actual process of launching, and the tacit consent of every man on board. Nevertheless, there was one final safeguard – a large polished truncheon which hung prominently in the Missile Control Centre, ostensibly to repel anyone who tried to interfere with the launch or to assault Joe or any other member of the launching team. Sam had always thought of it more as a symbol than an actual weapon. He knew that the ship's company, who were all aware it was there, were never sure whether or not to take it seriously. The sailors made jokes about its phallic appearance and properties, and advised newcomers to the boat to go and inspect it. One young Able Seaman, on his first Polaris patrol, had once been told to polish it because, he was told, the missiles would not launch properly unless the truncheon was polished. Leading Seaman Basing, with his inimitable gift for the apt phrase, called it the MoD PloD RoD.

'Intruder in the Missile Control Centre!' The Captain's voice betrayed nothing of the drama of his statement. 'Unship the truncheon!'

Unship the truncheon? Sam sensed the collective raising of eyebrows all round the control room, and hardly knew whether to laugh or not. *Unship* the truncheon? Every submarine captain was entitled, indeed expected, to go off his nut for five minutes in every day. But *unship* the truncheon? Nobody could ever remember exercising such a thing before. Besides, the thing was probably not designed to come off its hook, or rest, or whatever it was that supported it. It was only there to impress the Chinese.

'Control Room? Say again?' Joe's voice was indistinct and it sounded, most unfortunately, as though he were trying to muffle his laughter.

'Give me that!' The Captain seized the microphone. 'I say *again*, there is an intruder in the Missile Control Centre, *unship the truncheon!*'

This was the loudest roar, so far, of the whole Index. It seemed to stun Joe into silence for several seconds. But when he spoke again, the amusement in his voice was unmistakable.

65

'I am afraid our deterrent is not on its hook, sir.'

'*What!*'

'We're just getting it, sir . . .' There was the sound of other voices raised in the Missile Control Centre, and then Joe again. 'There it is. It's here, sir. It was in the ready use locker, sir. In position now, sir. And my Chief EA has it in his hand, ready to repel intruders, sir.'

Sam carefully positioned himself on the other side of a periscope from the Captain, so that its great gleaming column of steel was between them. It was important not to catch the Captain's eye at this juncture. There were two ways, in Sam's opinion, in which the Captain could now play this next coming scene, so as to save face. He could shrug off the Great Truncheon Drama, as being trivial, or he could become even more violent and roar even louder. Sam was relieved, and surprised, that the Captain chose the first alternative.

'Very well. Consider the intruder repelled. But have that truncheon on its hook next time.'

'Aye, aye, sir.'

That, Sam considered, should close the incident. But the Captain returned to it, when Sam reported Rounds of the submarine to him in his cabin that evening.

Though small by surface ship standards, the Captain's cabin in a Bomber was enormous in submariners' eyes, especially to anybody brought up in the old diesel-electric boats. But, even so, there was really room only for a bunk, a desk, a wardrobe and a chest of drawers. On one bulkhead were some indicators and a gyro compass repeater, showing the submarine's depth, shaft revolutions, course, rudder and hydroplane angles, and main engine telegraphs.

On another bulkhead were some framed photographs of submarines, obviously the Captain's previous commands. There were only three – not as many as Sam might have expected. Perhaps it was just another sign of the Polaris programme's voracious appetite for manpower. It sucked up men just out of training class, officers after only a few months in their first boat, COs after only a couple of commands, sometimes after only one. Even the Perisher these days, Sam had heard, was being split into two, so that some of the newly qualified COs would go straight into Bombers as Executive Officers, without any first command of their own.

Sam was surprised to see a photograph of Rosemary, wedged into the bookshelf. Otherwise, the shelf was jammed full to overflowing with paperback books – other people's paperbacks. The Captain was notorious for borrowing paperbacks and not returning them.

'Rounds correct, sir.'

'Thank you, Sam. No, don't go. Hold on a minute, you can take my night order book with you when you go.' The Captain signed the page, held the book up, blew on his signature, and then handed the book to Sam.

'What was all that about the truncheon today, Sam?'

Sam blinked. That was a question he might have asked the Captain.

'I don't know, sir. I suppose somebody forgot to put the truncheon up in its place when we went to sea.' Sam forbore to mention that it was some time since the Captain had visited the Missile Control Centre and that the truncheon might not have been in place for weeks. In fact, they could well have done the whole of the last patrol without it. Nobody was ever likely to notice it. Certainly nobody in their Port Crew ever gave it much thought. Maybe the Starboard Crew were more conscientious about it. In any case, all this was not Sam's part of ship. Joe was the man to ask.

The Captain seemed to sense Sam's lack of concern about the subject. 'Well, I thought it was a very poor effort. And typical of this whole Index. I don't know about you, Sam, but I am not pleased. Not at all pleased.'

Sam waited before he replied. He knew the Captain had this inner nervous tension which drove him on, and caused him sometimes to lash about him. Some of the wardroom – Danny, for instance – were almost immune. The Captain's ill humours seemed to bounce off them. But Sam was especially vulnerable, and the Captain knew it. The Captain was in a position of particular power and importance so far as Sam's immediate recommends for promotion went. But that was not all, not nearly the whole of it. Sam would have been vulnerable to the Captain's personality, whatever their present professional relationship.

'Are you feeling all right these days, Sam?'

'Of course, sir.' Sam recognised, with a feeling of dread, the opening gambit of a familiar mode of attack. 'Why do you ask?'

'It's just that I get the feeling sometimes that you are losing interest in us all.'

The Captain was, of course, notorious for this kind of psychological badgering. It sometimes made a patrol seem intolerably long. It was like being married to a quarrelsome and jealous woman whom one could never physically get away from, ever. The problem was to know how to react. Sometimes the safest way was to go along with it. Other times, the only way to survive was to counter-attack.

'You're not having one of your fits of conscience, are you, Sam? It's nothing to do with these weapons we've got on board, is it? Do you agree with these weapons we've got on board here, Sam?'

Sam blinked again, realising too late that he had waited too long before replying. In any case, it was an absurd question. *What* fits of conscience, anyway? As the sailors would say, all this was completely out of order.

'I haven't thought much about them, sir.'

That was true enough. He had not considered it for years, if at all. It was certainly not the kind of question a Captain should ask his Executive Officer, straight off the bat like that. Sam had certainly never had it put to him as bluntly as that, if indeed he had ever been asked it. The answer was, the received official answer, was that you should be willing to use whatever weapons the Navy has and gives you to use. It was not for you to say, I'll use that and not that. As the old saying went, 'You've been drawing the Queen's money all this time, now's your chance to front up and earn it.'

68

That would be all right if it was the old kind of weapon, if it was a 'one on one' confrontation, firing a gun at another ship, or a dog-fight between aircraft. Even firing by radar had at least some personal element in it, no matter how remote. Nobody else in the Navy's history had so far been asked to do as the Bombers' crews might have to do, to fire a giant missile off to a target nobody knew where, to destroy unknown people and places two thousand miles away. Fire and forget, it would have to be. Only nobody could forget. If there was one thing the sailors were all agreed upon, it was that their main concern would come after the missiles had gone. Before, it would be a matter of training, a piece of drill. This firing might be a drill, it might be real. Nobody would know until afterwards. *After*, then would come the awakening and the reckoning. For in that sleep of death what dreams may come, to give us pause.

'*Don't* start quoting *Macbeth* at me, please, Sam.'

Sam realised that he must have been muttering aloud. That was a very bad sign.

'Actually, it's *Hamlet*, sir, actually.'

'I forgot. You fellows with degrees these days. What did you read, by the way, Geography at Hull?'

Sam thought it advisable to let the Captain see him wince, although it was an old and unfair jibe, which had long since lost most of its sting. It was a custom, which had now almost become a cliché, for naval officers without degrees to disparage those who had them.

'I took a general course, sir, at the City University, in London.'

Which biographical fact, the Captain knew very well.

'One thing I will admit. With degrees, you do get a better class of complaint in the mess suggestion book inboard. Some of them can even spell properly.'

Sam had to admit the Captain did have a sense of humour. It might be somewhat pawky and warped, and some might even call it black. But it was a sense of humour. It was his main, some would even say it was his only, redeeming feature.

69

'Now what's this about Able Seaman Draper? I gather he says he's been having dreams. He's been watching too much TV about life in submarines, I'd say.'

'Well, sir, we have to deal these days with ship's companies who all watch TV. And wardrooms too.' Sam was relieved to be able to change the subject.

'I gather he says he feels he's being put upon.'

Sam would have liked to have been able to say that he knew that very feeling.

'Is he trying to work his ticket, do you think?'

'Possibly, sir. I know he's applied to buy himself out. It's wife trouble, sir. Or rather, mother-in-law trouble. He's basically a good lad. It would be a pity to lose him.'

'Maybe. But we can't have somebody going around the boat muttering that he's claustrophobic. It might give other jack-the-lads the same idea. In any case, Hamish says that claustrophobia is such a rare condition that if he ever came across a genuine case he'd write it up for *The Lancet*. Make his name. He'd be famous. Mind you, I think you only get any medical problems in a submarine when you have a medical officer on board. I know the American Bombers all said they never had any psychiatric problems until they had psychiatrists riding them. And even then, most of the problems were the psychiatrists.'

It was, Sam decided, a black sense of humour. The Captain definitely had a black sense of humour.

'You have a word with young Draper, Sam, and let me know, and then I'll have a word with him. With a patrol coming up so close, I don't want to mess about with somebody who might be likely to cause unnecessary trouble. Although I don't want to give everybody the idea that it's dead easy to work your ticket. Let's hope we have a better day tomorrow. We could do with it.'

'Aye, aye, sir.'

Sam saw Draper the next morning, by accident, as he was passing one of the sonar compartments. Sam usually walked

70

through the boat, slowly, so that he could see what was going on and who was doing what, on most forenoons at sea. Everybody including watch-keepers turned to for a couple of hours in the forenoon, unless the boat had been working particularly hard or the weather was particularly bad – although that was hardly ever a problem in a Bomber. There was no actual physical difference between forenoon and afternoon, even between night and day, in a nuclear submarine. All times were the same. But the traditional shape of the day was preserved, with breakfast in the 'morning' and supper in the 'evening'. The lights were lowered and everybody went to bed at 'night', as though it were nighttime – 'We're just like battery hens' as Leading Seaman Basing had once remarked. Sam often thought of the preamble to the Naval Prayer – 'who hast compassed the waters with bounds until day and night come to an end'. The worthy seventeenth-century bishop who wrote that would never have believed that it would actually come to pass. But day and night had indeed come to an end in a Bomber at sea, although they did have a Church Service every seventh day.

Draper was a sonar rating, and a good one. He was a capable man, in a branch of the Navy which was currently much in demand. He should have had a future in the Service. Draper was using a polishing machine on the compartment deck. This was not an aspect of the Navy which featured strongly in the recruiting advertisements. But at *Raleigh* at Torpoint, where the sailors did their basic training, there were lectures and demonstrations, seemingly a whole academic discipline, on how to clean a ship. There was even a display room, with every sort of brush and scrubber, polisher and cleaner, so that the trainees could get some practical experience. Because that, even now, even in a Bomber, was how the sailors still spent a good deal of their working time.

'Hear you've been having dreams, Draper?' Even as he said it, Sam realised what an unusual form of address it was. He noticed that Draper did at least have the grace to look somewhat abashed.

71

'Yes, sir.'

'What sort of dreams?'

'It's difficult to describe, sir.'

'Try.'

'Well, sir, I don't get them often . . .'

'How often?'

'Well again, it's very difficult to say, sir. I might go for a fortnight without having one, and then I might have them two nights running.'

'Have *what* two nights running?'

'Well, sir, as I said, dreams of being covered up, buried, for ever. Of just dropping down and down and never being able to get back up again.'

'That sinking feeling, you mean?'

'Yes sir, something like that.'

'You're trying to buy yourself out of the Andrew, aren't you, Draper? You're having us all on, about these dreams, aren't you?'

'Oh no, sir. I am trying to buy myself out, sir, but that's got nothing to do with these dreams. Or at least, they *may* be connected, sir. I am determined to get out, sir, that's true enough, I won't deny that. I'm willing to try anything to get out. Even standing for Parliament, sir.'

Sam had to laugh despite himself. 'I don't think that one holds anymore. It used to. But now I think if you lose the election you have to come back. That's if ever they let you go to fight the election in the first place.'

Sam paused. Draper should not have let it slip that he was willing to try anything, even a frivolous by-election candidature, to escape from the Service. But it was clear that he was determined, as he said. This sort of case, when a man genuinely wanted to leave, was comparatively rare. Many sailors talked about 'going outside'. They painted idyllic mental pictures of Civvy Street as a land flowing with milk, honey and unemployment benefit. They often pleaded, loudly but rhetorically, 'Roll on my Twelve'. But fewer sailors these days said that, and even fewer, especially amongst submariners, actually meant it. Even the non-volunteers for submarines, the so-called 'pressed men', generally knuckled down to the life when they got used to it.

'Dreams are not a good enough reason to leave the Navy, Draper. They're not even a good enough reason for leaving boats. Have you seen the Doctor about them?'

'Yes, sir.'

Actually, that in itself meant that Draper took them seriously. It was not every sailor who would go to the sickbay to complain of bad dreams. He would be laying himself open to too much unfriendly messdeck chiyacking.

'*Well*? What did he say?'

'Just gave me some pills, sir.'

'I see. Did you ask what sort of pills they were?'

'No, sir. Placebos, probably, sir.'

'I see.'

In its way, it was a significant reply. It showed Draper's level of education, and his sensibly cynical attitude towards the doctor and, through him, the wardroom as a whole. This was a new kind of sailor. That was hardly a new thought. In fact, it was now a very tired cliché. But it was still true, none the less. Sailors like Draper had passed examinations at school. They were highly qualified by the standards of the old Navy. Some of the weapons and electrical Polaroids in Joe's department, so Joe said, had A-levels in maths and physics. Draper's wife had a job. A well-paid one, so Sam had heard. Market research, or something like that. It was the wife's job that was, in fact, a main part of the problem.

But there might be one other aspect.

'Is it the . . .' Sam found that he hardly knew how to phrase the question. It was, he realised with surprise, the first time he had ever asked it of anyone. 'Is it the weapons we have on board that's bothering you?'

'Oh no, sir. Not at all.' Draper's laugh was obviously genuine. 'They're all full of Smarties anyway, aren't they, sir?'

'All right, carry on.'

'Aye aye, sir.'

Draper restarted his polishing machine. Sam could hear its characteristically low, melancholy, moaning noise for some distance as he walked on. It sounded just as though the deck-polisher had also had enough of the Navy.

It was going to be difficult to know what to do for the best about Draper. It would be bad for everybody if it were to be seen that it was very easy to work one's way out of the Navy. On the other hand, it would be equally bad to keep someone on board who had a grievance, who might not be absolutely reliable.

It was some time after stand-easy when Sam returned to the wardroom, and it was empty except for Hamish, who was having a cup of coffee and reading that day's news sheet. The W/T Office normally took in a twice-daily news broadcast when the boat was at sea and produced a news sheet, sometimes called the Polaris Post, with such items as the football results, a motorway pile-up, the weather, the winner of a big race, a rise in rates, sometimes a parliamentary report. It was the small change of news from home which preserved at least the semblance of normality, although, towards the end of a patrol, the news items often began to seem unreal, as though from some other planet.

'Morning, Hamish. Busy day?'

'*Comme d'habitude*.' Hamish did not look up from his reading.

Sam poured himself some coffee. He could understand why a young doctor came into the Navy: the experience, the ready money, the chance of some travel, even to gather some anecdotes to bore his family with for the rest of his life. But Sam could never understand why any doctor stayed in the Navy, where his practice would almost always be amongst young men and women who were, almost by definition, very fit. It must be professionally enervating, like being an officer in a ship which seldom went anywhere and where hardly anything ever changed. Polaris patrols were dull for everybody. For a doctor, they must be almost intolerable, until near the very end, when people often started to have fits of the 'glooms' and

74

suffered from depressions. Even then, there was nothing much a doctor could do, when the real cure was fresh air, a change of scenery and company, mail, and women. No doubt there was a case for having a qualified medical officer with every Polaris crew, but Sam had sometimes wondered how often the presence of a doctor on patrol had been vitally necessary, as a matter of life and death. Sam had a vague memory that one boat on one patrol had once had an outbreak of something, measles or mumps, or something like that. Maybe the doctor was just there to reassure the sailors that if anything went seriously wrong, they would be properly looked after.

'These dreams of Draper's, Hamish . . .' Sam sat down at the wardroom table opposite Hamish. 'What about them? Is there anything in them? *Is* he trying to work his ticket, do you think?'

Hamish deliberately finished what he was reading before looking up. 'Could be. But that doesn't mean the dreams are not genuine. They could be linked in some way.'

'Well, I don't know. I've been in boats for nearly eight years and I can't remember anybody suffering from this sort of thing before.'

'That still doesn't mean they've never happened, just because *you've* never come across them. Does it?'

'No, I suppose not. If you put it like that.' Sam wondered why Hamish was always so prickly. Possibly because he suspected Sam's doubts about the real necessity for a doctor in the boat.

With that awareness of the boat's attitude given him by long experience, Sam felt the deck tilting the slightest amount. They were coming up from deep this forenoon, probably to periscope depth. They might even be about to surface. Some submarine captains always ordered Diving Stations for diving or surfacing, making sure that they had all the most experienced people, the First Eleven, closed up. But this captain normally preferred to dive and surface off the watch, saying that he wanted everybody on board, no matter how junior, to get some practise in playing his part to the limits of his responsibility. Sam acknowledged that there was a great deal to be said for this point of view.

The Captain had been all smiles this morning. Perhaps his set-to with Sam the night before had cheered him up, but the Roaring Boy of the past few days had given way to Bonnie Prince Charlie, and all was sweetness and light. Sam was grateful for the respite, although he knew from experience that this change of role might not, in the end, be for the better. Besides, submarines had a way of punishing cheerfulness. Just as one thought one had all one's problems hacked, something unexpected happened. *Hubris* often had a way of being followed by *nemesis*.

As though in response to Sam's very thought, there was the lightest of shudders underfoot. Sam jumped up at once and pushed past Hamish's startled face. He could already hear the Captain's voice from the control room. There were hard words and harsh words.

There, it came again, the faintest trembling, and the deck was tilting down again. Something had gone wrong.

When Sam reached the control room, he saw the Captain still at the after periscope, which was still raised, although the deck had a steep angle now and the boat was passing one hundred feet.

'I daren't lower it! It may be bent!' The Captain was shouting at Sam as though it were his fault. 'Some bloody thing up there! We must have grazed it!'

The Roaring Boy was back again, and on full song.

'Did you feel it?'

'Yes, sir, I did.'

'Must be some bloody fishing boat . . .'

Sam pursed his lips. There were precious few fishing boats about these days.

'. . . Or some bloody yacht. Whatever it is, it must be stopped, and it must be small.'

Coming from deep to periscope depth was always a delicate process for a submarine; there was only one manoeuvre more hazardous, and that was actually surfacing. Checks had to be made, by listening carefully all round, that the submarine was not about to rise directly underneath a vessel on the surface. Even when there were no sonar contacts nearby, it was still possible to come up under a stationary ship.

But their sonar gear was superb. It could detect a shrimp farting at a hundred miles.

The Captain had obviously had the same thought at the same time as Sam. 'Sonar, this is the Captain, who is on watch?'

'This is Sonar. Draper, sir.'

Draper! Sam could not avoid catching the Captain's eye. But the very notion was fantastic. Nobody but a lunatic would hazard the whole submarine because he himself wanted to leave the Navy.

'This is Sonar. There are no contacts other than those already reported, sir.'

'Very good.'

Sam was already regretting the unworthy thought he had had about Draper. He hoped the Captain had, too.

Jimmy the Sonar Officer was officer of the watch in the control room. He was standing, looking at the Captain's face, waiting for the Captain's decision.

'One hundred and fifty feet, sir.' The planesman was reading off his depth gauge.

'Very good. Keep two hundred feet.'

'Two hundred feet, aye, aye, sir.'

Sam pulled at Jimmy's sleeve. 'James, tell me one thing. Why is Draper on sonar watch? He was polishing the deck up forward only a short time ago.'

'He's relieved Wrigley, who had the forenoon.' Jimmy did not take his eyes off the Captain's face. 'Wrigley's got Captain's requestmen in half an hour's time. For his Good Conduct badge, remember? He had to go away and clean.'

'Oh yes, I remember now. Got it.'

'Although whether it'll actually happen now, in view of all this, I don't know.'

The Outside Wrecker had arrived in the control room and

was looking up at the raised after periscope with a paternal but aggrieved look on his face. He always took any defect in any part of his department as a personal affront.

Chief, too, had arrived from aft, in response to some summons Sam had not heard. The Captain beckoned to him, and nodded to Sam to join them.

'What do you think the damage is, Chief?'

Chief shrugged his shoulders and gestured helplessly in the general direction of the periscope. 'I honestly don't know, sir. We'll have to have a look.'

'Did you hear anything back aft?'

'Not a thing, sir.'

'Will it affect the patrol, that's the question. Do you think it will?'

'Once again, sir, we won't know for certain until we've had a look.'

'I suppose we could call off the rest of the Index programme and go back now. One day off the Index wouldn't matter all that much. I want to give the periscope boys inboard as much time as possible, in case it does affect the sailing date.'

'We could change the periscope in a forenoon, given a bit of luck, sir. Once we get under the crane. Then all we have to do is line it up with the torpedo tubes. Should be no problem, sir. That's if there is anything wrong with it. Which we don't know yet.'

'We could send the divers out to have a look, sir?' Sam thought his suggestion an excellent one, considering they were on an Index. It would tell them what they wanted to know about the periscope, and exercise the divers realistically at the same time. But the Captain appeared to regard it as frivolous.

'No, no, no, no, that won't do. We'll go back. Fetch me a signal pad. Pass the word, the boat will be surfacing in twenty minutes' time.'

'Aye, aye, sir.'

'And, Jimmy . . .'

'Sir?'

78

'Have Draper relieved on the sonar.'

'Aye, aye, sir.'

The Captain turned, to face Sam squarely. 'That does it. Dreams or no dreams, Draper's had his time in this boat.'

CHAPTER 4

THERE WAS, SAM DECIDED, definitely an air of spring about the place, as they turned the corner to head up the loch. There were still very few leaves on the trees, but then they always were later in this God-forsaken part of the world. But the hills on either side were definitely a different, lighter colour, and the air temperature was certainly milder. As Leading Seaman Basing would say, even the rain was warmer.

Sam looked up at the after periscope, which was still raised, as a precaution. There seemed nothing much wrong with it, at least nothing visible. But there had been no question that some part of the boat had hit something. That slight shuddering had been like nothing Sam had ever experienced before, but he had known at once what it was. It had been an omen, a harbinger of a much more serious collision, a reminder that, after all, it was only a thin skin of metal that kept the water out. There had been some very concerned faces in that control room.

It was extraordinary how quickly, once the decision had been made, they had started for home. It seemed only moments ago that they had been at sea, dived, looking inwardly upon themselves, preoccupied with all the problems of working up the submarine for its next deterrent patrol. Now, here they were, on the surface, in the fresh air, with an unexpected weekend in harbour.

Clearly, they were also unexpected by the base. As the tugs pushed the submarine's hull closer to the jetty, there seemed to be only one man there to greet them and Sam recognised him as one of the periscope department. Verily, in this base, the right hand knoweth not what the left hath been doing since stand-easy.

But, in time, more figures appeared, with wires, and a sack of mail, just as though the message had at last passed around the local grapevine. There was the duty staff officer and somebody from the base maintenance office. Slowly, the base was reacting to this unlooked-for and unwelcome arrival. It was, after all, getting towards evening and this submarine base was known to function much better during normal working hours – normal base working hours, that is. Like some giant saurian, its blood always began to run more slowly as the sun went down.

The first hour after entering harbour was often the busiest of all for Sam. But on this occasion the general air of lethargy seemed to come up the gangway with the mail. Unusually, there seemed to be no urgency about anything. The Captain disappeared inboard at once, to make his peace with the operational staff, and to scotch any false rumours before they could gain currency and credibility. There were some sailors who wanted to take advantage of an extra unexpected weekend at home with their wives. There were some possible weekend trot movements for the periscope change to be organised, or at least pencilled in on the programme. There were some odds and ends of stores and paperwork, but then, there were always those.

But otherwise, there was nothing to stop Sam walking ashore, as he always did when the boat came in. It was not so important now, after only a short Index, as it would be after a patrol, but still Sam liked to get ashore first thing, before he even telephoned Janet, and simply stretch his legs. For the first time in days and often in weeks he could take as many and as long strides as he wished. He could run a hundred yards flat out in a straight line if he wanted to, although he would probably not be able to.

But first there were the MoD PloD, with a sergeant, on the gate.

'Got your base pass, sir?'

The sergeant's actual words were correct enough. But the manner was surly and aggressive. Sam looked down as the sergeant examined his pass minutely. What an exquisite joy it would be, Sam thought, to be able to kick that fat farting MoD PloD bum clear across the road.

The sergeant handed the pass back without a word. Sam set off up the approach road. He broke into a trot. He stopped, breathing deeply, in and out, in and out, with exaggerated curling of his nostrils. He set off again at a very rapid walk, swinging his arms ostentatiously high. He knew that the MoD PloD were watching him curiously. The hell with them. He started to trot again and, as he did so, he became aware of the uproar at the end of the approach road. It sounded almost as though it were coming from the main road, from the peace camp.

His jogging became running. He ran, as fast as he could, round the corner to a point where he could see the peace camp on the other side of the main road. There were figures running through the camp. One of them stopped, put both hands against the side of a caravan and began to rock it so violently that a washing line stretching from it to a tree broke and all the clothes fell to the ground. Sam could hear the angry shouts, as he came closer. He saw Mary Carmichael appear, running and being chased by a man in a blue bomber jacket.

He stepped on to the main road and at once the loud blast of a horn made him stop and draw back, as the car rushed past him, only a foot or so away. He had to wait while two more cars passed before he could start across the road. The man in the jacket put his arms around Mary Carmichael and lifted her bodily off the ground. He saw El Tel emerge from behind the main communal caravan, in pursuit of another man. But when El Tel saw Mary Carmichael's struggles, he stopped in his stride, clasped both fists together and brought them down on her assailant's head. The man let her go and ran off to join some others. There seemed to be several of them, and as they went off they seemed to join together in a bunch, and then separate,

82

and then join together again, like a family of starlings on the wing.

Sam stepped off the main road and up on to the grass beside the camp caravans.

'What's going on?'

El Tel glared at him. 'Who wants to know?'

Sam realised, and was faintly disappointed, that El Tel had not recognised him. But there was not much reason why he should, after such a brief encounter last time.

'Oh, I remember you.' His Cockney accent was still very noticeable. Maybe it always would be, up here in Scotland. 'It's our *punctured* friend, from the Bomber. Sam, Sam, the nuclear man, ain't it? You're back early, aren't you? Thought you weren't due back till next week?'

Sam forebore to comment upon El Tel's information or its accuracy. 'What was going on here? I heard a sort of furore and the next thing I knew I could see people running amuck through your camp. I came across to see if I could help.'

'Extremely good of you, I'm sure. It was just our usual Bank Holiday visit from the Scottish Nazi Party.'

'Ye ken there's no such a thing!' Mary Carmichael's evident indignation at El Tel's suggestion made her accent much more noticeable.

'Well the English Nazi Party, then. It's all the same thing.'

'Good God, is it a Bank Holiday?' Sam had completely forgotten it.

'Yes. It's the merry month of May. Don't you keep Bank Holidays in your line of business then?'

'Yes we do, of course we do. It's just that one gets sort of disorientated once one gets on board. The seasons don't seem to mean so much.'

'What a hell of a life *one* must lead. I'm glad I'm not you.'

'Well, I'm glad I'm not you.'

'Well, we're both satisfied then, aren't we?'

Over El Tel's shoulder Sam could see more of the members of the camp. They were all wearing similar clothes, blue anoraks and jeans, like a kind of uniform. One of the men had a

83

beard. Somehow, Sam had expected all the men to have beards. They were beginning to clear up, picking clothes off the ground, re-erecting the canvas shelter which served as a porch for their main caravan, straightening a bench, retrieving a cooking pot which had been kicked over. There seemed to have been very little harm actually done, in the end. Nor did the campers appear very much ruffled by the disturbance. Obviously, such things were an occupational risk for them.

'Are you going to tell the police? Report this?'

'No fear.' El Tel grimaced. 'Fat lot of good they would do. We've got a pact with the plod. They don't bother us, we don't bother them. Besides, we know who's behind all this. Some yobbos in Glasgow. They get stroppy from time to time. They feel the spring coming on.'

Sam looked at the tall trees on the other side of the road. Not a vestige of a leaf on any of them. Why were Scottish trees without leaves so peculiarly depressing? Sam felt melancholy just looking at them.

'Not much sign of spring here.' The tops of the trees were moving now, to a wind they could not feel down here.

'Reminds me of "That time of year thou may'st in me behold, When yellow leaves or none or few do hang . . ." '

' ". . . Upon those boughs which shake against the cold." Go on.'

' "Bare *ruined* choirs, where late the sweet birds sang." '

'I didn't know you would know that.'

'Why not? We're not *all* yobbos, you know. I didn't expect *you* to know it, come to that.'

'Why shouldn't I? *We're* not all yobbos, either.'

'Would you like a cup of coffee? I think we deserve it, after that. You, certainly. What do you think, Mary? After all, you were going to help us, weren't you? You would have done, wouldn't you, if you hadn't nearly been run over.'

So El Tel had noticed his episode on the main road. Evidently he did not miss much. El Tel would have made an excellent officer of the watch.

A car hooted its horn as it passed on the road, and the driver

84

held up his thumb and grinned at El Tel. El Tel held up his thumb in salute and waved.

'If you think the same way we do, hoot your horn.'

'A cup of coffee would be splendid. Thank you very much.'

'Would you like to come into our caravan then?' Mary Carmichael was gesturing towards their communal van.

'Yes please. Are you all right now? I saw one of those fellows handling you rather roughly.'

'Och yes, I'm fine. It takes more than that to bother me.'

Their caravan was rather bigger and much better furnished than Sam had expected. There was a large table at one end, with a tartan rug spread over it as a table cloth, and benches round the walls, giving seating for at least eight or ten people. By the door was a cooking stove, with Calor gas cylinders beside it, and a rack for plates, and a shelf stacked full of pots and pans. There was a cupboard, painted baby blue, with a glass front, through which Sam could see tins of soup and ravioli, and pots of jam, and a rack for eggs. On the other side of the cupboard, next to the table, was a very large refrigerator, with a deep freeze compartment below. Sam had half-expected the atmosphere of a gypsy encampment. But not at all. Quite the contrary: the whole kitchen area, with its economical use of space, and its air of practical utility, reminded Sam, in some odd way, of the galley on board.

On the opposite wall, there was a noticeboard, a bookcase and a wardrobe, and more benches set out from the wall. The noticeboard was fully papered, leaving not a fraction of a square inch of spare space, with, Sam could see, a curious mixture of the domestic and the didactic. There was, for instance, a printed timetable of the buses to and from town and beside it a portrait of the Prime Minister, disfigured by a ridiculously gigantic red clown's nose. There was a cutting from a newspaper, with a photograph of somebody, obviously a peace protester, struggling in the arms of the police. Beside it, and partly obscuring it, was a letter carefully written in what looked like a child's hand. Sam stood up close to read it: it was from a schoolgirl in Weston-super-Mare, asking for information on peace camps for her school project.

Sam's eye moved to the bookcase. He was astonished to see three copies of *Jane's Fighting Ships*, one of them the latest edition. The shelves below were crammed with books and with various issues of magazines on defence and naval subjects. Sam could see a row of copies of one particular magazine which he knew was officially classified as 'Restricted' and was thus supposed to be made available only to those authorised to see it. It was never to be communicated to the press or to any unauthorised persons – amongst whom, Sam was certain, the Ministry of Defence would undoubtedly have included El Tel and his fellow protesters.

'Surprised? You should see your face, mate. It's a picture. Know your enemy, that's what I always say.'

'Yes, indeed. I was surprised, but I suppose I shouldn't be.' It was, Sam supposed, only to be expected, now he came to think of it.

'We've got lots of books on submarines, too.'

'Yes, I see them.' They had, indeed, as good a library on the Trade as Sam had ever seen in one place, certainly better than the base wardroom library. There were books on submarine policy and tactics and weapons, books of wartime reminiscences by submarine COs, recognition books with photographs and silhouettes of submarines of all nations, studies of nuclear weapons and the strategic balance between nations, and even some copies of Hansard, probably with some parliamentary debate on submarine nuclear weapons. But after all, Sam reflected, there was nothing surprising in this. These people had books on submarines, just as people who hunted acquired books on venery.

'Who reads them all?'

'I do. We all do. Who do you think reads them?'

Sam looked at Mary Carmichael. 'Do *you* read them?'

'No. They're mostly Terry's books. In fact, they're *all* Terry's books. I don't read them. They're too gloomy for me.'

86

'Hear hear.' Sam clapped his hands together briefly. 'Submarines can be gloomy.' He wanted to bring Mary Carmichael into their conversation, and he was suddenly conscious that his first-hand knowledge of the world of submarines would enable him to score over El Tel.

'Well, I didn't say we *all* read them.' El Tel was flushing a little. Not for the first time, Sam noticed that where Mary Carmichael was concerned, El Tel became suspicious and defensive and prickly.

While El Tel still had his anorak on, Mary had taken hers off and hung it carefully on one of a row of hooks by the door. She was wearing a plain white T-shirt, with no design or device or slogan on it. It was crisp and clean, somehow innocent, almost virginal. She had a very full figure, which the anorak had hidden. So many of these Scots girls were big-breasted. But Mary did not also have the correspondingly large hips, under her blue jeans. It would be very pleasant to see her naked.

'Again, you should see yer face, mate. I know what you're thinking. Don't.'

'I'm sure I don't know what you mean.'

'You do.'

'Here we are. Here's the coffee.' Mary was pouring boiling water from an electric kettle into some mugs. The mugs were of thin, fine china, with a striking design of rainbow-coloured humming birds on them. Sam noticed for the first time the carpet on the floor, which had a deep pile and a distinctive Persian pattern. The whole caravan was almost luxuriously fitted out, absolutely different to anything he had imagined.

There was no sign of the bearded peace protester Sam had seen outside, but there were two others sitting at the table. They had not said anything at all since Sam had come in, but had just stared at him intensely in silence. He was reminded of young children in the presence of strangers in their home, and he also had a memory of a television programme he had once seen, of some primitive native tribe in the Amazon who had to watch strangers for some time before they could communicate with them.

Mary put the mugs down in front of them. 'Gillie. Desmond. Here you are.'

Gillie was a huge slut of a woman. She was wearing a crumpled and grubby-looking Disneyland T-shirt over her bulging figure. She had long straight dark hair, and a pasty puffed face, with the marks of pimples on her chin. She scooped three heaped spoonfuls of sugar from a bowl into her coffee and stirred it with the spoon. She continued to stare steadily at Sam whilst sipping her coffee. He noticed that her forefinger was heavily nicotine-stained. Gillie, he decided, was much more like the image the submarine base had of 'those women'.

'Desmond's our climber.'

Desmond was a little man, almost bald, with a chirpy manner. He wore a red-and-white checked shirt and brown braces. When he grinned, he showed he had a front tooth missing.

'Climber?' Sam looked at Desmond sharply. 'What sort of climber?'

'Anything you like, Guv.' Desmond, too, was a Cockney, or at least his accent was definitely from somewhere in the south.

'Can you climb the wire round the submarine base?'

Desmond laughed, evidently expecting that very question. '*Especially* the wire round the base. Many times.'

'Have you tried this new wire?'

'Not yet. But it won't be no problem.'

'I wouldn't be so sure, if I were you. It'll cut you to pieces if you get tangled on it.'

Desmond ducked his head, as though in modesty. 'I won't. It'll be worth it, just to show the plod as the stupid pricks they are.'

'It was the plod who knocked out Dessie's tooth.'

'Oh? When was that?'

'Right outside the gate 'ere. Last autumn. And then they had *me* up on a charge of assaulting a policeman. The plod swore blind they never touched me and the magistrates believed them. They fined me, said I was lucky not to go to jail, and commended the fat lying plod. And afterwards, d'you know what that copper said? He said he wished it had been *both* teeth. That's the reason I'm 'ere, to get me own back on those stupid fucking coppers.'

'Well, *that's* not a very profound reason for protesting against nuclear weapons, just because you don't like the police, is it?'

'There's more to it than that.' Once again El Tel was their chief spokesman. He might disclaim the leadership of this camp, but clearly he was their leader in all but name. 'There are all sorts of reasons for being here, and all of 'em complicated.'

'How many are there of you? There always seem to be a lot of you, that's the impression you give, but perhaps that's because you make yourselves very visible. How many are here on a normal day?'

'That's classified. But I'll tell you all the same. There's no set figure. It varies. Sometimes, when we've got something special on, there might be a couple of dozen actually here, with more staying around the place. Other times, it goes down to four or five, depending on who can come here. Sometimes it's just Mary.'

'What, all by herself? Is that safe?'

'Quite safe.' Mary spoke for herself. She seemed the only other one there who was up to El Tel's stature as a personality. 'It's never bothered me, and anyway it's only a day or two at a time.'

'And when have you next got something special on, as you call it?'

'I'm not telling you that, mate. You'd go straight to the fuzz.'

'I doubt if I would, actually.'

'Well, as a matter of fact, we usually tell them beforehand ourselves. It's as much to our benefit as anybody.'

'It's funny, you've got this attitude towards the police, and yet you rely on them for law and order so you can do your demonstrations.'

'You're learning all the time, aren't you, mate? Since you're so interested, I'll tell you. We have got something on this weekend. We've got some people coming up from the south and the Midlands today. They're hitch-hiking, so we don't know when they're arriving, or how many of them there are. When they get 'ere, *if* they get here, we'll decide what to do. But the fuzz already expect us to do something this weekend. This is the weekend we always remember somebody.'

El Tel reached up to the bookcase and took down a very large book which had been lying on the very top. He put it on the table and opened it. Sam could see that it was a scrapbook, full of newspaper cuttings, some pasted in, some loose, and some photographs.

El Tel had the book open to show the photograph of a fair-haired young man, wearing a sweater. Sam could see at once that he did not look at all like a peace protester. He clearly was what Sam's mother would have described as 'a cut above that sort of thing'.

'That's Martin. He was killed at a demonstration during this Bank Holiday three years ago.'

'Where was that?'

'Right here in town. Under the eyes of the good solid Scottish burghers of this good solid Scottish burgh. You could say the fuzz killed him.'

'I don't believe it!'

'There was a scuffle in the road. I myself saw a policeman grapple Martin and trip him up. Martin fell and hit his head on the kerb. Knocked himself out and never recovered consciousness. They took him to the Infirmary in Glasgow. They operated on him. They did everything humanly possible, as the saying goes. But he died. So every time this Bank Holiday comes round we remember him.'

'But that could have happened anywhere, any time, an accident like that.'

'It could. But it didn't. It happened here. And it wasn't an accident. That policeman is still on the force here. He's up here at the camp whenever there's any trouble. It's as though they send him specially, just to remind us.'

'I don't believe it! The police don't behave like that!'

'If you really believe that, then you know sweet eff-all about the plod, mate, let me tell you.'

El Tel tipped the book up, so that he could study the photograph. Sam saw that the letters R.I.P. had been written underneath it. 'He was a nice bloke, Martin. I admired him. Eton and Sand'urst. Royal Green Jackets. 'Is old man was a general. Spoke with a *very* far-back accent. But he got fed up with the army, and weapons and all that sort of thing, and one day he just joined us. Sent in me papers, old *boy*, he used to say.'

The mimicry of the accent was so brilliant, the intonation so eerily accurate, that for an unnerving moment Sam wondered whether it was El Tel's Cockney accent which was assumed.

'It must be nice to be able to do that. Just send in your papers, and go. Old *boy*.'

It was almost as though El Tel were actually mourning a lost leader. It could even be that El Tel himself had been trying ever since to live up to that dead man's image. Sam guessed that Martin had already become part of the peace protesters' mythology. Like everybody else, they needed their heroes, their lost leaders, their legends and their mythology. Maybe it was not so surprising, after all.

'What else have you got in that book?'

'Have a look. See for yourself.'

It was just like a family photograph album. There was even an invitation to a wedding, at the register office in town, with pictures of the happy couple and their guests, amongst whom Sam recognised Mary Carmichael, and El Tel, and Desmond.

'Is this two of your camp mates, getting married here?'

El Tel leaned over, to squint at the pictures. 'Yep. Marlene and Tartan Tommy. They met here at the camp.'

The groom was indeed wearing a kilt.

'I must say, it's rather sweet. A camp wedding.'

'Very sweet. They're divorced now. Tartan Tommy still campaigns a bit. He might even be coming up tonight. But

Marlene . . . God knows what's happened to her. Just dropped out. I think she was only here for sex. Men used to come round enquiring for her, and she used to give *massages*, she called them, in her caravan. She gave the camp a bad name.'

It was interesting that El Tel should attach such importance to the camp's reputation. It gave a clue to the word Sam had been searching for in his mind, to describe the peace camp and its inmates. The word was *respectability*. The camp was intensely *respectable*.

Sam turned over more of the pages. There was a copy of the 'Wishing you all a Merry Prixmas' Christmas card. There were photographs of the various stages of the building of the base, and pictures of the wire barriers, getting higher and higher and more formidable as the years went by. Nobody had watched the building of the base more closely, or recorded its growth more carefully, than the campers at its gates.

There was even a picture, taken from the roadside, of Desmond, grinning triumphantly from inside the wire as the police led him away. In a sense, this scrapbook was valuable local history. It constituted the peace camp's newspaper, its archives, its parish records, its Squadron Line Book.

There were newspaper cuttings by the score, filling most of the book: protesters being carried away by the police, people laying down in front of cars, politicians, some of them very well known and including two Secretaries of State for Defence, quite patently being booed and jeered and heckled.

There were countless reports of court cases. Sam looked at one picture of a girl coming out of court, with a scarf hiding her face. According to the cutting, she had refused to give her name, insisting on being addressed as 'Number Fifteen'. Under that pseudonym she had been bound over to keep the peace.

'You must be popular with the local newspaper. You've given them any amount of stories, and cracking good pictures, over the years. It looks as if you're nearly always on the front page, whenever you've done something, or anything's happened.'

'Too right. I know for a fact that one of the reporters is on our side. But like everybody else round here, he's in two minds about it. He's agin nuclear weapons, but they bring the money in, and the roads and the schools and the Royal Family. They come up here now, which they never did in the old days. And, as you say, we give 'em some good copy. Poor local Scots buggers, they dunno what to make of it, do they?'

'Don't you dare call them poor local Scots buggers, a cocky wee Cockney like you.' But Mary Carmichael was smiling as she said it. It was obviously part of a game the two of them played together.

Something in the shape of her face caught Sam's attention. He looked down at the scrap book again. 'You wouldn't be Number Fifteen, by any chance, would you?'

'Of course. Very clever of you.'

'But why did you hide your face and refuse to give your name?'

'But why not? It's all a farce anyway. That was one case where the local reporters were on our side. They all knew who I was, but none of them let on in print.'

'Even though you were local? That would have been an even better story. You *are* local, aren't you?'

'Even though I was local. Yes, I'm from Alexandria. Me father used to work in the torpedo establishment.'

'Good heavens! That *is* a turn-up for the book! What does *he* say about your presence here?'

'Oh, he died.'

'What about your mother, then?'

'Oh, she's gone to live with ma elder sister in the south. I've never discussed it with her.'

'What is this, "This Is Your Life"?' El Tel had been showing signs of growing impatience. 'Can we break up this edition now, do you think?'

'Och, don't be so mean. It's nice if someone shows an interest in you. I'm flattered.'

'Oh, cor blimey O'Reilly!'

Sam finished his coffee. It was supermarket instant stuff, but it was hot and good and very acceptable, much better than Pussers. 'Thanks for the coffee. I was going to wish you all luck but in view of what you say you may be up to this weekend I don't think I can.' Sam looked at Desmond. 'Best of luck with the wire, anyway. I have a feeling you'll need it.'

'Not luck, Guv. Skill.'

'Okay, have it your way. I'll watch the news broadcasts.'

'Haven't we managed to convince you of anything yet, then?' That aggressive look was back on El Tel's face.

'About your opinions? On nuclear weapons and all? No, you haven't. Well, you haven't really tried, have you? Besides, my opinions and yours are so far apart, there's not a great deal of point in discussing it. I always think the Bomb is one of those subjects like fox-hunting and putting fluoride in the drinking water and bringing back capital punishment. Everybody's made up their minds about it years ago and they're not going to change because of anything you might say now. So there's absolutely no point in trying to talk to closed minds. You're wasting your breath.'

'Do you agree with fox-hunting and bringing back hanging then?' It was the first time Gillie had opened her mouth. For such an unpleasant-looking woman, she had a surprisingly pleasant and melodious voice.

Sam gestured, trying to register his helplessness at being asked to debate such things at such a time. He stood up. 'One thing I will say, because I believe in it passionately. It's a cliché but it's true, none the less. The Bomb has kept the peace for the last forty years . . . No, it's *true* . . .'

He simply had to pause, in the face of their expressions of disbelief and contempt. The bearded protester had just come in and stood by the door, with a smile on his face, as though Sam had just succeeded in fulfilling his most dire predictions about him.

'. . . There you go, you see. Closed minds, just as I said.'

'Nuclear weapons . . .' This time it was Mary Carmichael who was the speaker for them all. 'Nuclear weapons are morally wrong. Utterly and morally wrong.' Curiously, she had entirely lost her Scots accent. It was as though speaking of what they believed in divested their voices of all traces of their background. 'They are sinful in the worst possible way of being sinful. They offer man no hope of salvation and redemption. It is no good telling people they should not have them. We must do something else. We must make the first move. Somebody has to start somewhere. We decided that we must make a start.'

The others all made gestures and murmurs of approval. But Sam just stared at Mary. All this talk of damnation and hell-fire, it must be the old Scottish Calvinist feelings coming out. Perhaps anti-nuclear sentiment had a base in puritanism. That would make it even more difficult to debate against.

'But you've just said it yourself. It is no good telling people they shouldn't have nuclear weapons, you said. You must know they won't take any notice of you. You're going against basic human nature, you must know that. In war and politics, nobody ever does anything, ever, unless there's something in it for them, or unless they're frightened that something will happen to them if they don't.'

'What about love?'

'What about it?'

'Fear and greed. Just greed and fear. Is that what you think?'

'Well, yes, if you put it that way. But that's putting it far too simplistically.' Sam had the eerie feeling that he could hear himself actually speaking, as though from some distance away. He had not meant to broach this subject. He did not want to talk about it, not to these people. But it seemed to have arisen all by itself, like a squall arriving out of a clear blue sky. 'I don't care what you say, nuclear weapons *have* kept the peace for the last forty years or so, in a way conventional armies conspicuously failed to do before there were such things as nuclear weapons. It would be madness to give them up one-sidedly, unilaterally, as they call it, while your enemy still has them and while you cannot trust your enemy or his long-term intentions. We can't trust Soviet Russia. They have said all along they're going to try and bury us. They make no secret of their

95

intentions of making the whole world a single undivided Communist entity. That is what I sincerely believe. I respect your right to have an opinion. You must respect mine.'

'We do, we do. But all they want is peace.'

'Yes they do. That's quite right. They do want peace. But what they mean by *peace* is a state of affairs where all resistance to Communism has ceased, worldwide. That's what peace means to them. It is not what peace means to us. Not to me, anyway.'

'Don't you ever worry that you may one day have to fire one of those weapons on board your submarines?'

'Never.'

'*Never?*'

'Never. I've never lost a wink of sleep over it.' Well, hardly ever, Sam added to himself. It would be an insensitive and blockish man who never considered such an eventuality. Once again, he wished the subject had never arisen. He had never wanted to discuss it, and especially not here, amongst these people. It was as pointless as arguing against fox-hunting before an audience of Masters of Foxhounds. Sam felt his temper beginning to rise. He resented being spoken to in this way and made to justify his own existence.

'Nuclear weapons . . .' This time it was Gillie; as a group they were obviously practised in ensemble playing. '. . . Are the abomination of desolation, spoken of by Daniel the prophet, standing in the holy place. Whoso readeth, let him understand.'

Sam looked at her. 'I understand what your words sound like, but I don't follow their drift, exactly. Could you be a little less . . . Delphic?'

'Delphic Gillie!' Anything further she might have said was drowned by El Tel's laughter. 'I like it, I like it. Cap'n . . . Skipper . . . Number One . . . Sam, Sam, the nuclear man . . . whatever yer mates in that hell's torpedo call you, let's forget morality just for the moment. Let's get down to practical politics, since that is what our guest is interested in. Yours is a second strike weapon, right?'

'Right.'

'You'd never fire it first, right? Only in retaliation. That's what your book of rules says.'

'Right.'

'But can you imagine any possible state of affairs where the United Kingdom would use its nuclear weapons alone, without the United States?'

'It's difficult to say . . .'

'It's bloody impossible to say, mate.'

'No, what I meant is, that wars have a way of happening in a way you would never have anticipated. They say that you must always remember that if your enemy has three possible courses of action he can take, he will always choose the fourth. No plan of action survives contact with the enemy.'

'*Very* good.'

'Don't be so damned condescending! What the hell have *you* got to be so condescending about?'

Sam regretted the words as soon as he had said them. To lose one's temper was to lose it all. El Tel was clearly delighted by his palpable hit. '*I* say that the chances of this country ever using its independent nuclear weapons independently are nil. Zero. Zilch. It don't make sense. Our so-called independent nuclear deterrent is neither independent nor a deterrent. And think of the cost, mate! The cost of this base up here, and all the future buildings, and the cost of the boats themselves. You've got two crews, eating their heads off. Think what the Navy could do with the money they put into Polaris. Think of all the brand new toys you could buy . . .'

'On the contrary, Polaris costs less than two per cent of the defence budget.' Sam was glad to be on the rock of hard fact. 'It's extremely cost-effective.'

'*Cost-effective?*' There was what almost amounted to a growl around the table. 'Are you saying that after a nuclear exchange the last survivors on earth, if there are any, will be sitting in their fall-out shelters, congratulating each other and saying "Well, we certainly did *that* cost-effectively. Nobody could blow up the world cheaper than we did!" '

'No, that's not what I meant at all.' Sam stood up. 'I knew there was precious little point in discussing this. I said so.'

'Oh, I dunno about that, mate. I have the feeling you and I are going to have some *very* interesting conversations in the future.' El Tel was following Sam to the door. The bearded man looked as though he might stand in their way. El Tel waved him aside. 'It's okay, Josh. Did you find anything? No, I thought you wouldn't. They're back in Glasgow by now.' He turned back to Sam. 'You got off lightly, this once, mate. You must have something about you, that we all listened to you for so long without rushing your platform. But there'll be other times, I'm bloody certain. I'm looking forward to it. I'm very interested in submarine psychology.'

'Submarine psychology?' Sam grimaced. 'Didn't know there was such a thing. *Kiddology*, more like.'

'Kiddology! I like it, I like it!'

Sam turned at the door, to say goodbye to Mary. But she was already coming towards him. 'I'll come and see you off.'

El Tel was pulling another face. 'Like a good little hostess.'

Sam looked at the yellow van with the Gerard Manley Hopkins inscription, which was set back amongst the birch trees. The random placing of the caravans, as though they had all been driven up off the road and on to the grass and had just settled wherever they happened to stop, nevertheless gave them a functional but very pleasing appearance, almost as though the camp site had been carefully positioned, in a deliberate act of landscaping.

'Long live the weeds and the wilderness yet. Who thought of the Gerard Manley Hopkins?'

'Hey, you *are* a clever little know-all, aren't you? Sam, Sam the literary man. It was Martin's van once. He wrote that on there. He said his father used to quote it to him whenever they went shooting. Pheasants, that is, not people. *We* all 'ad to go and look it up, all us working class ignoramuses. Mary and I live there now. That is, whenever I'm up here.'

Sam had a sudden aching desire to look inside the yellow van. But he could not possibly ask. He walked on, feeling that

98

he had been excluded from something which might be of importance to him.

'I touch it up from time to time, when the weather looks as if it's going to rub it out. Keep it fresh-looking.'

'As if it's Martin's memorial?'

'Hey, watch it.' There was genuine alarm on El Tel's face. 'You're getting too close, mate.'

'Well, it's obvious you miss him. You don't have to be very clever to see that.'

'I do miss 'im and that's a fact. It grieves me to say it, but I miss 'is leadership, although that really isn't the right word. It churns me up inside, but it makes me think there might be something in this class business after all. People do look up to a certain kind of person. Somehow he could lead, without even thinking too much about it, because it was something he was always going to do. Family.'

'And now you're the leader.'

El Tel grunted. 'As I said, we don't have leaders. One or two of us give the thing a sense of direction, that's all.'

'And organise the protests, and all that. Looking at some of those pictures in that book, you're pretty violent sometimes, for people who call themselves peace protesters.'

'Ah well.' El Tel grinned. 'There's violent violence and there's peaceful violence. Nice to meet you, mate.'

Sam was surprised to see El Tel holding out his hand. He shook it.

'You may be somewhere to the right of Vlad the Impaler, mate, but it was nice to have something even approaching an intelligent conversation with somebody new.'

'I'll take that as a compliment.'

Sam looked over El Tel's shoulder. Mary had put her anorak on again and was standing behind him. 'Thank you for coffee and sympathy.'

'Och, yer welcome. Come again sometime.'

'Well, I'm not sure . . .'

'I suppose the base wouldn't like it, you hobnobbing wi' folk like us.' Her accent had returned in force.

99

'Well, I don't know, I've never asked them . . .'

'Yer doctor's been here.'

'*Has* he? When was that?'

'Some time back. When Marlene was having one of her turns. Tartan Tommy rang up the base and next thing we knew, there was this doctor. Very good-looking, too, in his uniform. We all wished we were ill, too. You must wear your uniform next time. I'd like to see you in it. Have you got any medals?'

'No. Nobody has, these days. Very few, anyway.'

'But you've got some gold lace on your sleeve?'

'Oh yes.'

'Good. I'd like to see it.'

'Well, as I said . . .' Sam wondered what the Captain's reaction would be, if he said he was going to call on the peace camp in uniform.

El Tel had been growing visibly restless, as he always did when Sam addressed himself to Mary. When there was a hoot from a passing car, he swung around as though glad of the interruption, to hold up his thumb.

'That's it. If you think the same way we do, hoot your horn.'

Sam looked at the car. 'I'm afraid that's not one of your supporters. That's my wife, coming to collect me.'

CHAPTER 5

'BUT WHAT WERE YOU doing there?'
'I was just visiting.'
'But why? For Heaven's sake, why?'
'You know I normally go for a walk as soon as we get in. I'd just reached the road opposite the camp when I saw there was a row going on or something, so I crossed to see if could help. Then I stayed for a cup of coffee.'
'*Coffee!*'
There was not a great deal of point in carrying on the conversation in this vein. 'Can you take me back to the base, darling? Drop me at the main gate, then hang on while I change, and collect my gear. I won't be long.'
'Was that the girl I saw on TV? That protester, one of those women?'
'Yes it was.'
'What were you doing with her?'
'I wasn't doing anything with her. Just drop me here, please. I won't be long.'
In fact, it took much longer than Sam had forecast. The Captain was back down in the boat. It seemed there was nothing amiss with the periscope, but they had decided to change it as a precaution. The final day's programme of Index was cancelled, but Der Tag for the patrol stood as originally arranged. There would be leave for the Bank Holiday weekend.
It was nearly an hour before Sam was able to return to the car, but any hopes he had that the atmosphere might have

cleared a little were dashed by one look at Janet's face. In fact, his very appearance and his apologetic manner as he made his excuses seemed to activate her anger again.

She started the car and drove off without saying a word. The camp appeared deserted, but while Janet was waiting for the traffic to clear before turning into the main road, the bearded one, Josh, came out of the main caravan and stood for a moment looking at them. Seeing him, Janet sounded her horn furiously.

'Oh, don't do that . . .'

But Josh had already acknowledged the salute, with a grin and a raised thumb. Janet gave him and the camp a venomous look.

'Cheek!'

'It's not cheek, darling, it's a recognised code. If you sound your horn, it means you agree with what they stand for. He was giving you the thumbs-up sign to show that he had heard you and was acknowledging you.'

'Quite the expert, aren't you. I don't know why I was so annoyed to see you standing with those women. It's so unlike you.'

'I told you, I happened to be passing and there seemed to be some trouble so I went to help. After all, they did help us change our tyre the other day.'

'Yes, but staying for *coffee* and all that . . .'

Janet was driving much faster than she normally did, sitting up closer to the wheel than usual, with a deep frown on her forehead, which showed how upset she was.

'Do slow down, darling. It's thirty-mile limit now.'

'I know, I *know*. What were they like, anyway?'

'Very pleasant. Very sociable. But argumentative.'

'I bet!'

But, as she turned into the bottom of their own road, Sam could sense that her anger was passing, and her curiosity was getting the better of her. Janet was never angry for long. Sam had learned, like his children, to wait until what his late father-

102

in-law had always called 'the crockery-throwing stage' was over.

'But really, what were they like?'

'Well, as I say, really quite sociable and pleasant. Mary, that's the girl you noticed on TV, made some coffee and . . .'

'*Mary*. So we're on christian name terms now, are we?'

'Well of course, darling. There's really nothing to it. As I say, they were quite hospitable. A *bit* stroppy, but no more than one would expect. After all, their whole lifestyle is protesting about something. At times I did feel a bit outnumbered. They did try to discuss nuclear weapons, but it's like talking about foxhunting or hanging. People have made up their minds and they're not going to change them because of anything you say.'

'You told them that?'

'Yes I did.'

'What did they say?'

'Well, I don't think they quite took it in. One of them did say . . . that chap you saw on the box, the fellow who mended our tyre . . . that I was somewhere to the right of . . . what did he say now? . . . I was somewhere to the right of Vlad the Impaler, but otherwise I was really quite a decent chap.'

'Oh, did he now? That's very big of him.'

Sam put his grip down in the middle of their hall, and stretched. Janet put her arms round his neck and kissed him.

'I'm sorry I was a bit offhand with you. Somebody rang me to tell me you were back and I thought I'd go and pick you up and give you a surprise and, lo and behold, there you were, hobbing and nobbing with the raggle taggle gypsies, oh.'

Sam found himself inwardly objecting to that phrase. But this was not the time to mention it.

She sniffed at his lapel. 'No matter what kind of submarine you're in, you've always got that same submarine smell when you come home.'

'Attar of diesel, we used to call it. I'm going to have a bath and then . . . where's Alice?'

'Over at Morag's.'

'Somebody bringing her back?'

'Yes. Mr Morag, when he gets home.'

'I tell you what, let's get hold of that babysitter and go out this evening. Have dinner at that hotel along Loch Lomond side.'

But when Alice had been delivered home and told them about her day and had been put to bed, and Sam had bathed and changed and fetched the babysitter, and Janet was just getting ready, the telephone rang. It was Danny Bennett, who was duty officer on board.

'I'm very sorry to disturb you, but I just thought I'd tell you there's a report of an intruder in the base.' Danny's voice was calm and unexcited. This did happen from time to time. 'I gather he may be making for the boat.'

'Have you seen anything down there?'

'No, not a thing. It's a message from the main gate. And the Royal Marine patrol is out. They've got their rigid raiders in the loch and we saw some of the patrol on the jetty just now.'

'Have you told the Captain?'

'No, I can't get hold of him. He's having dinner with somebody up at Arrochar and I can't find the number.'

'That's all right, now you've told me I wouldn't bother trying to find him. Do you want me to come down?'

'Well, that's up to you, Sam.'

There was a set routine laid down for this sort of occurrence and it seemed that everything was being done that ought to be done. Danny was perfectly capable of handling anything that might come up. There was no reason for Sam to go down. But he had the feeling that this was somehow connected with the peace protesters.

'I'll come down.'

The sun had set and it was now quite dark, but there was still that lovely turquoise blue and deep pink after-glow in the sky above the hills on the other side of the loch. It was too dark to see the small rigid raider craft but Sam knew they would be there. There was no sign of light or life at the peace camp as Sam passed. But the submarine base was ablaze, and the main gate was swarming with people, just as though somebody had kicked an anthill into life.

Sam stopped his car at the barrier, where the MoD PloD had signalled. There was some scuffling going on about twenty yards inside the base. Marines and PloD were struggling with somebody. It seemed they might even have caught the intruder. Sam got out of the car and stood beside it, to see better.

They had indeed caught somebody. As they came under the full glare of a floodlight, Sam saw the captive's bald head was gleaming and he realised with a shock that it must be covered in blood. The man was still wearing his braces. It was, as Sam had already been half-expecting, Desmond the climber.

Sam turned to get back into his car, but Desmond had already seen him.

'They've done it again, Guv!' Desmond had ducked down and Sam could see his head under the arm of the policeman holding him. He was not tall enough even to reach the shoulders of the police. He was shouting now, quite clearly at Sam. 'It weren't the wire. I got over . . . Let *go* of me, you poncey great Plod. Clean as a whistle. Not a mark on me. *They* did this . . .'

A policeman bent Desmond's body forward and pushed him into the back seat of a police car. By some trick of the floodlighting, Sam suddenly caught sight of the top of Desmond's head and saw the nature of his head injury. It was a great, slashing cut across the centre of the scalp which could never in a million years have been caused by a wire fence. Sam could hear Desmond still shouting 'Not the wire not the wire!' until the car door slammed shut.

The police car drove past Sam so slowly that he could see Desmond looking directly at him, with his mouth still working silently, mouthing something inaudible. Sam watched the car go, with the strange, sick feeling that he had just betrayed a friend. His mouth filled with saliva. Sam swallowed. What *could* he have done?

One of the MoD PloD was motioning him to get back into his car. 'Where are they taking him, do you know?'

The PloD shook his head.

'Is he going to get some medical treatment for his head?'

'I don't know, sir.' The tone of voice and the dismissive tilt of the head said I don't know and what's more I don't care and anyway it's none of your business, *sir*.

Everybody there must have heard Desmond addressing himself to Sam. But to Sam's surprise and relief, nobody asked him whether or not he did know the man. It seemed that it was of no interest to anybody in the base that a peace camp protester who was already known to the police and who had just been apprehended inside the base should apparently know an officer from a Polaris submarine.

Driving through the base, Sam saw two groups of Marines, one group actually wearing steel helmets. There were helmeted figures standing in the shadows, and vehicles parked without lights in entrances. Every boat in the base had its trot sentry on deck and clearly visible. The whole place had been thoroughly stirred up, and all because of Desmond the climber. Wee Desmond, as Mary Carmichael would say. Desmond's only motive would have been to ridicule the PloD by showing that their precious wire was not invulnerable. Had he been inside the base, Desmond would have felt exactly the same compulsion and would have done exactly the same, but he would have climbed the wire to get out instead.

Sam felt guilty about his knowledge, that he actually knew who the intruder was, had spoken to him, and knew something about him.

Danny himself was on the casing when Sam reached the tip of the gangway.

'Seen anything?'

Danny shook his head. 'Not a brass sausage. Disappointing really, it all helps to pass the time.'

'They've caught the chap. Well, they've caught a chap, I should say.'

'Oh good. Who was it?'

106

'Somebody from the peace camp.'

'Not the chap who changed my wheel . . .'

'No, no, somebody else, quite different.'

'D'you know, I'm quite glad it wasn't him. In some strange sort of way I didn't want him to be caught. He was quite a good bloke.'

'Yes. Yes, he was. Look, there's no point in me hanging around any longer. I'll push off now. Let you get your head down.'

'Oh yes, funny joke.'

The camp was still dark and deserted. Sam wondered what had happened to the extra protesters who were supposed to be coming up from the south that evening. It was curious that he now knew so much about the camp and its people. He would very much have liked to stop at the camp now, and try and check on Mary's safety. But that would simply not be possible.

Hardly knowing what he was doing, he drove past the camp, stopped, parked his car in a bus-stop lay-by, and walked back. He had had an excuse for what he had done before. He had no excuse for what he was doing now.

There was no sign of anybody at home. He was about to turn away, ashamed of himself, and relieved to have seen nobody, when the door of the Gerard Manley Hopkins caravan opened. Mary Carmichael was there, silhouetted by a single light shining from behind her.

'Och, it's *you*. Back again. Are we that fascinating? Could you not drag yourself away at all?'

'No, it's all this turmoil and uproar that's been going on down in the base. I was just passing and I stopped to see if you were all right.'

'Well, that's very decent of you. I hadn't heard anything.'

'Are you by yourself?'

'Gillie's around somewhere, I think, or she may have gone into town. Terry and Josh have gone into Glasgow to see somebody, or meet somebody, I'm no' sure. Desmond's gone down to look at the wire and prowl around. Case the joint, he says. I thought that was him coming back when I heard somebody.'

Sam could not bring himself to tell her about Desmond. He would have had to try and explain why he had done nothing, why he was still doing nothing. For the second time, he felt a traitor.

'Come in or go away, but just don't stand there. It's awful cold.'

He had longed to see inside the yellow van. Now that he was invited, the light was so dim he could hardly see anything. But it was tiny, with only two bunks, a folding table, a minute wardrobe, and a Lilliputian wash-basin. It was the smallest, barest, most chillingly cold and deeply depressing dwelling place he had ever seen. There was no room for a chair. They sat facing each other, one on each bunk, so close together that he had to sit sideways on the bunk to prevent their knees touching.

'Very cosy.'

'Och, it's okay for two. Terry's away a lot. And I know what you've been wondering.'

'What's that?'

'What does Terry mean to me . . .'

'There's no need to be so direct about it!'

'I do sleep with him sometimes . . .'

'Really, it's none of my business, and there's no need at all for you . . .'

'I do fancy him. But it's nearly always when *I* need to. Not him. He thinks he's in love with me. He's no'. He's in love with his campaign. It gives him a chance to be somebody. Organise things. Organise people.'

That, Sam reflected, was a very true and a very perceptive observation.

'He told you he had a garage. Did he tell you he gave it up to come here? He did work in a garage. But it wasnae his garage. He was just an employee. Now, Terry wants to make something of himself.'

'Good for him. Although I can think of better ways of doing it, and ones with rather more prospects.'

'He wants to go into politics.'

'Yes, I can imagine he would. But what about you? What do *you* want to do?'

She leaned back against the wall of the caravan and drew up her legs, so that her heels rested on the side of the bunk, and clasped her knees with her fingers. It was a gesture of withdrawal, as though she wanted to preserve her privacy.

'Let's not get talking about *that* just now, if you don't mind.'

'But I'd much sooner talk about you than about El Tel.'

'Oh you would?'

'Yes I would.'

'Have you got a wife to go to, at home?'

'Yes. Yes I have.'

'Well, you should go home to her then. And let me give you some more advice. Don't come round here any more.'

'You mean about El Tel . . .'

'No I *don't* mean about El Tel. I mean about *you*. This camp will do someone like you no good. This camp, the people in it, they're not for you. They'll do you no good at all.'

'Does that include you?'

'Aye, it does include me.'

'I was hoping it wouldn't include you . . .'

'Now you look here.' Sharply, she put her feet back on the floor again, and rested both hands, knuckles down, on the bed on either side of her. Bracing herself she glared at Sam with a look of contempt. 'You'll have to change your ideas about us, and sharpish, too. You belong on the *other* side of that road. You think you can just come round here and patronise us and look around you, saying "Good *Lord*, do look at that", like some sort of tourist, and play games with Terry and make eyes at me . . .'

'For heaven's sake, there's no need to . . .'

'You think I don't know what you're thinking when you look at me? Do you want me for . . . what do you call it . . . yer wee bit of *rough*, isn't that the phrase?'

He shook his head, although he was obscurely, shame-facedly, pleased by the word. It assumed a degree of social difference between them which he knew did not exist.

'Well, all you have to do is just say so. Do you want to see me? Do you want me to strip naked, for you to look at? Because I will. I'll do anything you ask. Just say. It doesn't matter a damn to me. Which do you want? Do you want to see me topless first?'

'No, I don't want you to do anything.' He could not have explained even to himself why her outburst had made him so sad so suddenly. Perhaps it had crushed hopes he did not even know he had had.

'Just as well. Now we understand each other, maybe you'll go.'

They both stood up and in doing so they collided. Involuntarily he put his arms around her. To his surprise, she kissed him.

'There.' She tilted her head back. 'You're no' such a bad sort, after all. Away ye go now, away home to your wee wifie.'

Her choice of words, and even more her tone of voice, maddened him. He tightened his grip on her body and kissed her, pressing down on her lips until she wrenched herself away.

'Brother.' She wiped her mouth with the back of her hand. 'That's enough, and more than enough. Now you'll go from here.'

Some spark of anger, or mischief, or resentment at being rejected, made him kiss her again, as roughly as before. Once more she pulled her body backwards and away from him. 'D'you *mind*. Now *go*.'

A third time, he bent down to kiss her, with the same violence. This time he fancied her body relaxed slightly, with the hint of submission.

'I'm not one of your sailors. Do this, do that. You can order people about on that side of the road. But not this side, understand what I'm saying? You don't belong here. This is another world.'

'Yes. I was aware of that, thank you.' He could not

110

understand why she had made him so angry. 'You could take it as a compliment. Some girls do, when they're kissed. To tell you the truth, I'm surprised at myself. I never thought I would ever find myself kissing you. When I first saw you I thought you were a bit of a bundle, though maybe worth unwrapping . . .'

'And I thought you were a self-conscious, pompous twit of a naval officer. But unlike you, it seems, I havnae changed my mind . . .'

'Self-conscious?' The word stuck, it was so unexpectedly insulting.

'Aye, you didn't know where to put yourself, or where to look, even.'

'Oh, didn't I?'

'But nae matter. I quite like you, for all that.'

'And I quite like you, too.'

'We both agree then.'

His blood had cooled. He bent forward again and this time he did not force, nor did she recoil. 'There.'

'Away with you.'

'I hope we meet again.'

'No' if I see you first. Hang on, I'll come with you. I wonder what's happened to Desmond, he's such an idiot in so many ways.'

Again, it was on the tip of his tongue to tell her, but if it had been difficult before, it was impossible now.

He left her standing on the grass in front of the caravans, staring across at the lights shining from the base. He saw her, still there, in his car mirror, as he rounded the bend and went over the brow of the slight hill and drove out of sight.

Janet was standing in their hall, with her coat on, and looking as if she had been waiting for some time, as indeed she had.

'Trouble at mill?'

'Yes, but all sorted out now.'

'Are we still going?'

111

'Of course. We've got the babysitter, you, the night and the music. Babysitter okay?'

'Yes. Watching the telly.'

'Let's go. I said we'd be there about eight o'clock. It's not too late.'

They went to the Tower o'Lomond, where they had sometimes been before on semi-special occasions. It had originally been the home of a wealthy Victorian Glaswegian businessman, who had evidently been reading, or had heard about, Sir Walter Scott. It was a great pile of a place made of stone faced with granite, with battlements, a vaulted archway over the front door, Italian marble tiles on the hall floor, a huge sweeping staircase, and a minstrel's gallery, bell-tower, and narrow, echoing corridors. The Glaswegian and his family had long gone, the first son and heir killed at Loos, and his great-nephew gone to San Francisco in the Sixties to practise flower power. The house had been a military hospital during the war, then a sanatorium for the shell-shocked, and finally a terminal home for aged gentlefolk.

Lately, the house and grounds, which were still famous for their rhododendrons and their views of Loch Lomond, had been bought by an entrepreneur from Leicester, who had plans to transform the property into a Leisure Park, with wild animals, a narrow gauge railway, a garden centre, motor cycling scrambles, a restaurant, and, it was rumoured in the local press, international nudist conventions.

Of these schemes, only the restaurant had been completed and was open for business. But clearly its new owner suffered from restaurateur's schizophrenia. The pictures on the walls of the main dining-room were vivid, even lurid, gouaches of Spanish street scenes and flamenco dancers, with large pale patches around them, showing the outlines of where the original "Monarchs of the Glen" and "Stags at Bay" had hung. The great fireplace, with a centrepiece medallion engraved with somebody's coat of arms, was piled with logs, but there was a fan-heater in front of them, and electric storage heaters around the walls. The tables were solid oak or elm, obviously original furniture bought with the house, and one of the tables would seat at least twenty people, but the table cloths were red-and-white check, as from a French bistro. The waitresses wore kilts, with long-sleeved white blouses, matador's waistcoats, and plastic roses in their hair. As the Captain was reputed to have said when he first saw it, 'It certainly had style'.

They had the table Sam liked and had asked for, by the window looking out on the loch, but there was not much competition. There were only three or four other couples eating, and one party of six.

The famous view of the loch was framed by two massive fir trees and by a bank of rhododendrons. The water was dark, with the sun long gone from it and from the hills behind. There were a few lights shining on the far side and the faintest silhouette of a small island, probably only visible to somebody who knew it was there and who was used to looking out over water by night.

A waitress brought them menus which had broad tartan borders and, in each corner, a picture of a set of bagpipes. As Sam studied his menu, the piped music began, seemingly directly over their heads.

'Bloody music. Even that can't decide what it's supposed to be. Like the whole place. Is it supposed to be Spanish or Scottish or what? Do you know what the Captain calls this sort of music? Ochayesak.'

'Shut up, darling, and order. She's coming back.'

'I'll have cock a leekie soup, just to be patriotic, and then I'll have steak au poivre. And I'd like mine rare.'

'You always have steak. You study the menu for ages and then you always have steak. I don't know why you don't just order it right away.'

'Got to keep up the suspense.'

'I'm going to have steak, too. Steak Diane. And I'd like mine well done, please.'

They brought the soup and Janet's whitebait, and a decanter of house red wine, which again, Sam said, was not sure whether it was Spanish or not.

113

'Well, at least that can't be Scottish.'

'Do you know the first time I ever came here?'

Janet methodically squeezed her slice of lemon over her whitebait. 'I believe you have told me.'

'It was years and years ago. Long before this owner, in fact it was probably two or three owners ago. In those days it was much more up-market than now and much more expensive. You really only came here if you'd just won the pools. I was fourth hand in my first boat, more or less day-running from here, and then we did Perisher running for a spell. I met this girl at a dance and I invited her on board the depot ship for something, supper and Sunday cinema or something, and ever afterwards her father kept on inviting me and another bloke, he was third hand of another boat, out to dinner. He had two daughters and he was quite clearly trying to marry them off. He must have spent a small fortune wining and dining young naval officers and generally taking them out and about. Because we weren't the only ones. He was always inviting blokes out with his daughters. Talk about baron strangling! Here was a baron absolutely asking to be strangled.'

'It was probably much cheaper than sending them to finishing school or university. Marriage may have been the best career for those girls. Maybe the only career.'

That was a very true and perceptive remark. And it led to another thought.

'Would you say I was self-conscious?'

'No. Would you?'

'No. Not at all.'

'Well, you're the best judge.'

'What would you say if I said I wanted to give up the Navy?'

'That's a bit sudden, isn't it? Now come on, darling, this conversation we've had before. We have it every now and again. I would say as I have said before, don't be silly.'

'What would you say if I said I was beginning to have doubts about nuclear weapons? If I said I was beginning to think the whole policy is a nonsense.'

'Well, there I'd tend to agree with you.'

Sam put his spoon down in astonishment. 'You *what*! You'd agree with me? But you've never said anything!'

'It wasn't for me to say anything.'

'Even though I was a volunteer?'

'Especially when you're a volunteer. It happens that I do think nuclear weapons and our nuclear deterrent are, well, not dangerous *nonsense* exactly, but a dangerous irrelevance.'

'Well, this is certainly a night for revelations. You've never said anything before?'

'You've never really asked me before. But in any case, what I think about it is really not relevant in the end. That's not because I think my own opinions are not important. It's because in this particular case we're talking about your job. You're a professional naval officer and you have to do what the Navy tells you. I realise that. I agree with that. And if the Navy tells you to serve in a Bomber then you serve in a Bomber. That is as it should be.'

'But you're my wife, you're entitled to say what you think. Maybe I would have done something different.'

'Do *you* think you would have done anything different, if I'd said anything? There'll be other jobs and other ships, which don't carry nuclear weapons.'

'But this will overhang everything, every other job. You can never get away from them. You can never ignore them.'

'I can. What do you think I do all the time?'

'Maybe. But that's not possible for me.'

'True. But, as I say, you have to do what they say. You have obligations.'

'Obligations!' Something about that word touched Sam on the ready raw, as though he had actually been waiting to hear it. 'I've had obligations up to here! All my life I've had *obligations*. I'm sick of obligations. Sometimes I wonder, why can't I just do what *I* want to do for a change? I'm absolutely sick of it.'

'Maybe. But the obligations are there and you can't escape them just by saying you're sick of them.'

'You know, there's something very old-fashioned about you.

115

You talk just like your father used to talk . . . And your mother too, come to that.'

'Now I *know* we've had this conversation before.'

'Things aren't the same today as they were for him, you know. He had a sort of . . . romantic? Is that the word?'

'Romantic was the word the last time we had this conversation . . .'

'He had a very romantic view of the Navy, a tremendously affectionate philosophy about it. I'm not knocking it. It suited him. It did his generation very well. But people of my generation don't feel that anymore. They don't talk like him anymore. They really don't, you know. Something has gone from the Navy. But something else had taken its place. For a start they pay people a half-way decent wage nowadays, which they never used to.'

'Is pay really all that important?'

'You and the rest would be the first to complain. As it is, we're a bit pushed. You'd be on to it like a flash if the pay didn't at least keep up with inflation.'

'No, I wouldn't, I'd get a job.'

'What, up here? In bonnie Scotland? There aren't enough of that sort of job for the native tribesmen, let alone Sassenachs like you. A job doing what, may I ask? You, and all the other wives who'd all be in the same boat. You'd all be literally taking in each other's washing.'

'You needn't be so dismissive about it. You're very good at putting me down. Sometimes I think you spend so much time and energy trying to understand that Captain of yours and his funny little ways, you've nothing left for me.'

'I'm sorry.' That, too, was an uncomfortably accurate accusation. 'But to get back to . . . We're a new generation now. We don't go for the sort of romantic stuff your father and his generation did. We just don't. It's the Navy that's just a job now.'

'I would have said that was ridiculous if I didn't know that you really believed that. I've known all along that you and my father had different views about the Service.'

'Now you're wearing your Celia Johnson hat. Don't you think all that "In Which We Serve" guff is a little old-fashioned now? That went out with the Ark. Did you know we showed it on our last patrol? Black-and-white. Noël Coward and Company.'

'Didn't you enjoy it? My father thought it was a masterpiece.'

'Well, he would, wouldn't he?'

'Oh don't be such a . . . But didn't you think it was good? Still?'

'Yes, in a funny sort of way. But it was old-fashioned. The accents so sort of cut glass . . . And Celia Johnson's speech about her great rival, the ship . . . It made me feel actually, physically uncomfortable. The Captain lapped it up, of course. I think his main feeling was that he was sorry he was not able to take part in it.'

Sam caught a glimpse of a kilt out of the corner of his eye.

'Was your soup all right, sir?'

'Yes thank you, lovely.'

'And you, madam?'

'Very nice, thank you.'

Sam watched the waitress bearing their plates away. 'It's all out of tins.'

'Oh don't be such an old misery-boots. Something's upset you and I wish I knew what it was.'

'Nothing's upset me.'

There was the light of a boat moving slowly across the lake. It was the tiniest pinprick, hardly visible through the window and from a lighted room such as this, Sam was pleased that he could see it so clearly. There was nothing wrong with his night vision. There seemed to be many more headlights on the lakeside road, just beyond the rhododendrons. They were much more noticeable, even obtrusive, than they had been.

Their steaks arrived. They both watched in silence as the waitress served the vegetables. The girl was using a spoon and fork in one hand, in the proper manner as she had clearly been taught, but she was not expert. Sam watched her vainly chasing vegetables round the dish for some time before he picked up a spoon and began to help himself.

'You don't mind, do you?'

'No, sir. I'll bring the mustard.'

Sam prodded the steak. 'Bet it's not rare.'

'Oh do get on with it and stop criticising. Mine looks delicious.'

'Have some more vino. It's dreadful, but it's cheap.'

'Just a little, a very little. I'm going to drive you back, remember.'

'I don't think the PloD will be waiting to ambush us when we get home.'

'Never mind, I'd rather not. Well?' Janet was staring at him intently.

'Well what?'

'*Is* the steak rare, or isn't it?'

'Yes it is.'

'Well don't sound so reluctant.'

'You know, I meant what I said earlier when I was talking about my doubts. I've got this patrol coming up. I'm going to be sealed away for weeks, with all the time in the world to wonder whether it's all worth it. For weeks you look at bulkheads, up close to you . . .' He held up the palm of his hand, close to his eyes. ' . . . Until your eyes start going round and round. And your thoughts, too. You know that song, "The Windmills of your mind"? Well, that's it. I'll be honest with you, I am having doubts. It's difficult to put into words. A lack of commitment. A lack of something, anyway. A feeling that it's not worth going on with it.'

'Oh Sam, let's not go on talking shop, please?'

'If I can't talk like this to my wife, who can I talk to? In any case, it's not shop. Well, if it is, it is everybody's shop. That is the curious thing. Until we had nuclear weapons, what sort of ships and guns and everything the Navy had were not ordinary people's concern. Oh, they might read about them, and some of them might be interested and queue up to go and see the ships on Navy Days and all that, but in the end what the Navy did was the Navy's business and only the Navy's business. But you can't say that any more. Can you imagine people a hundred years ago demonstrating and setting up a peace camp outside a dockyard where they were building one of those Victorian battleships with those huge guns? Or even fifty years ago, come to that. I was reading somewhere, do you know what Mr Gladstone said when they were showing him round the guns on one of those ships? Portentous weapons, he said, I really wonder the human mind can bear such a responsibility. You can just hear him, can't you? Portentous weapons, ye Gods. What would he say if he could see Polaris?'

'Your steak is getting cold.'

It was true, and Janet had nearly finished. Sam began to saw at his meat, consuming it in great lumps.

'Darling, the funny thing is, I agree with you. I agree with everything you say. But it's your job we're talking about. Your job. I'm glad you have these doubts. I'm very pleased you're sensitive enough to have them. I wouldn't like to think of you as some sort of macho man, all gung-ho, and bombs away. But in the end we come back to the same thing, it's your job, which you chose.'

After that, there seemed no more to be said. Janet drove home. Sam only broke the silence once.

'*Not* one of our better evenings.'

'Oh, darling, don't say that. I enjoyed it.'

'Good. I'm glad of that. It's just that I'm having one of my shivery "This could be the last time" sort of feelings.'

'If *that's* all you've got to worry about. You remember you had that premonition when we were going skiing? You nearly didn't go at all. And then nothing happened and we had a splendid time.'

They were turning into their road when Sam saw the police car.

'Good God, it's a PloD car, outside our gate! Just as well you're driving. I had most of that bottle.'

The police wasted no time. There were two of them and when Janet stopped the car in the short drive, they were already standing by the car's front windows, one on each side. They came to the point at once.

'Do you know a Mr Desmond Townsley, sir?'

Sam shook his head, pursing his lips. 'Nope. Never heard of him. Why?'

'He was apprehended in the submarine base earlier this evening, sir . . .'

Desmond! *That* Desmond. Desmond the climber. So that was his surname.

'He says you know him, sir, and would vouch for him.'

Sam looked at the policeman's face, and beyond him, at the implications of the question, and the dangers in it that lay ahead.

'Excuse me, I must get out.' Janet half-opened her car door. 'Our babysitter will be all of a twitter with all this going on.'

The policeman on that side of the car bent down to speak to her. 'Have you been drinking, madam?'

CHAPTER 6

'My GOD, I HOPE I never have another weekend like that. It was supposed to be a Bank Holiday. Some holiday.' Sam looked at his watch. 'What time's the Boss due?' He already knew the answer himself, but asked just the same, for something to say.

'Any moment now.' Jimmy the Sonar Officer was huddled, like Sam himself, in foul-weather oilskins. So, too, were the casing party, barely visible in the darkness forward and aft. It was a terrible evening, of wind and driving rain. White water was actually breaking over the bows of the two tugs, waiting in the middle of the loch. But otherwise all that could be seen of them were their steaming lights and their silhouettes, outlined against the lights on the far shore.

'What about that periscope?'

'Nothing about it. We've got it back, in the end. They can't find anything wrong with it. We must have all been mistaken. I'd swear we hit something. But there you are. The phantom collision.'

'Funny things happen at sea. I wish he'd hurry up.'

'Just giving the staff office inboard his *Nunc dimittis*, I suppose. Why does it always have to be such bloody awful weather whenever we sail on one of these?'

'Dunno. Sod's law. Feet are cold.' Jimmy was jumping up and down, lightly, on the balls of his feet.

'Did you know Janet was breathalysed?'

'Heard.'

121

'In our own drive!'

'Bloody disgraceful. Didn't know they could do that.'

'Neither did I. It seems they can.'

'She passed, though.'

'Yes. Bloody rozzers, they're always complaining about lack of manpower. They've got the men to do that when they want to. But if we were burgled, there wouldn't be a policeman for miles. I suppose you can't blame them. Most of the PloD up here, you wouldn't pay them to go on the dole, they're so thick and useless. But they join up, why not? Nice blue uniform. Eight to ten grand a year before too long, and all sorts of other financial perks, housing benefits and such-like, which they don't publicise much when they're talking about policemen's pay.'

'Well, we get some allowances, too, which we don't stress in public either.'

'Yes, I suppose so. I'm just getting all bitter and twisted.'

The encounter with the two policemen in their driveway had been just the start of it. Sam had had to go down to the police station, give his name and address, and submit to a series of questions which had seemed to go on interminably. The police had kept him waiting for twenty minutes before they even began to question him. Sam could still remember his rising resentment at the tone and manner of the interrogator, some young Inspector with a Glasgow accent you could have cut with a flick-knife.

Then there was the confrontation with Desmond, who had at once claimed a very much closer and longer-lasting acquaintance with Sam than was anything near the truth. He had actually met Desmond once, and briefly. But to hear Desmond, you would have thought that he and 'Guv', as he persisted in calling Sam, were old friends and even fellow-protesters. With the sensation that he was being drawn down into something, he knew not what, Sam had noticed the expressions of suspicion and contempt on the police faces, as they listened to Desmond's outbursts. They had treated him like a suspect. When he did get back to his house, he felt like a criminal, who had done something wrong.

Janet, still sore from the implicit guilt of being breathalysed in her own driveway, had waited up for him, and he had had to deal with her sense of puzzlement, that she had been excluded from something. What *had* he been doing at that camp? He had eventually placated her, but only at the expense of feeling that he had committed yet another betrayal.

From there, as Leading Seaman Basing would have said, the weekend had gone on downhill. Janet's mother had rung to say that she had fallen and bruised her hip. Alice woke up on Saturday morning sickening for something which the doctor said was very probably measles. On the television on Saturday evening, the peace camp was back in the news. The people El Tel had said he was expecting from the south had clearly arrived and it was obvious what they had come prepared to do. Sam sat and watched the pictures of the whole disorganised chaotic scene, of protesters struggling with the police, banners raised and torn down again, the figures, running and pursuing, the hostile, uncomprehending faces and the seemingly meaningless violent movement, with a sick dismay, as one who knew more than he should about such matters.

It was not a time to leave Janet on her own to cope with everything, although she seemed capable of doing it. But she was used to it, and there was no help for it. The boat had to sail. The Patrol must go on.

'Here's the Captain now.'

The Captain came up the gangway with his shoulders hunched and his head down, with his briefcase and his characteristically unbalanced, almost crab-like strides, swinging his right arm forward with his right leg instead of his left.

'Good evening, Sam.'

'Sir.'

'Nice night for it. Bit too much moon, though.'

The night was pitch black. To suit the Captain's peculiar sense of humour.

123

'Everybody on board?'

'Yes sir.' Strictly speaking, the Captain should have waited, to allow Sam to report everybody on board. But it was like him to preempt the normal routine. The sailors had all, every one of them, returned to their leave, but to Sam's intense annoyance, the Navigating Officer had been adrift. He had gone down to see his MoD Wren and his car had broken down on the motorway on the way back. He had only been an hour adrift, but an hour was an hour. It was just one more of that weekend's irritations. Sam knew he should tell the Captain. The Captain had insisted that he must be told whenever anybody overstayed their leave. But Sam wondered whether this was the moment.

'Everybody back from their weekend all right?'

'Yes, sir.'

'Right. Let's go then.'

There was a well-defined ritual of departure. The casing party formed a line to receive the Captain and then, as soon as he had passed them, began to slip the securing wires one by one as they were ordered from the bridge, and pass them ashore. A Bomber had no need of wires on a deterrent patrol. Murdoch the Petty Officer Steward was waiting at the base of the fin, with foul-weather clothing for the Captain. He helped the Captain on with the gear and then took the briefcase below. Sam followed the Captain up to the bridge. The tugs were closing, ready to haul the Bomber off the jetty.

The Navigating Officer was already on the bridge, with the signalman. 'Obey telegraphs has been passed, sir.'

'Very good. There's nothing to keep us here any longer, is there?'

The Captain picked up the microphone and blew experimentally on it. Sam knew how the rasping noise of the Captain's breath would grate on the nerves of the electrical department in the submarine below. There had never been anything wrong with the microphone in the past, but nobody in the submarine service would ever trust a microphone to work without testing it.

'Let go aft.' The first, time-honoured, move was to go slow

ahead on the forward spring, to swing the stern out, away from the jetty.

Sam caught a movement on the jetty out of the corner of his eye. Somebody was waving. He waved back. There was quite a farewell committee there. Sam could just see them in the lights. A Bomber was always accorded a respectful, almost reverential leave-taking. It was like a senior diplomat being ushered out of his embassy, on his way to some important conference abroad.

The rain stopped and the wind dropped as the Bomber moved towards the middle of the loch. Sam could see the shore lights reflected in the black water between them and the jetty which appeared by some trick almost flat, like a mirror, but flecked with tiny whirls of moving water, the eddies set up by the screws of the tugs and the Bomber itself.

The respite from the rain was only brief. Sam bent his head forward as another squall hit the fin and poured a torrent of rain over the bridge rail. There were thumps and bangs from below, as the casing party thankfully came in out of the weather, shut the outer fin door behind them, and climbed down the tower into the control room.

Ahead was the single stern light of the police launch. Somewhere out in the middle of the loch, unlit and unseen, were the Marines in their rigid raider craft. The tugs were backing off. There was a final swirl of water around the Bomber's stern. The Bomber was lined up now for the passage down the loch and out to sea.

Once again Sam wondered, as he always did when they sailed, who was watching from the shore. There were, he knew, preparations ahead. There would certainly be enemy watchers and listeners out in the Irish Sea and beyond, endeavouring to pick up the Bomber and follow it out to sea. So, the sea, and everything on it, below it and above it, had to be inspected and cleared, as though they were to be disinfected – indeed, 'deloused', the word the intelligence spooks themselves used, was the best description.

The Bomber would have helicopter surveillance overhead until it reached the open sea. There would be a mine countermeasures vessel, to see the passage was swept clear. There would be another submarine, an attack boat, waiting to act as a decoy, to attract attention, and to divert any possible pursuit. From now on, the Bomber would be less like a diplomat and much more like a burglar – a large and very obtrusive burglar, who had somehow to be smuggled out of his gaol and allowed to get clean away, with no pursuers of any kind, and no trace of him once he had made his escape.

The boat was already swaying to the lift of the sea as Sam climbed down the tower to meet the Outside Wrecker and open up for diving. The tower always smelled of seawater – 'fishy' was the word. It was the most claustrophobic part of the submarine, and the most difficult to keep clean.

At the bottom of the ladder, Sam looked briefly around the faces in the control room. He had often tried to find a word to describe the predominant feeling on board when they set out on one of these patrols. People were not apprehensive, but certainly they were not looking forward to the next two months. Perhaps wistful was the best word. Everybody was still mentally at home, but aware that the hull was sliding away from the mainland. They could feel the shore receding in the distance astern, although Leading Seaman Basing had an often-expressed theory that they never actually went anywhere and the entire patrol was actually spent off Campbeltown.

The transition from shore to patrol life at the start of a patrol was always deceptively easy and gradual. There was fresh salad with the first meal and for the first day or two the food did seem fresher – not pre-frozen, then thawed, and then cooked. The newspapers were only a day old and then only two days old, but soon they were crumpled and creased with repeated opening and folding, and all the crosswords had been filled in, except possibly one or two clues which remained unsolved, sometimes for an entire patrol, to irritate the crossword addicts. The magazines, too, were new and shiny, and that month's. But soon they too would become battered and dog-eared, and eventually Murdoch would carefully fold them and stow them away.

The letters, the photographs, the thoughts of home, were still new ones. On the last patrol, Sam had heard, one just-married stoker's new wife had written him a letter for every day of the patrol and given them to him before he set out. She numbered all the envelopes. He was supposed to open one a day, in the right order. But, so the Chief Stoker said, he had opened them all and read them before the end of the first day.

Sam waited in the control room until the Captain came down from the bridge. The first encounter with the Captain at sea normally indicated which role the Captain was playing for the time being. Last time, it was the Roaring Boy. This time it would probably be something different, although it could conceivably be the Roaring Boy yet again. Such things were not unknown.

The Captain came down the ladder without commenting on the weather, or the time before the next meal. He silently studied the chart on the chart table for a few moments and then stood, without speaking, behind the helmsman for an equal length of time. Then, without looking at Sam or addressing a word to him, the Captain went to his cabin.

There was nothing hostile or admonishing about the Captain's manner or his silence. It was just, as Sam was quick to recognise, that the chosen role for today, and perhaps for the next few days, was the Trappist Monk. It could have been Bonnie Prince Charlie, or the Senior Statesman, or the Political Pundit, or the Wartime Submarine Ace, or any one of about half a dozen. But, unmistakably, it was the Trappist Monk. Sam welcomed the choice. At least it was quieter than the others.

The days began to slide into each other, as they always did, as though, just as the Bomber was steadily distancing itself from the land, so its crew were gliding away into a state of suspended time. In every patrol, it seemed that many days had passed, but the calendar showed that there had been only a few. Some of the sailors actually had calendars, and crossed off the days of the patrol, like boarding-school boys crossing off the days left of the term before they could go home for the holidays. In the earlier part of the patrol Sam was always surprised when he looked at one of these home-made calendars and saw how few days had actually passed. It must be like the beginning of a long prison sentence, when a prisoner had served several years and then realised that he was still not even half-way to his release. That, they said, was when a man first began to take the weight of his punishment.

The watches changed, mealtimes came and went, the lights dimmed and brightened again. There were the first missile drills, and the first issue of Polaris Post. Danny Bennett and Chief Bluntstone organised a programme of inter-mess quizzes in the evenings, and there were film shows, and a brains trust, and tombola, and gramophone requests, with Leading Seaman Basing as disc jockey.

Some sailors, a few, spent their spare time studying for higher educational qualifications. This was an aspect of life in the Polaris boats which had been greatly exaggerated in the early days, when almost every off-watch Polaris sailor was supposed to be taking an Open University degree in economics. In fact, the studious and the ambitious studied to improve themselves, just as they had always done in the Navy. The rest did as they had always done – went on watch, and ate, and slept, and went on watch again.

On the first Saturday, the first Familygrams arrived. These were short messages, from wives and girlfriends, transmitted periodically to the submarine whenever signal traffic permitted. Every man on board was allowed a Familygram. They were discreetly handled, inboard and on board, by as few people as possible, and they were vetted, to prevent undue stress. Before sailing every man had to decide what action he wanted taken: should he or should he not be informed, in the event of a family emergency, such as a death, a serious accident, or an illness of a near relative? Some sailors opted not to be told. They reasoned that they could not personally do anything about the emergency and the knowledge of it would only distress them unnecessarily.

For himself, Sam thought this was false reasoning. He had

watched the looks of badly concealed relief on the faces of sailors who had opted not to be told, when they returned to find that all was still well. Nor would he ever forget the expressions, of astonishment and shock and grief on the face on one sailor, years ago, in his first Polaris boat, when the man was told that his wife had died while he was away, that she had died soon after they sailed and that she had, in fact, been dead for some weeks. It was possible that wondering whether something had happened in one's absence might actually be worse than knowing what had happened. That was one question the psychiatrists could address themselves to, if they really wanted to make themselves useful. For himself, Sam felt that it would be the worst of all worlds, to spend weeks wondering whether anything had happened and then to come up the ladder after a patrol and receive the bad news. He himself had opted to be told, no matter how bad the news.

In any case, this was not the first time, nor were Bombers the first ships, when sailors had been in the position of knowing bad news and not being able to do anything about it. That had been the case for much of the last war. Sam's father-in-law had been serving in the Pacific when his father had died. He had been given just the bare, bald signal, with no possibility whatever of going home until the war was over. That was in wartime. This was peace. But one could certainly argue that a Bomber was at war, in the purest sense, and wartime conditions should prevail.

'Alice measles. Mother here recuperating,' said the Familygram from Janet. 'Johnny second Eleven.' Of course, it was now the start of the cricket season. Sam's thoughts had been lingering on the football season and he had been expecting news of Johnny's goals. 'Simon monitor his class.' That had been on the cards last term. Simon was a very responsible little boy. He would make a good class monitor. 'Raggle taggles in the news again.' Raggle Taggles? The need for brevity sometimes lent wives an epigrammatic wit when composing their Familygrams, but Sam was baffled by the reference. Who on earth were the Raggle Taggles? Was it some TV programme

Alice was watching?. 'All well here. Love you very much. Janet.'

On the first Sunday forenoon, there was church service in the senior rates' lounge. All the departments in the boat took it in turns to organise the service, to rig chairs and an altar for church, choose the hymns, and read the lessons. Very few sailors attended, unless it was their department's turn, but most of the officers went every Sunday.

This Sunday it was the Supply Department's service. In this boat, Sam had noticed, as in very many ships in the Navy, the Supply Department had a curiously close-knit *esprit de corps*. They had all turned out, the whole department, and Sam gave them credit. Murdoch and the PO Chef, with the Pecos Kid, the Main Man and Boxcar Wilfred, were all in attendance. The Petty Officer Jack Dusty and the Leading Jack Dusty gave out the hymn sheets. Forsyth, the Leading Steward, provided the accompaniment for the hymn-singing with his squeezebox.

De Lacy Brown, the Supply Officer, led the service. He looked the part, and he had the voice. The wardroom always said he should have been a parson. The unkind even said he would have made a much better parson than he did a Supply Officer. But such a service needed somebody to take the lead and, with De Lacy Brown and the Captain both singing, the hymns went very well, indeed much better than usual.

They ended, as always, with the last verse of 'Eternal Father, Strong to Save' which over the years had become the unofficial naval hymn. Sam had sung it in every ship and shore establishment he had ever served in, and he had always thought it a much better structured hymn than perhaps the Navy had ever noticed. The first three verses, one each for Father, Son, and Holy Ghost, had appropriate allusions to the Creation in the Book of Genesis, to the calming of the storm and the walking on the water from the Gospels. The fourth and last verse summed up the previous three. O Trinity of love and power. Our brethren shield in danger's hour. From rock and tempest, fire and foe, protect them whereso'er they go. There were no rocks here, except thousands of feet below, and the boat and everything and everybody inside it would have been crushed by the sea long before they reached them. Tempests were no problem either down here, except internal ones, although fire was always possible. And there were certainly no foes. That was the eerie part of it. This had to be the sneakiest way of going to war. Thus evermore shall rise to Thee, Glad hymns of praise from land and sea. They ended, Amen, with a praiseworthy *glissando* from Forsyth.

It was the church service which, ironically, put an end to the Trappist Monk. The Captain had, as usual, sung the hymns with gusto. Afterwards, he was clearly in a much more chatty mood. The Captain very rarely drank at sea, but he offered Sam a glass of sherry, 'as it's Sunday morning.'

'Thank you very much, sir.' Strictly speaking, Sam was President of the wardroom mess, not the Captain, but this distinction of protocol was always a very fine one in a submarine.

'You know, you really should have told me about Pilot, Sam.'

'Pilot, sir?' Once again, Sam realised that the Captain had his own lines of communication. He seemed to know what was happening without ever reading a noticeboard or gossiping at the bar inboard.

'I think you know what I'm talking about, Sam. Adrift coming back from his dirty weekend down in the smoke.'

'Well, sir . . . Of course I meant to inform you . . . What with sailing and all the other problems . . . It just slipped my mind . . .' Sam always resented the way the Captain so effortlessly succeeded in making him feel like a guilty school-boy.

'You know I like to know these things. I don't want ever to hear about anything to do with my own boat or the people inside it at second hand. And that's for everybody's benefit, not just for mine. Self-defence.'

'Yes, sir, aye aye, sir.'

'Us, *contra mundum*.'

'Yes, sir.'

'Well, if I've got that point across, at last, I'll say no more about it. You can tell young Pilot he's a lucky man.'

'Yes, sir.'

'When we've finished this, I want you to come with me to my cabin. There are some things I want you to read.'

Sam knew, from his own days as a submarine CO, that there was a certain extra secure cypher, addressed for the eyes of the Commanding Officer only. Few things were secret in a Bomber on patrol. Sam had known, as everyone who kept watches in the control room or the main communications centre could not have helped knowing, that ever since they had sailed on this patrol they had been receiving a slow but steady trickle of extra signal traffic in the Commanding Officer's own cypher. Sam had shared the general curiosity about this volume of traffic which, in his experience, was unprecedented. Normally, a signal in the CO's cypher was a comparatively rare event.

'Here you are, Sam. Read, mark, learn, inwardly digest.'

Sam took the leaded file, and began to turn over the signals, with their colour-tinted edges.

His first reaction was disappointment. The signals were all about the Middle East crisis, which had been on the television news and in the newspapers constantly in the weeks before they sailed.

'We've been through all this before, you know, Sam. I remember years ago when I was Third Hand in . . .'

'Yes, I recall, sir.'

The Captain had turned so as to show his profile. With his puffy cheeks, protuberant lips and noticeable flattened nose, the silhouette was markedly non-heroic. Nevertheless, Sam recognised the signals. The Trappist Monk had gone. Fast emerging in his place was the Wartime Submarine Ace.

There were two very long signals, the two latest to be received, on the top of the pack. At first, they seemed merely to be repeating the news broadcasts, but when Sam had read them both through, he realised that their tone, and the detail of the intelligence information contained in them, were very much graver than the news available to the general public. It seemed that the intelligence spooks who interpreted the international situation, and whose reading of events gave rise to this sequence of signals, worked on a system of triggers. They watched for certain events, certain trends, which acted like trip-wires; as each of these trip-wire events occurred, so the chance of a crisis was considered to have increased. Some of them, like the movement of spot prices for oil in Rotterdam, were logical enough. But others – Sam had heard that somebody actually noted the number of lights burning over-night in the office windows of the Pentagon – seemed far-fetched. Maybe it was the job of some little boffin in some little office to note these events. Maybe he was next door to the boffin who studied acoustics in submarine control rooms. But whatever the indicators were, and whoever it was who watched them, it seemed that everything now pointed in the direction of a grave crisis.

But it was still difficult to relate this news to themselves, out at sea, miles from anywhere, in a Bomber.

'What does this mean to us, exactly, sir?'

'I don't know, *exactly*. It's early days. But it's just possible, just conceivable, we may be called upon to use these weapons we have on board. Believe it or not. I think it's possible. Just possible.'

Sam saw the Captain staring hard at him, as though to impress upon him the gravity of what he was saying, as well as trying to gauge the effect of his remarks.

The effect on Sam was one of sheer incredulity. To him, it was, literally, incredible that they would ever launch their missiles, or even come close to it. Sam simply could not believe that their Bomber and its missiles could have the slightest effect upon a crisis in the Middle East. There was a theory of a sliding scale of deterrence. Sam subscribed to it. One needed to be flexible. One could never know at what point on the scale, by the fear of which precise weapon and what precise threat of retaliation, an enemy would be deterred from attacking. But to imagine that these missiles had any relevance to the content of those signals was simply unbelievable. It was nonsense and even, as Janet would say, dangerous nonsense. Yet here was the Captain, clearly flexing his muscles, and preparing for doomsday. The Wartime Submarine Ace was now fully in charge.

'I see you don't believe me.'

'Believe you, sir?' Once again, Sam knew that he had been unable to conceal his thoughts from the Captain. His face had given him away again. 'Anything's possible, of course. I suppose we must go on preparing for the worst, whilst still hoping for the best, sir.'

'Let that be the thought for today. Have it broadcast through the boat I shall be talking to the ship's company in five minutes' time.'

'Aye aye, sir.'

Sam sat in the wardroom to hear the Captain's speech. It was Sunday forenoon. Sunday morning in early May. Janet and her mother and Alice would be just coming home from church. Blossom would be out, even in Scotland. Much of the snow would have gone from the hills, even up there. Alice would sit down to half an hour's homework, before lunch, to have it all ready for Miss Farquhar first thing on Monday morning. His mother-in-law would read the book reviews in the Sunday paper. They would most probably have roast lamb for lunch, which Janet always did deliciously, with some herbs. Meanwhile he was sitting out here in the middle of the ocean, waiting to hear his Captain talk about missiles and crises and eventualities.

Hamish had come in and was gloomily looking through one of the magazines, which he must have looked at a dozen times before. Hamish no longer had a Story for the Day. They invariably dried up, about a week into a patrol.

'D'ye hear there?'

Hamish looked up. 'Oh? What's this?' Hamish always seemed to switch his ears into neutral on a patrol. He never seemed to hear anything.

'Speech from the Throne.'

'. . . Captain speaking. I expect most of you were following

134

events in the newspapers and on radio and television before we left and have been reading Polaris Post, and you are now wondering what is going on in the Middle East and worrying about how it is going to affect us.'

Sam doubted that. He would be surprised to learn that anybody in this boat apart from the Captain cared a damn about the Middle East or ever gave it a thought. Even Hamish had gone back to his magazine already.

'. . . I know there have been lots of crises in the Middle East since the war. You could almost say there's virtually been a permanent crisis there ever since the war ended. I myself, in one submarine I was in, was involved in one of these crises . . .'

Oh *no*. Sam gritted his teeth. Not the Great Middle East Crisis again, and How I Personally Foiled King Farouk With My Bare Hands. Not again, please.

'But this one is rather different. This time it seems that all the other times they were crying wolf. But not now. From my reading of the signals we have had and are still getting, and from the briefing I had before we sailed, it seems that what we are looking at is a possible invasion of Iran by Soviet Russia. That is the bottom line at the moment.'

The Captain paused, as though to let his words sink in. Hamish was still studying his magazine. Danny Bennett had come in and sat down and was staring up at the loudspeaker on the bulkhead, as though expecting the Captain to materialise out of it.

'Now you will all be asking yourselves, how does this effect us out here? The answer is that it might, sooner than we expect. We might just have to use those weapons we have on board. Naturally, I hope and pray not, as we all do, I trust. But I have to warn you that there is now a greater possibility than at any time in the past. We have trained and prepared for this for years. We may now be about to be put to the test and have to prove the worth of our training.'

And you, good yeomen, whose limbs were made in England, show us here the mettle of your pasture.

135

'My message to you is that you have all been drawing the Queen's money all these years. This might just be the time you have to front up and earn it. I know I can rely on you all. That's all for now. I will let you know as soon as things are clearer. Meanwhile, we shall have a full missile launch drill this afternoon. That's all for now.'

'Missiles on the Sabbath?' Danny Bennett grimaced. 'What would the Moderator of the General Assembly of the Free Churches of Scotland say to that? Do you think the Boss has gone off his rocker?'

Hamish looked up from his magazine. 'Clinically, no.'

Sam could not stop himself from bursting into laughter. It was such a sheer relief to hear them talk like that. So he was not the only one.

'He does have these short sharp fits of the Gunther von Priens occasionally. I think he's permanently cheesed off because he was too young for the war. Torpedoing things, and surfacing close to an enemy shore and shooting up enemy trains, and landing secret agents with rubber boats on beaches, all that sort of thing would have been pure heaven for him. As it is, all he does is stooge around the ocean practising to fire missiles which nobody in their right senses wants to fire. We're training for something we know will be the end of us all if we ever have to do it. We're a floating paradox. No wonder the Boss wants to win the Victoria Cross occasionally, out of sheer frustration. Don't blame him.'

'Danny, I think those the most sensible remarks I've heard from anybody in a long time.'

Danny Bennett shrugged. 'Aw shucks.'

During the drills that afternoon, Sam watched and listened closely, to see if the Captain's speech had had any noticeable effect on the ship's company. There was no sign of it, not the slightest hint of any extra tension or apprehension. Sam was surprised. Surely they were not so insensitive? Surely they thought about what they were doing? But it seemed not. Everybody concentrated, as usual, upon their own roles in the launching drill and upon playing their roles as well as possible. Sam was chilled by such emotional detachment. It took professionalism to submerge personal feelings so comprehensively. But, he had to admit it, there was also one small part of him which was proud.

'Sir, sir, it's the Captain on the broadcast, for you, sir.'

Sam had been so absorbed in his own thoughts, he had no idea what stage the current launch drill had reached. He could see Joe and the others looking at him, obviously expecting something or some word from him. But he did not know what it was. It was like an actor drying up, forgetting everything, even what act of the play they had reached. It was like waking from a bad dream to find oneself on a strange stage, with everyone else on it waiting for their cues.

Sam heard the Captain's voice on the broadcast. The Roaring Boy was back, temporarily at least, and at more than normal strength, several decibels louder than usual. But Sam could make nothing of the words. He could tell they were impatient, angry words, but they had no meaning for him. They were just incomprehensible sounds. Once more, people were looking at him, and he had nothing to contribute.

Sam did not know how he reached the end of the drill, or what he did, or how or whether anybody covered up for him. But when the drill was over, and people were putting the gear away, locking up books, switching off consoles, and leaving the Missile Control Centre, Sam stood for a few moments, just where he was, without moving.

He now knew for certain that he could not go on. This must be his last patrol, even supposing he could somehow get through it and survive to the end of it. It was not a matter of politics, or morals. It was just there in his genes, a deep down sense of revulsion and repugnance, bred in the bone.

Sam stood stock still, almost dazed by this new knowledge. There was a word for this sensation. The Greeks had it. It was called *anagnorisis*, the moment in the play when the tragic hero realised what was happening, what was being done to him. But perhaps this revelation was nothing new. Perhaps the knowledge of it had been there all the time and he had subconsciously repressed it. Whatever it was, it had escaped into the open now. He knew now that in all conscience, and conscience maybe was the right word, he could not, as a matter of honesty and honour, continue to serve in a Bomber.

'Sam, Captain wants to see you. *Sam?*' Joe was standing right in front of him, staring into his eyes. 'You okay, Sam?'

'Sure.'

'You just look a bit dazed.'

'No, I'm fine. Never better.'

The Captain was still in his towering rage, indeed he seemed to have worked himself up into a greater rage while waiting for Sam to arrive. There was spittle on his lip, and choler in his cheeks, and he spoke with emphasis as though he wanted to spit each word down Sam's throat.

Sam did not understand what the Captain was saying, nor did he know what he had done wrong, or why the Captain was so angry. He was numb, indifferent to whatever the Captain said. Maybe ignorance really was bliss, of a kind. He kept on saying 'I'm very sorry, sir' and 'Aye aye, sir' and 'I'll see to it, sir', whenever the Captain seemed to pause for breath. This repetitive catechism of penitence seemed eventually to have its effect on the Captain, who suddenly turned on his heel and walked away.

There were several people sitting in the wardroom. Sam did not recognise them. They must have heard every word. The whole boat must have heard.

'So, have we have left undone those things we ought to have done, and done those things we ought not to have done, and is there no health in us?'

Sam did not know who had spoken, nor did he care.

'Not to worry.' He meant it. It was, indeed, not to worry. He felt buoyed up by his new knowledge about himself. A whole load of cares and responsibilities seemed to have dropped away from him. It no longer mattered what the Captain said or thought, or indeed what anybody else said or thought. He knew the way forward.

But he had forgotten that there would be more launching drills, a seemingly endless succession of them, day after day, until the end of the patrol. He discovered that he was not brave enough to disobey an order directly and refuse to take part in any more drills. He told himself, again and again, that if he was sincere, if he was genuinely sure, he should tell the Captain and step aside, accept the arguments, the remonstrances, reprimands, even close arrest, or whatever penalty the Captain decided on. But he simply could not bring himself to do that. Thus, he had to continue to play his role, an important, leading role, in an elaborate ritual ceremony of preparation and launch. Each time, he was reminded of his own indecision, each time he was confronted by his own dishonesty and cowardice.

Sam noticed that, as the news from the Middle East continued to deteriorate, the drills were beginning to take on a fresh and horrifying dimension of reality. Certainly, the Captain was behaving as though he fully expected one of these drills, one day soon, to be a real launch. Sam, who knew the Captain so well, could tell what he was thinking, by the sound of his voice. It had a new, rasping certainty about it, which eventually began to affect some of the launching crew. Once or twice, Sam caught a look on a face which suggested that he was not alone in suddenly realising that he might any day now have to 'front up and earn the Queen's money'. At last, even Sam's incredulity began to give way. It was inconceivable, it was impossible, that their missiles might ever be launched, but every time he closed up for drill, Sam asked himself 'Is this the one?', 'Could it be real this time?'. Suppose, feeling as he did now, he actually took part in a hot launch?

If there had been only one more drill, or even just two, before the patrol ended, he could perhaps have steeled himself. But they went on and on, the familiar rehearsed words and actions repeatedly jabbing at his conscience, as though at a sore wound. He became more and more morose and depressed, said less and less at meals in the wardroom, and spent less and less time there. He suffered violent changes of mood, at one moment longing to talk to somebody, the next resenting any approach from anybody. He wanted help, but behaved in such a manner as to make it impossible for anyone to offer it. He found Janet's Familygrams, which he knew she took such care to compose, almost unbearably painful to read. Three successive Familygrams he put away unread in a trouser pocket, and it was two days before he could bring himself to look at them.

Sam knew his behaviour was making unreasonable demands upon the rest of the wardroom's good nature. But even in his depression he was sufficiently detached to be able to observe himself and he could see that they were responding with that magnificent forbearance of submarine crews who knew that, as a necessary part of their normal existence, they had to get on with each other. They were, after all, accustomed to 'nursing' one of their number through a black patch of what they called 'the glooms'. Many people suffered from them, some more than others, and it did not matter who they were, high or low in the Bomber. The 'glooms' were a fact of life and not at all uncommon, although this was the first time anybody could remember Sam falling a victim to such a prolonged bout.

One night he had one of Able Seaman Draper's dreams. He called it that because he recognised it at once, from Draper's descriptions. There was the sensation of helpless falling, the awareness of a black and bottomless abyss waiting below, the knowledge that the steep-pitched sides were advancing and closing in as he fell, the terror of falling into a tunnel from which there would never be any way back.

When Sam woke he could feel the sweat running down the side of his neck and already cooling in his hair. There was a figure standing by his bunk. It was Chief, bending down to look at him.

'Did you wake me? Is it time to turn out?'

'No. You sound like a Chief Cadet Captain. And no. The answer both times is no. I just stopped because I could hear you.'

'Hear me?'

'Yes. Sounded as if you were *crying*. In trouble, anyway.'

'No trouble. I'm quite all right.'

140

'You've been a bit down recently, Sam, haven't you? Not your usual bouncing cheerful self.'

'I'm perfectly all right.'

'Okay, I take your word for it. You didn't sound all right just now.'

'Why, what did I sound like?'

'I don't know. As if you were calling for somebody to help you quick, and they wouldn't come.'

'That's ridiculous.'

'I know it's ridiculous. But you asked me what you sounded like, and I'm telling you. It sounded as though you wanted help. Was it one of those dreams?'

'What do you mean, one of those dreams?'

'Well, we all get them occasionally. Par for the course. It's a funny existence and the mind plays funny tricks sometimes.'

'Do you get funny dreams, Chief?'

'Yes, of course I do. I'm normally looking for something, searching through the boat. It's a cliché really, the original psychiatric dream. Getting more and more anxious and uptight about it all. And yet, secretly, I don't want to find it, whatever it is. Or I'm trying to fix something, a camera or something, or fasten something, before something else happens, and whatever it is is getting closer and closer, and I still can't fix it. In the end, I just tell myself it's only a dream and I wake up.'

'You can do that?'

'Oh yes.'

'Lucky you.'

'It's all in the mind, Sam.'

Sam lay back in his bunk, finding unexpected comfort in the knowledge that Chief, than whom there was nobody in the world more prosaic, pragmatic and matter-of-fact, also suffered from bad dreams.

He was still thinking of his dream the next morning, when he met Draper, who was still onboard, despite the Captain's remarks after the periscope incident during the Index. Draper was coming down the passageway, head bowed, and muttering.

141

'How are the dreams now?'

'Much better, sir. They seem to be easing off, sir.'

That, Sam thought, probably proved they were genuine. Had Draper been swinging the lead he would have continued to exaggerate his dreams. This might be Draper's last patrol, as he devoutly hoped it would be his own. Sam wanted to reassure Draper, to put him out of his uncertainty, but of course he could not do that.

'Were you muttering something to yourself just now, Draper?'

'Yes sir. Not talking to meself though, sir. Learning me part for the ceremony, sir.'

'Of course. What is it this time?'

'Crossing the Line, sir. I'm the Clerk of the Court, sir.'

'Crossing the Line, of *course*! I'd forgotten!'

They were approaching the mid-point of the patrol, when the sailors celebrated with an elaborate fantasy. Last time it was a Nature Ramble. Parties of ramblers set off for a tour through the boat, taking with them packets of sandwiches and Thermos flasks of coffee. Some wore stout walking shoes, and carried binoculars. One even had a haversack. On their way, they observed and logged the local flora and fauna. They went bird-watching in the Missile Room. Somebody claimed to have seen a tree-creeper on one of the missile tubes. There was a swan's nest in the Health Physics Lab, natterjack toads in Manoeuvring, a fox's earth in the motor room.

This time it was Crossing the Line. It was appropriate. It was a line in time they were crossing. The mid-point was, in a way, a kind of solstice. From now, the number of days left in the patrol would get shorter.

A loud hail was heard in the fore ends on the previous evening. King Neptune, in the person of Chief Bluntstone, carrying a gold trident, wearing a breast-plate of sea-serpent scale armour, and trailing a sarong decorated with seaweed and fish-scales, had boarded the submarine, now proclaimed that he was Sovereign of the Seas, and demanded due obeisance from all his subjects. Accompanied by Queen Amphitrite,

142

thinly disguised as Leading Seaman Basing, in a green frock embellished with cardboard seashells, His Oceanic Majesty was conducted to the control room, where he was respectfully welcomed by the Chief Bear and the Pirate Coxswain, inspected a guard of Bears, Pirates and Maids of Honour, and announced that it was his Royal Intention to initiate all nozzers into his realm with proper rites and ceremonies on the morrow.

The following midday the Bomber crossed the 'Line', went a hundred feet deeper, turned through 180 degrees and re-crossed the 'Line', came up to the original depth and crossed the 'Line' for the third time, thus tying the 'Line' in an imaginary loop.

A canvas bath was prepared in the control room and half-filled with seawater. King Neptune and His Court took up their positions. Bears and Pirates searched through the submarine for miscreants, finding them hiding in the bilges and in the remotest parts of the boat, and dragged them struggling and protesting to justice. They were shaved with a noxious mixture of soap, paraffin, paint and gravy. Anybody who opened his mouth to protest had the shaving brush thrust into it.

The ceremony had an anarchical, saturnalian freedom which went back to the days of sail. The Captain was seized, charged, convicted and summarily ducked for acting in a manner prejudicial to good order and naval discipline in that he whispered in the control room. Hamish, the tallest man on board, was shaved and ducked for damaging the deckhead. Likewise, the Petty Officer Chef, the shortest man, was ducked for being a 'Shortarse' and damaging the deck. The Outside Wrecker was convicted and severely ducked for conceitedly, in the eyes of the Court, claiming that he had already crossed the Line, the *proper* Line, that is, the Equator.

Some were also ordered to carry out an appropriate forfeit. Sam was left with mixed feelings about his own charge, conviction and sentence. He was ducked for acting in a manner prejudicial to good order and naval discipline in that he had been too cheerful and had cracked too many jokes with His

Oceanic Majesty's subjects. He was sentenced to find the marbles he had lost.

Looking over the heads of the milling crowd of Bears and Pirates and Barbers, to the other side of the control room, Sam saw the Captain smile at this. He kept his mouth firmly shut, so that he escaped the shaving brush, as he was determined to do. But he could not escape the foul stuff daubed on his face. The Captain's ominous grin was the last thing he saw before he was tipped over backwards into the evil-smelling water.

He was not surprised, when the ceremony was over, to get a message that the Captain wanted to see him.

CHAPTER 7

'NOW I'M NOT PSYCHIC and I can't read tea-leaves, Sam, but I'm not daft, either. Just what has been going on with you recently?'

'I don't know what you mean, sir.' Sam had not meant to reply so predictably and so unconvincingly, but once again the Captain had managed to throw him off balance from the very beginning.

'Oh come off it, Sam, don't come the old three-badge AB with me. You've been moping around the place the last two weeks or so. Even the sailors have noticed it. In fact they were the first to notice it. You were even moping around the place when we were crossing the line just now, when you should have been enjoying yourself like everybody else was. There's something going on and I want to know what it is. You're the Executive Officer of this boat. Anything that affects you affects the boat and anything that affects the boat affects me. So I want to know what it is. Is it to do with your family, perhaps? Something in one of those Familygrams that somebody ought to have spotted and cut out? I didn't know you had any particular . . .'

'I haven't.'

Sam paused, before saying any more. He was already regretting having replied so brusquely. The Captain had inadvertently offered him a convenient way out and without thinking he had slammed it shut. This was an important moment, one of the most important of his life. It was still possible to draw back. It would be difficult but it would still not be impossible to convince the Captain, or at least to tell him and hope he believed it, that the trouble was that he had been physically out of sorts recently. Sam recognised that he would have to give the Captain some reason. He was not the sort of man to rest until he had been given a reason. But Sam could still avoid giving him the real one. But if he ever did give him the real reason there could be no going back.

'I just find that . . . I find nuclear weapons repugnant, sir.' Even as he said the word, Sam knew how pompous and unlikely it sounded. 'I don't wish to have anything more to do with them. I would like to wash my hands of them.' He had not intended to use Pontius Pilate's phrase, but it had slipped out.

Sam watched the first incredulity on the Captain's face giving way to an amused relief.

'Good God, is *that* all? My dear Sam, none of us want to have anything to do with nuclear weapons. Is that really all that's worrying you? Thank God for that! I thought it was something serious!'

'It is serious, sir.'

'Of course, of course. I suppose it is serious, although you're a bit long in the tooth for this sort of thing, aren't you, Sam? After all, you'd expect every curate to have doubts about his vocation once in a while, wouldn't you? But you wouldn't expect the . . .'

'That is nothing to do with it, sir. That does not describe how I feel.'

'Well, how *do* you describe how you feel?'

Sam could not help noticing that the Captain's tone of voice was exactly the same as he had himself used towards Able Seaman Draper.

'I have decided that I do not wish to have anything more to do, personally, with any nuclear weapons.' There. Sam had to admit to himself that, put just like that, it sounded trite, and bald, and unconvincing, and even ridiculous.

'You decided . . . Just like that. You had a blinding flash of light, on the way to Damascus . . .'

That, Sam conceded, was a very apt comparison.

'. . . And as a result, you decided you wanted to . . . wash your hands of them all . . .' The Captain had been studying the backs of his hands in a seemingly abstracted manner. Now he suddenly put his hands down and looked directly, and menacingly, at Sam. There was a correspondingly menacing note in his voice.

'Now let's cut out all this demeaning and school-girlish crap. I think you *are* serious. You and I have never been in the habit of exchanging jokes together. We're not on those sort of terms. So let me tell you one or two things, for your own benefit. You're no great shakes as a submariner, Sam. Never have been, never will be. As an XO of a Bomber, you're certainly not God's Gift to any CO. But you agreed. You took the money. You've been taking the money for years. Now the very first time you read in the news that you might have to *earn* your money, you turn all squeamish. Please, sir, no, sir, can I go, sir, I didn't really mean it, sir. That's really what you're saying, isn't it . . .'

'No, not at all . . .'

'Well, it's not good enough. I'm not going to let you get away with that . . .'

'I'm not trying to get away with anything . . .'

'Yes you are! What this amounts to is a con trick on the public purse. What are you suggesting, that we stop your submarine pay, as from today? Because that's the other side of the coin. If you're not going to do the job, *all* the job, the whole of it, you shouldn't get the pay. That's the implication of what you're saying, if we carry it to its logical conclusion. Now, before we go any further, let me make you an offer. Let me say that I'm prepared to behave, now, from this moment, as though this conversation had never happened. And that's a great deal more than you deserve . . .'

'I'm serious, sir. I wasn't sure when or how I was going to tell you. You've rather rushed things, as it happens. But I was going to inform you sooner or later, and I certainly don't want

147

to behave now as though this conversation had never happened . . .'

'You realise that the launches can still go ahead, the missiles can still be fired, with or without you?'

'Yes, sir, I know that.'

'So your protest, if that's what it is, will have no actual effect whatsoever, except on you?'

'Yes, sir, I realise that, too.'

'And on me, too. I'm telling you, I will not have any XO of mine refuse his duty. You will carry on as normal. You *will*.'

Maybe the Captain's main motivation was pride, and fear of the effect this might have upon himself and his reputation. Perhaps he was afraid of guilt by association, wondering whether the shame could ever rub off on himself.

'I'm not having one of my officers behaving like one of those gypsies at the main gate.'

Now, suddenly, Sam understood Janet's reference to the Raggle Taggles. She had used the phrase again, in a second Familygram, and, of course, she meant the peace protesters. He ought to have twigged that before.

'I am prepared to continue to take part in drills, sir, and carry out the rest of my duties on board.'

'But won't that go against your new-found scruples?'

It was interesting to see the Captain changing the ground of the argument, shifting his stance, like a wrestler feeling for a more effective hand-hold.

'Yes, it would, sir. But I'm prepared to do it.'

'Very big of you.'

Having got clear in his own mind where he stood on the central question, Sam now felt confident enough to make concessions. They were unimportant, set beside his central confession.

There was a knock on the cabin door. The door, Sam now noticed, was actually open, with the cabin curtain pulled across for privacy.

'Come in.'

The curtain was jerked aside. It was Danny Bennett. He

148

could have been standing outside for some little time. He might have heard at least some of their conversation.

Danny Bennett had some report for the Captain, about a temperature rise in one of the missile tubes, which had now been corrected. He looked at Sam as he turned away, but Sam could not read anything in his expression.

'Have you ever discussed this with your wife, what's her name, Janet?'

'No, sir.'

'Have you ever discussed this with *anybody* else?'

'No, sir, never.'

'Nobody, except me. Nobody knows except you and me. So there's still time, and no harm done yet.'

'It wouldn't make any difference, sir.'

'Oh yes it would. You wouldn't believe how much difference it makes.'

No, Sam thought, I probably would not. But there was a basic illogicality in the Captain's behaviour. If he had such a low opinion of Sam's worth, if he really believed – what was the phrase? – that Sam was no great shakes as a submariner, then why was he bothering to argue? If Sam was not God's Gift as an XO, then surely the Captain ought to be celebrating, and forwarding his application to leave the Polaris programme with the greatest alacrity and enthusiasm? Perhaps the Captain was arguing because of the intellectual stimulus he obtained from it, for nothing more than the sheer pleasure of arguing. Perhaps the Captain was just playing with him, after all.

'I am sorry you have such a low opinion of me, sir. I feel it would have been fairer if you had told me before where I was letting you down.'

It would not only have been fairer, it was unequivocally laid down in the Navy's regulations, that a Captain *must* inform any officer of how and in what respects that officer was, in the Captain's opinion, not performing his duties satisfactorily. One of the objects of this regulation was to warn a commanding officer against behaving towards a junior exactly as the Captain had just been behaving towards Sam.

The Captain had clearly grasped the implications of what Sam was saying.

'Now don't you go bandying words about with me. I can break you, do you understand? I can make sure you never go to sea in another boat, ever again. I'm not having it, you understand me?'

'Yes, sir.'

There was a silence, during which the Captain pulled at his fingers and cracked his knuckles. Sam could see that the Captain was slowly, painfully, trying to arrange his features in an expression of conciliation.

'I suppose it's no good using words like honour, and duty, and responsibility?'

It might have been, Sam thought, if you had begun with them instead of descending at once to personal abuse.

'All the arguments about deterrence, and the free world, and it being a second strike weapon, I agree with them still, sir. But I can no longer carry them out, on a personal level. I can't do that any more. Other people can. Good luck to them. I can't, and that's that.'

'That's that, eh?' I'll say this for you, Sam, you're the most selfish bugger I've ever met. All you can talk about is yourself.'

To Sam, that was the unfairest and most hurtful remark of any the Captain had made. But it was the end of their interview. Sam left the Captain's cabin, surprised by his own lightness of heart and spirit. It was, just as they always said, as though a heavy load had been lifted from his shoulders. He was also now aware of a more subtle change in his situation. He had been regarding the remainder of the patrol as an ordeal, to be survived somehow. Now he understood that the patrol was, in fact, a respite; his real test would begin when it ended.

That evening, as he was doing rounds, he met Hamish in the passageway. Hamish stood at attention, but spoke as Sam passed him. 'A word with you, when you've finished, Sam, please?'

The Captain received Sam's report of rounds correct without comment, or indeed any remark of any kind. He signed his

Night Order Book and gave it to Sam to take into the control room, again without comment. The Trappist Monk was clearly once again in firm control, so far as Sam was concerned.

Sam found Hamish in the sickbay. It was obvious what he wanted to talk about.

'The Captain has asked me to see you, in a professional capacity, Sam. I suppose I must, as it's an order.'

'You don't sound very interested.'

'I'm not. This is not a medical problem, as I have already tried to explain to the Captain. It's nothing to do with me, none of my business. In many ways, I agree with your new point of view. But I think it's irrelevant. The only point I would make is that I don't think this came to you suddenly, as a sudden revelation. I don't believe it did. I believe you've always felt this way, as you say you do now. But until now, you've managed to rationalise it, conceal it, cover it up, whatever. You may be congratulating yourself on coming clean at last, bringing it out into the open, being honest with yourself, or however you may choose to express it. I would say that, on the contrary, you should now be admitting to yourself that you've been *dis*honest all this time.'

'Well. Thank you for that consolation.'

The wardroom was empty except for Danny Bennett. Once again, Sam knew what was coming.

'I'm sorry I overheard some of what you and the Captain were saying today, Sam.'

'That's all right. Wasn't your fault.'

'I found myself standing outside the curtain, and I could hear what you were saying plainly and I was afraid I couldn't leave without making a noise and giving myself away. Silly, really. So I just stood there, trying to decide what to do. Then I chose a moment to break in.'

'That's all right. As I said, that's all right. Everybody will know sooner or later. You just happen to know sooner.'

'If I can give you some advice, Sam. Just put in my penny-worth?'

'Go ahead. It's open season for giving me an earful.'

151

'Well, I think you're too honest for your own good, Sam . . .'

'*Honest?* That's pretty rich! I've just been officially diagnosed as being *dis*honest. It seems I've been dishonest for years. I've been kidding myself.'

'No, I don't think you have, Sam.' Sam had never seen Danny looking so earnest, so obviously desperate to get his point across clearly. 'Sam, why don't you just keep quiet, and go on? Why not treat it all as what it is, the whole Polaris set-up, the boats, the machinery, the missiles, the whole bang shooting match, the whole thing, as a professional challenge? Which is exactly what it is.'

'But that's not all it is . . .'

'No. True, but that's the way to look at it, surely? It's one of the most challenging professions in the world. It is not easy to do what we do. Those rockets are just an irrelevance. We all know they're never going to be used . . .'

'Do we?'

'Of course we do. They don't matter. They're just complicated pieces of highly technical bits of metal. They're just *kit*. That's how we salve our consciences, those of us who do have consciences. It's only the challenge that really matters.'

'Is that what you really feel, Danny?'

'Yes it is.'

Sam now recognised that his new situation was providing revelations not only about himself but about his friends and fellow officers, men he had served with for years. It was as though he had come out from behind a mask, and found everybody else doing the same. Or perhaps they were now wearing different masks.

As Sam had expected, his interview with the Captain and its outcome were soon common knowledge throughout the boat. There were some curious glances when he closed up for the first launch drill. It was almost as though some peculiar behaviour was expected of him, and the sailors were looking forward to seeing him go berserk and run shrieking and gibbering through the boat.

If so, they were to be disappointed. Even the Captain's voice, level and neutral, revealed nothing of his thoughts. After those first lurid expectations, it seemed that everybody tacitly decided that, provided Sam continued to carry out his normal duties on board in the normal way, the questions of his conscience and his private decision could safely wait until the patrol was over and the Bomber had returned to harbour.

After Hamish and Danny Bennett on that first night, nobody referred to the matter again, except Able Seaman Draper who, in a sense, was in a privileged position.

Draper was polishing the deck again, and stopped his machine when he saw Sam approaching.

'How are the dreams, Draper?'

'Much better, sir. Haven't had one of those for quite a time, sir. I think things are really improving, sir.'

'Good. Are you still going to leave? Or does this mean you're going to stay on?'

'I don't know, sir. I'll have to talk it over with the wife.' Draper's manner changed in an almost comically theatrical way, becoming wary and confidential. 'I heard about your . . . spot of bother, sir.'

'Oh yes? I expect everybody has.'

'I think it was very brave of you to say what you did. If I may say so, sir. It's always easier to just go along with the rest and say nothing. In a way, I know how you feel, sir.'

'Yes, I suppose you do, Draper. Well, thank you for your support.'

'Thank *you*, sir.'

There, Sam thought, is someone who has managed to hack his personal problems. He had to give Draper due credit. Draper had started the patrol in a mental mess. But he had sorted himself out in his mind and had got a grip on himself.

Ironically, the political storm in the Middle East had begun to subside from the day Sam saw the Captain. As so often in the past, the crisis seemed to resolve itself, or at least put itself into a state of suspension without any specific action being taken, as though it were a meteorological phenomenon, gathering and

153

deepening when conditions were right, filling and dispersing when conditions changed. The crisis dropped further and further down the items in Polaris Post, until it disappeared altogether, as it also did from the signals from Northwood.

The end of the patrol was now only a few days away. It seemed to come unexpectedly much closer, as though appearing into sight suddenly over the brow of a long hill. On the home-made calendars around the boat there were now great blocks and entire rows of dates, all crossed or scratched out. Appetites fell off, and there were more grumbles about the food than usual. No matter how skilfully De Lacy Brown and the PO Chef rang the changes on the menus, familiarity at last bred complaints. There was a kind of end-of-patrol lassitude on board. Men tended to sit longer in thought, staring at the bulkheads. Hamish had more patients as the end approached, complaining of headaches and feelings of inadequacy and depression.

For Sam, the last few days were, strangely, some of the happiest he had ever had on board. He felt as though he himself were in some care-free state of limbo. Limbo was a good choice of word: the arrangement Dante's Christian beliefs had had to concede to the realities of history, the region allotted to virtuous pagans, the good men who did not know any better, those who had never had the chance to learn the true faith. He still had his responsibilities, but the main burden had been lifted. The future had still to be faced. There were sure to be difficulties. But the most important decision had been taken. He realised he had taken a step, which would certainly affect Janet and the children, without consulting her. But he had not had a chance to consult her. And had she not said, many times, over a long period, that Polaris was dangerous nonsense.

At last, there came Surfacing Day, with the usual cheers in the control room, the expectancy, the decisive tilt upwards towards the open air, and the seemingly violent but welcome movement of the deck underfoot, after weeks of slow shiftings and stirrings, as the boat swung to the real sway of the sea. There was brilliant sunlight from the top hatch and, when they

154

started the diesel to aid ventilation, the clean, pungent, unbelievable smell of fresh air which came flooding down the tower in a great refreshing gale. Some of the sailors in the control room held their noses in mock dismay, as though this new air was too much for them.

When Sam reached the bridge, he discovered the most perfect summer's morning, with a brisk breeze and hot sunshine. The hills and slopes of the Clyde shoreline were an astonishing green. The light made his eyes ache. He could not stop himself blinking. The wind filled his nostrils with cold pure air, as though he were on an Alpine mountain. The air felt so cold it burned the lobes of his ears and he was soon blinking tears away.

The Captain was still on the bridge. He, too, was blinking and taking deep draughts of air, and there were tears, created by the wind, streaming down his cheeks. In recent weeks, he had been behaving towards Sam with a studied, punctilious politeness, exchanging what words had to be exchanged between them in the course of their duties, but nothing more. But Sam knew that the Captain would have something more to say before they entered harbour, and he could guess what it would be. Nor was he disappointed.

'I suppose there's no point in asking you, Sam, but I'm going to all the same. I suppose you're going to go through with this? There's no chance of you changing your mind?'

'No, sir. I am going to go through with it.'

'I was afraid so. I have to say I think you're making a big mistake. I don't think you really realise yet how big a mistake.'

'I don't think it is a mistake, sir.'

The Captain paused, to put his binoculars to his eyes and study an approaching ship.

'It's funny, we've never had any trouble like this before, until you.' The Captain put his binoculars down. 'We always thought we were going to have problems with conscientious objectors and such-like, but we never did. Well, nothing serious. One or two minor ones in the very early days, with people whose wives got at them. But nothing serious. Until you

155

came along. I must say you're an unlikely one, to be causing all this trouble. I always thought you were sound, through and through.'

There was no reply to that, so Sam let it go.

'In a way, I can see what an effort it must have cost you. It is always easier just to go along with the crowd. To stand up for what you believe in takes guts, and I admire you for it . . .'

'Thank you, sir.'

'. . . But I also despise and loathe you . . .' The Captain's voice hardened under the weight of his contempt '. . . For taking the Queen's money all this time and then, when it boils down to it . . .'

'Excuse me, sir, may I go below now, and get ready for Harbour Stations?'

The Captain stared hard, as though awakening from a dream.

'Yes. But I want to see and approve your letter before it leaves the boat.'

'Of course, sir.' Such letters, applying to leave a particular ship, or branch of the Service, or even to resign from the Navy itself, had to be written with care and in conformance with a strict Service formula. The Navy knew, from long experience, that such letters were not always what they seemed. A competent and keen officer, who had no real wish to leave the Navy, could be driven to write a letter of resignation by particular circumstances or personalities in one ship.

By the time Sam returned to the bridge, the Bomber was already well up the Clyde. The Captain and the Navigating Officer had both put on sunglasses, and Sam wished he had remembered to bring his up with him. He had forgotten how bright the light of day was, after such a long time below in artificial light. He was surprised by the number of yachts and motor-boats. But, of course, this was the summer holiday now. They had sailed just after one Bank Holiday at the beginning of the summer season and they were returning just before another which would mark the end. It was one of those time-warps people in the Polaris programme had to endure.

156

Some of the people in the small boats waved as the Bomber passed. Others stared, as though they had just seen the Loch Ness Monster. Perhaps, Sam supposed, that was not such an outlandish comparison, after all.

Sam stayed on the bridge, after the Captain and the tugs had brought the Bomber alongside, to supervise the final placing, tautening and turning up of the wires. He saluted from the bridge as the Captain went ashore to be greeted by Captain S/M and his staff. Sam could guess at one of their main topics of conversation in the next hour.

Members of the Starboard Crew were coming on board, and the turn-over from one crew to another had already begun. Chief and the technical officers would be conferring with the Starboard Crew's Chief and their technical officers, telling them of outstanding defects and problems. Sam himself would have to greet and brief the Executive Officer of the other crew. Beneath the bantering talk of 'what *have* you done with this submarine while you've been away?', this was always a curiously tense period, of meeting one's exact counterparts, as though encountering a mirror image, and suddenly, in a short space of time, sloughing off all one's responsibilities, washing one's hands completely of a giant submarine which had been workplace, hearth and home, for three months.

When Sam reached the foot of the bridge ladder, Jimmy the Sonar Officer was waiting for him.

'Don't suppose you've heard about Draper's wife, Sam?'

'No?' Sam had a cold foreboding feeling at the back of his neck. 'What about her?'

'Killed in a car crash.'

'Bloody hell! Why didn't they tell us before?'

'They waited until we got alongside. Obviously thought a few hours more wouldn't make any difference.'

'Why, when did it happen?'

'Weeks ago. Just after we sailed.'

'Didn't he . . .'

'No, he opted not to be told. This was actually the first patrol

157

he'd opted out. Thought it would help him with his dreams and all that . . .'

'And it did, too. Bloody *hell*, it *did*! He's hacked all that. Where's he now?'

'He's getting his gear together, before he goes ashore.' Jimmy read the look in Sam's face. 'It's okay, Sam, I'll see him off. I'm his divisional officer, and his departmental officer anyway. There's no need for you . . .'

'All that time ago! And there was Draper, happy as a sandboy. He was going to discuss his future with his wife. He told me so, only the other day, it seems. Do you know what happened?'

'Apparently she was taking the kid to school in the morning and somebody ran into them as they were coming out of their side road.'

'Oh good God. What a homecoming. Who'd have thought it?'

'Yes, it's bad.'

Sam stood for a few moments in the control room after Jimmy had gone. Already the compartment had lost its sea-going look. An electrician was just fitting a shore telephone and already somebody was dragging a heavy power cable through from forward. There were strange faces from shore passing by. There would be mail in the wardroom by now, and perhaps newspapers – that day's newspapers. All the everyday trappings of normal existence ashore were flooding back into their submarine.

Sam looked about him, at the busy comings and goings. He knew he had this nervous habit, close to a neurosis, of frequently wondering whether this would be the last time he ever saw or did something. It could well be that this really was the last time he would ever stand in this control room, having just come back from sea.

The shore telephone was ringing already. Sam waited for somebody to answer it, but when everybody continued to ignore it he finally went across himself. He picked up the receiver with no sense of forewarning.

'Sam?' The voice was unmistakeable.

'Sir?'

'Can you come up here? Captain S/M wants to see you.'

'*Now*, sir?' They might at least have waited a decent interval. He had not even had a chance to walk ashore and loosen up, as he usually did after a patrol. He had not thought of the peace camp for weeks. He had not even spoken to Janet. He was wearing an old uniform. His best reefer jacket was at home.

'Yes, *now*. Right away. Pronto. They're waiting for you.'

'Do you know what it's about, sir?'

'You know damn well what it's about, Sam.'

'Well, sir, I would at least like the chance to discuss it with my wife . . .'

'Captain S/M wants to see you *now*.'

'Aye aye, sir.'

Sam looked through the wardroom door. The Navigating Officer was there, sorting through the mail.

'Yours is in that pile, there.'

Sam looked through it. It was, as he expected, bills and official mail – except for one letter which he recognised. Janet always wrote him a letter, so that it would be waiting for him in the mail when he arrived. He picked it up, smelled the envelope and put it in his pocket.

'I'm off inboard, if anybody wants me.' There was no point in telling Pilot of his destination. Everybody would know soon enough.

The Starboard Crew's Executive Officer was just coming on board as Sam reached the gangway.

They shook hands. 'Good trip, Sam?'

'Not bad, Ralph. So so.'

'Problems?'

'*Pas de problème.*'

'Okay, I've got the weight then.'

'Look, Ralph, I've got to go inboard right now . . .'

'I know . . .'

How did he know already? This whole base was like a

159

whispering gallery. 'But I'll come back, soon as I can, and give you a debrief.'

The sun was uncommonly hot on Sam's back, as he walked up through the base. There was always something clammy about the air in a submarine, even with a Bomber's air-conditioning. He fancied he could almost feel the heat of the sun burning the dampness out of the shoulders of his uniform jacket. One or two people he passed called out 'Hi, Sam, back in the land of the living again?'

It was some time since he had walked as far as this and he found himself sweating. The glare of the light was very hard on his eyes, which normally did give him a little trouble on first returning from a patrol. It seemed that staring at bulkheads and gauges at close range for weeks on end in some way impaired his normal vision.

The phrase 'They're waiting for you' had sounded ominous. When Sam reached Captain S/M's office he saw that all that was missing was the court martial sword on the table, with the point turned towards him. S/M himself was there, in the centre, seated at his desk. Standing on either side of him were Commander S/M, two officers from S/M's staff, and, perhaps significantly, the PMO. This certainly was the full turnout, the First Eleven. Even the great bulk of the Captain, standing on one side, seemed diminished in such company. They must feel this matter was important. In a way, such an assembly was something of a compliment. For a fleeting moment, Sam even felt flattered.

'Come in, Sam, come in, let's get this over.' Captain S/M did not get up from his desk, nor offer his hand. 'I think we can sort all this out before it goes any further.'

Sam studied S/M's face closely. He had never served with him before, nor with Commander S/M either. Commander S/M had only joined the flotilla shortly before they sailed. So these two men, whom Sam now recognised as adversaries, were both almost complete strangers to him. That was compara-tively unusual, though by no means unique, in such a small and

160

closely-knit branch of the Navy as the Submarine Service. It would have been of some advantage to have known more about his opponents. Because opponent Captain S/M certainly was, as the interview soon made clear. Sam wondered what his Captain had said about him.

'Now, from what your Captain has told me, you did not directly disobey an order . . .'

'No, sir.'

'But you informed him that you did not wish to take part in any more launches, or drills, after this patrol was over?'

'That's correct, sir.'

'In fact, you now want to leave the Polaris programme?'

'Yes sir.'

'Why is that? Why do you want to do that?'

'Well, sir . . .' Sam paused. It was an enormous question to answer. In fact, it was impossible to answer. 'I would prefer to give my reasons in writing, sir, when I write my letter applying to leave, which I will do in the next few days, sir.'

'I don't want you to write a letter. That won't be necessary. I want to get this sorted out here and now, before this goes any further.'

That was twice S/M had used that phrase. He seemed uncommonly anxious not to let this go any further.

'The first point to be made is that, naturally, we don't wish to lose one of our best Polaris officers. You've got a lot of experience in the programme. You've got a good track record, with several patrols behind you.'

That statement, Sam thought, would have been a great deal more convincing had it not been for the memory, which still rankled, of 'You're no great shakes as a submariner'. Sam glanced at the Captain, who had the grace to look slightly sheepish.

'Don't you yourself feel you've done well in this boat?'

'Well, yes, sir, I do.' Sam did not look again at the Captain. 'I feel I've done my best.'

'Good. Well, having said that, surely you don't want to chuck all you've achieved so far down the drain?'

'I don't think I will be, sir. I hope to continue my career outside Polaris.'

Captain S/M did not reply for some time. The silence lengthened, in what Sam was sure was intended to be an ominous manner. Sam found himself resenting the implicit threat behind the silence. He simply could not believe that his own circumstances were so special, meriting such particular pressure. He would not be the first to apply to leave the Polaris programme, nor would he be the first to leave it. Others had had misgivings. One officer he knew of, with a reputation as a very able submarine commanding officer, had flatly refused to take a Bomber command when it was offered him. Admittedly he had not been promoted to any higher rank, not yet, but he had certainly not jeopardised his whole career thereby.

'What puzzles me, what puzzled all of us when we heard, is why you should reach this decision now? Why *now?*' Captain S/M had clearly decided to try another tack.

'I don't know myself, sir. I just made up my mind during this last patrol.'

'But you must have some idea.'

'No, sir. It is just a decision I came to.'

'You realise that it might have the most serious consequences for your future in the Service?'

Again, there was that implied threat.

'I do realise that, sir. But as I said, I don't see why it necessarily should.'

'Well then, let me tell you. If you do leave us, as I say, *if* you leave us, you will take this with you. The officers and ship's company in any other appointment you go to in the future will know that here is someone who was trained for a specific job, who volunteered for it . . .'

'I volunteered for submarines, sir, not for Polaris . . .'

'Well then, you volunteered to be a submariner, and you took the extra money, and you had the reputation of being a submariner, which we are all so proud of, but when it came to putting it to the test, when it came right down to it, you failed. You chickened out.'

162

'I don't think I did chicken out, sir.' The word had stung Sam more than he would have believed possible, and he replied more hotly than he knew was wise. 'In some ways it required much more to stick out and say no than it would have done to say nothing and just go on.'

The point was so obviously true, so palpable a hit, that Captain S/M was silent again. Sam expected somebody else to take up the questioning, but he was wrong. It was Captain S/M himself.

'I grant you that. But the broader question remains, that when it came down to it, you behaved like a conscientious objector. What they used to call a *Conchie*.'

Sam felt his cheeks beginning to burn. He was amazed and angered by the unexpected intensity of this attack on him. Nobody else he had ever heard of had been grilled like this. Others had been questioned about their motives and their reasons, certainly, but they had not been put under such immediate pressure. He was barely home from a full deterrent patrol, and had not even had a chance to speak to his wife, before being summoned to appear in front of Captain S/M and his staff and being called upon to justify his behaviour whilst being subjected to a disagreeable cross-examination.

'If I'm forced to explain myself, sir, I would say that my main feeling was one of helplessness.'

'Helplessness.' Captain S/M and the others grimaced at the word, as though at a sudden unexpected whiff of a sewer.

'Yes, sir. It suddenly came to me that what we were doing was daft. It was irrelevant. We're not deterring anybody. The other side are not daft. They don't want to commit suicide. The whole thing is a giant con trick. I don't know why I never thought of this before. I suppose I never stopped to think before. I think the whole thing, the whole Polaris project, is a huge and frighteningly expensive waste of time. In a most curious way . . .'

Sam was conscious that the others were all reluctantly, in spite of themselves, listening closely to what he was saying.

163

'. . . It was like that saying, the scales fell from one's eyes. As I say, sir, I don't know why I didn't think of this before. I suppose, when it comes right down to it, my opinions are not *moral* at all, they're *practical*. I just suddenly thought to myself what the *hell* is the point of all this? What are we *doing* here?'

Captain S/M had been drawing in deep breaths, his nostrils curled, like a runner preparing for the start of what promised to be a hard race.

'The Polaris programme, which you criticise for its *daftness* and its *irrelevance* has given the Submarine Service more money and submarines, more *kit*, than any of us would ever have dreamed possible in the old days. It has given our branch a marvellous professional opportunity, which *some* of us have taken with both hands. As a branch, we would never have had such a chance without Polaris. Now, the deterrent is going to be upgraded. We have the prospect opening before us of a new generation of submarines, with a new and more powerful deterrent. None of this is decided yet, but as you know there is a great deal of opposition to nuclear weapons in this country. I need not spell out for you the possible consequences of an officer like yourself making public his aversion to nuclear weapons, whether on *moral* or *practical* grounds, or whatever. You are not just any naval officer, not just any submariner. You are Polaris crew, and a very experienced and responsible member of it.'

As Captain S/M had said, there was no need to spell it out. Sam saw the point at once. He himself thought it ludicrous to suppose that his own private little crisis of conscience would have any public effect. But that was unimportant. What mattered was that Captain S/M thought it might have an effect. In his bitterness and anger, Sam could suddenly see it all clearly. Captain S/M's expressed anxiety not to lose him, because of his 'experience' and his 'track record', was just so much unctuous crap. Captain S/M did not care a hoot whether or not Sam stayed in the Polaris programme, or in submarines, or in the Navy. All that concerned him was that Sam should not embarrass the Navy in public.

Curiously, this sudden knowledge gave Sam an added reassurance. He might eventually, if Captain S/M had gone on long enough, have yielded to an appeal to his loyalty to the Submarine Service. Probably it was the only appeal that might have swayed him. But Captain S/M had let slip the truth. Sam had always felt that he was on his own in this matter. Captain S/M had just inadvertently revealed to him that he was nearer the truth than he knew.

'I see I'm not having any success in impressing you . . .'

Sam realised that Captain S/M was as good as his Captain at reading his face. He really must try and guard his expressions more carefully.

'. . . I'll give you a week to think it over.'

'I don't need a week to think it over, sir. I've already had weeks to think about it.'

'I'll see you in a week.'

Sam knew that the interview had probably ended earlier than Captain S/M had intended, and in a way which he certainly had not intended.

'Aye aye, sir.'

Commander S/M followed Sam down the staircase and into the sunshine outside the main office block. Significantly, his own Captain stayed behind with Captain S/M.

'I'm sorry about that, Sam.'

'Don't be.' This Commander S/M had started in boats one training class behind Sam but he had already outstripped Sam by some way. He had had his brass hat nearly a year ago. He was very junior for this job, and clearly he was a very able fellow. That was quite enough reason for disliking the man and for resenting this extra interrogation. Sam remembered this man's nickname when he had started in submarines: Mouser.

'I didn't know S/M was going to be so brutal about it. It's the political angle that worries him . . .'

'I could see *that*.'

'Yes. Look, don't be so bolshie about it. I think I know how you feel. But I just didn't know he was so concerned about it, was going to fly off the handle like that. As a matter of fact, I agree with a lot of what you say, especially about the practical angle. It's just that I don't see the point of making a stand like this. If it *is* a stand. At your time of life, that is. You're not the sort of person who should be saying this. You just annoy people. Get up their noses.'

'How do I do that?'

'Well, if a sub-lieutenant was saying what you're saying, somebody just fresh out of training class, somebody just about to start in the Polaris programme, it would be out of the mouths of babes and sucklings sort of thing, and might have a sort of credible innocence about it. Or, if you were a senior Captain or Admiral, people would have to take notice. But you're neither. You're neither junior enough nor senior enough. Furthermore, you've been in Bombers for a long time now and you've never breathed a dicky bird until now. D'you see what I'm getting at?'

'Yes I do.' Sam could hardly avoid seeing what he was getting at. Mouser was never known for his subtlety.

'Well, anyway, I just thought I would give you as much of a buck-up as I could.'

'Very good of you.'

'By the way, I hear you've been visiting that camp just outside?'

'Who told you that?'

'Security. They keep an eye on things.'

'We had a puncture once, and they mended it. One of them is a trained mechanic.'

'I thought it was a bit more than that. So I heard. But if that's all it was, not to worry.'

The sun felt unusually hot on Sam's back as he walked down to the submarine. This must be one of the west of Scotland's rare heatwaves. It made Sam feel almost faint with the unaccustomed heat. He could feel sweat under his cap and streaming down his back, under this shirt.

The Navigating Officer called from the control room as Sam reached the wardroom door.

'Janet's just been on the blower, Sam. She's coming down to

collect you in half an hour or so. She and the boys and Alice send their love.'

'Oh good, thank you.' Of course, the boys were at home now for their summer holidays.

Sam sat down in the wardroom. He remembered Janet's letter and took it out of his jacket pocket. She wrote such a letter, to welcome him, after every patrol. It was her own expression, in her own words, of love, and longing, and loneliness.

Sam let the letter rest on the cushion beside him. He leaned his head back against the bulkhead. He shut his eyes and soon felt the tears running down his cheeks and into the corners of his mouth. He could actually taste the salt. He had not cried like this since he was a little boy. It gave him the relief he needed.

He opened his eyes. Danny Bennett and Chief were standing in the wardroom, looking down at him.

'Sam, it's okay.' He did not know which of them was speaking. 'It's okay. Don't take it to heart so much, Sam.'

CHAPTER 8

I**T WAS ALWAYS HARD** for Sam to adjust to the sights and sounds of summer after a patrol, but this time it seemed harder than ever. The light was so bright, the sounds of traffic and road-drills so loud, the road up the hill so steep, the smell of earth and vegetation overpowering. He saw people playing tennis on his way up to the wardroom. To his eyes, they might have been visitors from Mars.

Janet and the children were waiting by the car on the forecourt in front of the wardroom. They all swarmed towards him.

Janet was wearing a bright striped cotton summer dress and sandals. She had what Sam always thought of as 'that peaches and cream' smell.

'Darling, you do smell of that submarine.' Janet sniffed deeply at his lapel. 'I don't know what it is. I always forget what it smells like until you come home again.' If she had noticed the stains of tears on his face, she said nothing. While walking up, he had screwed up his eyes, to hide the telltale signs, just as he used to do at school.

The children were clamouring round him.

'I want to smell Daddy's submarine smell . . .'

'No, I'm older, I'm first . . .'

'Alice, get back, you're only a *girl* . . .'

'Meanie . . .'

The 'submarine smell' was just a good excuse to put their

168

arms around their father. Simon had noticeably grown. He was just reaching the stage when he would begin to shoot up.

The boys fought each other to get Sam's grip and put it in the car boot.

'Hey, watch that thing! It's on its last legs, that grip.'

As Sam climbed into the passenger's seat, he saw the Captain standing in the wardroom doorway, watching them. Janet saw him, and waved. The Captain briefly waved back.

At the main gate Sam braced himself for the MoD PloD. One of them, in shirtsleeves, looked at him, and at Janet and the children, and waved the car through. As the car moved off, Sam leaned back in his seat and shut his eyes. The shock of new sensation, the vividness of the green leaves, the piercing light, his children's excited faces, were overwhelming. The country-side, the world outside the submarine, had a richness and a beauty he had quite forgotten. He felt the tears start again.

They had reached the road junction. Sam opened his eyes, feeling the wetness on his eyelids. The camp was much larger than he remembered it. There seemed to be more than twice the number of vans and caravans, and many more people walking about there.

'They've all been in the news, very much so.' Janet had followed his gaze. 'Three of them are going to try to take the Prime Minister to court for conspiracy to commit genocide, because of authorising nuclear weapons. So the local paper says, anyway.'

'What's that, Mummy?'

'It's when one lot of people try to kill a whole lot of another people.'

'That's what Miss Farquhar says the English did to the Scots.'

'Oh, your Miss Farquhar, what does she know about it?'

'More than you do, Clever Clogs.'

There was the thud of what sounded like a punch.

'Don't *do* that.'

There was no doubt Alice could hold her own in debate with

169

her elder brothers. And, if all else failed, there was always the last resort of physical violence.

Janet stopped the car in their drive. The boys jumped out, yelling and struggling, to open the boot and the garage door.

Janet kissed Sam on the side of the cheek. 'I've saved you the lawn to mow.'

'Oh goodie. I knew there was something I was looking forward to all through that patrol.'

'You okay, darling?' With one fingertip she traced the dry course of a tear down his face.

'Yes, sure.'

He had a long bath first, while Janet unpacked his grip. As usual, Janet came in with a big towel to dry him.

'You're very quiet, darling.'

'Well . . . Am I? I'm still winding down from the patrol.'

Looking down, he saw that, as usual, he had left a deep, dark 'tide-mark' on the sides of the bath. No matter how hard one tried, it was impossible to keep oneself absolutely clean on board; there was no substitute for a hot bath and a good scrub at home.

'Don't worry, I'll clean it, darling.'

'No, no, *no*. *I'll* clean it.'

'All right, darling, you clean it. I'll leave you to it. Don't forget the lawn.'

'I won't.'

It seemed to take a long time and a great deal of effort to clean the mark off. Maybe he was dirtier than usual.

When Sam came back into the bedroom, he could smell 'the submarine smell' himself, rising like some miasma of memory from the pile of his clothes. He changed into a clean shirt and trousers and mowed the lawn. It was only a small lawn, as befitted a small bungalow, but it seemed much larger than he remembered it. The odours of new-mown grass, with flowers and the petrol of the machine, were strong enough almost to be sickening. He would have liked another bath. It was illogical to have had one before cutting the lawn. He should have waited.

Afterwards, he took a can of beer from the refrigerator. It

170

was a Scottish beer and his favourite, which he knew Janet, who never drank beer, must have got in specially for his homecoming. But even the beer seemed to have a lingering taste of exhaust fumes from the mower. The beer on board had tasted better. That was something at least that was better on board. He poured half the can away, guiltily, down the sink.

There were three invitations on the mantelpiece. On two of them, the names meant nothing to Sam. But the third was to dinner with Captain and Mrs S/M. The date was a fortnight off. Probably it would all have been settled by then. He hoped so.

There was the usual assortment of mail in the desk. Plenty of bills, but nothing to worry about; Janet, as usual, had everything in hand. There was the latest issue of the naval history magazine he subscribed to, still sealed in its wrapper, because Janet knew he liked to open it himself.

Sam wandered restlessly around the living-room, as though still trying to accustom himself to strange surroundings. He could still hear the resonances of the submarine's machinery, the rhythms of footsteps in its passageways, the tones of announcements on the broadcast. He could rid himself of the Bomber's smell, but not yet of its remembered sounds.

They had a special homecoming supper, as a family, in Sam's honour. It was, as always, crowded around their little table, but the boys wore their school suits, with shirts and ties, and Alice wore her party dress. There were candles, which Alice was allowed to light. They had kebabs, one of Sam's and the children's favourites, and one of Janet's great specialities, with tomatoes and sauces, and a great dish of fluffy white rice. There was a long fresh French loaf, which Johnny cut and handed round. Sam and Janet had wine, which Simon poured for them. The children, even Alice, were allowed to have half a glass of wine, as it was an occasion.

As always, Janet's cooking was too good for anybody to waste any of their time or energy in conversation. Sam watched the children concentrating on taking the pieces of grilled meat, kidney, sausage and bacon off the skewers. Looking at his wife sitting opposite him at the end of the table, and at his children's bright intent faces, Sam had once again the terrifying thought, like an ice splinter in his heart: could this be the last time?

Alice was already asleep, with the bedroom light still on, when Sam went in to see her. He knew she had been bursting to talk to him, but she had simply not been able to stay awake. He was sorry. He kissed her and turned out the light.

The boys said goodnight in their various ways. Simon was quiet, Johnny was talkative. They were still not used to having their father at home and Sam was conscious that he was still exotic, to be stared at, with an unfamiliar voice, to be listened to with extra concentration.

Simon was reading. He put the book down as Sam came in. 'What's that?'

'*The Last of the Mohicans*, Daddy.'

'Good? I don't think I've ever read it.'

'Yes, I like it. My English master says it's a bit dated nowadays. He says it projects an essentially bourgeois view of the ethnic population. Elitist, he calls it.'

'Good Lord! I'm sure J. Fenimore Cooper would be surprised to know that.'

As usual, Johnny wanted to talk about the submarine. 'Did it all go okay, Daddy?'

'Oh yes. Box of birds.'

'I bet you all felt jolly pleased when it was all over safely.'

'Yes we did.'

'It's not dangerous, is it, Daddy?'

'Not at all. Like falling off a log.'

'Only . . .'

'Only what?'

'One of the boys at school was saying how dangerous submarines were.' Johnny's voice held a note of real anxiety. 'He said his father said it was a dog's life and that was why they had to pay you more, to get you to go down in them.'

'What does *his* father do?'

'I think he sells motor cars, or something.'

'Well, I would say that was far more dangerous!'

'Daddy . . .'

172

'Yes?'

'I don't care. I still want to be a submariner.'

'Good. That's *exactly* the right spirit. Now goodnight.'

'Goodnight, Daddy. We like it when you're home.'

'Oh good. I like it when I'm home, too.'

'They're so glad to see you. We all are.' Janet had her tapestry on her knee. It was the same piece, but now it was nearly finished. That was yet another sign of how much time had passed since he had last been at home. He thought of all the evenings she must have spent sitting alone by the fire, doing her tapestry, while he was away.

'Yes I know. But in some strange way I feel I'm not at home properly yet. I'm still getting used to it all.'

He switched on the television. It was a round-up of local news. Every other programme on Scottish television was a round-up of local news. That, or gangs of laddies and lassies Scottish country dancing.

To his amazement, there was a picture of El Tel, and then one of the wire fence by the main road running alongside the submarine base, and then a reporter standing facing the camera.

'. . . The Ministry of Defence's action was described as "monstrous". Next stop will be the House of Lords. But one thing is certain, this is going to run and run . . .'

'What's he talking about, do you know?'

Janet looked up and at the screen. 'Oh, it's probably the road. That's been in the news, too. There's been a great court case about it in Edinburgh, apparently. When they were building that new fence the Ministry shut off one lane of the main road, do you remember? Apparently the local council objected and said you can't do that because we own the road and you haven't asked us first and the Ministry said yes we can, we can do whatever we like because we're the Ministry of Defence and what we say goes and they've all been to court about it . . .'

'Oh yes I do remember now.' Obviously, the television people had asked El Tel to comment upon the verdict, as the

173

representative of the peace campers. El Tel was getting to be quite a television personality. 'So the MoD has got itself a thick ear.'

'It seems so.'

'I'm glad.'

'*Are* you? Whatever for?'

'I'm against the whole base and all its works at the moment.'

'Darling, whatever are you talking about?'

'Honey, I've got something important to tell you.'

'I rather thought you had.'

'It's quite serious, actually.'

'I guessed it was. I thought you had something on your mind. I know you're always a bit quiet when you first come back. As though you're mentally still back down there . . .'

'That's quite true . . .'

'But *today*. Darling, you've no *idea* how terribly sad you looked, sitting in the car today. As though the children were too noisy for you and it was all too much for you. Had you been crying?'

'Yes. Yes I had.'

'I thought so. Whatever for?'

'I've decided I don't want to go on serving in a Polaris boat.'

'Just like that.'

'Well, to begin with, just like that, yes. But I've had lots of time to think about it and it's not just like that any more. I can't bear the thought of ever having to go to sea in one of those things again. I don't want to see one or smell one, or even think of one, ever again.'

'Goodness. What's brought this on?'

'Yes, it does sound like a disease, doesn't it? Although I'm beginning to think of it as more of a cure. But I did feel a sort of sickness, it was while we were practising one day, I just looked around me, and I suddenly got a sort of gut feeling that I just didn't want to go on with this. I didn't believe in it. I didn't want to do it. I didn't think it was any good, that it had any relevance at all. I got the feeling we were all just posturing away doing something that was very dangerous. We were

174

actually being presumptuous in thinking we could go on doing what we were doing. As I told Captain S/M, it is not so much a moral thing, although I suppose morals must come into it to some extent, it's a matter of practicalities. It's all a big con trick. It's difficult to describe it, really.'

'Oh, I think you've described it well enough, darling.' She was looking at him as though she were not quite sure whether to believe him or not. 'So what now? How does this affect us?'

'I don't know. I've told them I don't want to go on.'

'But can you do that? *Can* you just say to the Navy, I don't want to go on with this? They must think it a bit odd, surely? They must say to you, what if everybody did this, where would we be then?'

'They didn't actually say that. In fact, that's about the only argument they didn't use.'

'Well, I must say, your argument doesn't sound very convincing, darling. It's not as if you're a new boy. Why this sudden change of heart? Why didn't you speak up before?'

'Now, that's an argument they did use.'

'Well, what did you say?'

'I don't know, really. I had to admit they were right.'

'You're serious about this, aren't you, darling?' Janet was looking directly at him now, every line of her body showing her alarm, like somebody suddenly alive to a real danger and ready to flee. 'Does this mean we may have to move from here?'

'As I say, I don't know yet, honey. They may not let me go anyway, even though they don't think much of me.'

'How do you know they don't think much of you?'

'Oh, I get up people's noses, they say. They say you're no great shakes as a submariner, Sam. That's what they tell me.'

'Who said that?'

'Well, the Captain, actually.'

To Sam's astonishment and chagrin, Janet began to laugh. 'He's a caution, that man. There's something about him. I know he's a great fat slob and a male chauvinist pig of the deepest dye. Those great rubber lips of his . . .'

'I'd no idea you studied him so closely.'

Janet did not reply.

'Just because I want to go, doesn't mean they'll let me. There's a sort of bloody-mindedness about the Navy. Like the appointers, they find out where you want to go and then make damn sure you don't go there. The funny thing is that more than one person has said to me that they basically agree with what I say about nuclear weapons, but they think I shouldn't say it out loud.'

'Well, I agree with that!'

'But it's you that's always said nuclear weapons were a dangerous nonsense. You've said that yourself, many a time.'

'Yes, but this is your *job*, darling. And our future as a family. Can't you explain it a bit more?'

'No, I don't think so. I think this was something I've felt all along. It's a kind of madness, and now I feel I'm coming to my senses again.'

'Darling, this is your life you're talking about. What happens if they do give you the sack?'

'Too bad. I'll do something else. Get another job.'

'You'll get another job. And what about me? I married a naval officer. Not an ex-naval officer who left of his own free will when he didn't need to.'

Janet did not actually spell her meaning out, nor perhaps did she even mean what her words had implied, but Sam took the implication at once. Sam as a Lieutenant RN had been worth marrying, enough of a 'catch', as they used to say. But Sam as a civilian, as a bank clerk, like his father before him, would certainly not have been considered.

'Darling, I just get the dreadful cold feeling that if we're not careful something awful is going to happen to us as a family, if you do this.'

'But surely you wouldn't want me to go on doing something I no longer wanted to do? Something I actually thought was wrong?'

She did not reply for some time, and when she did, it was as though she were reluctant to speak. 'But I thought you said it was not moral.'

'Well it is. Although . . . I'm really not sure.' Sam frowned. He felt that he had already exhausted all the words available to him on the subject. He would just be going round the buoy again. But he had the ominous feeling he would be doing precisely that in the future, again and again and again. 'All I *am* sure about is that I don't want to go on.'

'I can see that. Well, let's go to bed and sleep on it. Maybe it will look different in the morning.'

'I doubt it. I hope it doesn't. I've been thinking about this a long time, you know.'

'I know, darling. It's just all a bit new to me, that's all. I'll just go and check and see if Alice is all right.'

Janet got into bed unusually quietly. In the dimness, he could see she was naked. She lay beside him, motionless, for some time.

'Is something the matter?'

'Is something the matter?' She had turned suddenly towards him. 'Darling, that's something I could ask you. I'm terrified. For some reason, I'm absolutely terrified. And I don't quite know what I'm terrified of.'

'Well, don't be. It'll be all right. I know what I'm doing. I love you. Can I say that?'

'Darling, I've been waiting and waiting for you to say that.'

Her skin was smooth, delicious to touch, cool and yet hot. It was an act so often imagined during the patrol. It was fantasy now made real, but different from any fantasy, a reality forgotten but now instantly remembered. As always, he was aroused by her submission, and her willingness.

'I feel I'm really home now.'

'I *feel* it, too.'

'Oh don't be so coarse. Honestly, women. It's women who tell the dirtiest jokes. We've got nothing on you.'

'I've got *you* on me at the moment.'

'There you go again.'

'But it's good. It's very good.'

Afterwards, she only had one more question. 'Can't you give

177

up this idea of leaving? Is it too late to go back and just say it never happened?'

'I think it is, darling. And, anyway, I don't want to go back. Can we just leave it until the morning?'

Unusually, for the first night after a patrol, he went to sleep almost immediately and had no remembered dreams, until he woke and heard the telephone ringing in the hall. He got out of bed and put on his dressing gown. He sensed that his movements had disturbed Janet briefly out of her sleep.

'Telephone, darling, got to go and answer it.'

'I can't hear anything.'

It was very cold in the hallway and Sam shivered as he picked up the receiver. He could not recognise the voice, it was probably the duty officer of the Starboard Crew, but it had the same urgency as Danny's, on the night he telephoned to say that there was an intruder in the base.

'Sam? Could you come down right away? There's a fire on board.'

'Oh my God. Is it bad?'

'Quite bad, yes.'

'Have you told the Boss?'

'Not yet. We're sending a messenger up to tell him.'

'Okay, I'll come down right away.'

Sam put down the receiver, and saw Simon standing in his pyjamas in the bedroom doorway.

'Did the telephone wake you?'

'No, I didn't hear it, Daddy. I was on my way to the bathroom.'

'Well, hurry up and go and then get back to bed.'

Sam put on his uniform trousers and reefer jacket over his pyjamas. There was not time to dress properly. He pulled on socks and then shoes. On a peg in the hall he found a blue scarf and wound it round his neck. Nobody would ever notice that he had no shirt on, at this hour. He looked at his watch. Half past four. It was broad daylight outside already and the birds were singing.

In the bedroom, the curtains were still drawn. Janet would

178

not like them suddenly pulled back. Sam bent over and kissed her. She was always a heavy sleeper and a reluctant riser. Unlike himself, who always got up early by choice. Strange that he should marry somebody who was the complete opposite.

'Got to go now, honey. Fire on board the boat.'

'Oh good. So soon?'

Clearly she was still fast asleep.

'See you later.'

Outside, it was a perfect morning. The sun was up, and the sky was an unbroken blue, from horizon to horizon. In the low sunlight, the river looked as though it were made of multiple panes of shifting, shining glass. There were currents to be seen moving in it, and wide sheets of water which looked absolutely flat but then dissolved into thousands of pin-pricks of light, glowing and fading again. Sam drove down towards the bright river, and turned right for the submarine base.

There was not a soul on the road. Sam was vaguely puzzled. If there was an emergency of any kind at the base, he would have expected more activity, perhaps even a fire engine by now.

As he drove, Sam considered what sort of fire it might be. At sea, particularly in the earlier days of the Polaris programme, it would most likely be steam-pipe lagging in one of the machinery compartments aft which had become soaked with hydraulic oil. Or it could be in one of the diesel generator compartments, one of the main fire hazards; Chief always said they were like fire-lighters waiting to be lit. It was not likely to be the reactor compartment which was reasonably inert, so far as fire hazards went. At the worst, it might be a fire in one of the gas generators which actually fired the missiles out of their tubes. That would be almost as bad as a cordite fire in a conventional gun turret. Whatever it was, it must be serious for somebody to telephone Sam at his home, now that he was off-crew.

The main gates were still drawn shut at that hour of the morning. The MoD PloD on the gate had a ginger moustache and halitosis. He looked suspiciously at Sam's scarf. 'You got any means of identification, sir?'

'Look, haven't you received any report of a fire on board a submarine?'

'No, sir?' The MoD PloD's suspicions of Sam were clearly deepening.

The MoD PloD scrutinised the ID card which, providentially, Sam happened to have in his inside jacket pocket, apparently reading every word on it as though it were inscribed in some obscure foreign tongue. Sam wrestled with the almost overpowering urge to call this man the stupid, obstinate, time-wasting clod he was.

'Look, could you please hurry? There's an emergency. Somebody rang me at my home.'

'What sort of emergency, sir?'

Dear God, if there had been a burglary the burglar would be miles away by now. 'A fire. A bad fire, on board my submarine. I must get down there. Has anybody rung the fire station?'

'Not that I know of, sir.'

'Well, would you do it *now*, please? It's urgent.'

Their voices, raised as though in argument, had already attracted attention. As the MoD PloD at last waved him through, Sam saw the figures of Marines in the shadows. Judging by the silhouettes, they were armed. Well, at least it was good to know the boot-necks were awake and on the job.

Sam parked his car in the main car-park and, still wondering at the absence of any activity or urgency anywhere in the base, began first to walk and then to run towards the next gate, giving access to the inner high security area.

The hurried way he had parked his car, the slammed car door, his urgent running, at that hour, again attracted suspicion on the gate. The PloD faced him, with an impassive face. With a weird sense of playing a preordained part, Sam conducted much the same conversation again.

'. . . So could you *please* tell the fire station?' Sam nodded and pointed towards it. It was, after all, just behind the police station building.

He ran on, down between the buildings and across the pontoon to the loch side and the Polaris berth. At the gangway, he paused.

There was nobody on the jetty, or on the hull of the submarine. There was no sign of a trot sentry or anybody else. But, from the open fore hatch, a column of black smoke was rising, as though from a ship's funnel. Clearly, there was a major fire burning below, with not a soul anywhere to take any notice of it.

Sam fancied he could hear a siren sounding behind him somewhere in the base as he ran up the gangway. Looking down through the hatch, he thought he could make out the shape of somebody lying at the bottom of the ladder. But he could tell, from the density and smell of the smoke, that he could never get down there. It would be foolish to try. He would probably become a casualty himself. But he jumped down into the hatch recess, braced his back against the edge and pushed the hatch shut with his feet. It was not possible to shut it properly to seal it. That had to be done from below. But at least this would stop the air flow. Something left open on the submarine below was creating the draught which was fanning the fire.

The door leading into the fin was open. Sam climbed in and down the tower. He could feel air flowing past him as he descended. They still had the ventilation running. They seemed not to have taken the least fire-fighting precaution.

The control room was empty. Sam could hardly believe his eyes. Here was a Bomber with a major fire, and nobody round to take the slightest notice of it.

'Where the *hell is* everybody!' Sam could hear his own voice resounding back against him from the bulkheads.

At last, there were figures gathering at the after end of the control room. He could not recognise any of them. Of course, they were Starboard Crew. They might even be newcomers to the Starboard Crew, not only new to the boat, but strangers to each other.

'Where's the duty officer?'

There was no answer.

'*Who* is the duty officer?'

They looked at each other, still without replying.

'Are there any of your duty watch missing? Have you checked?'

Ye Gods, answer came there none. Sam paused. Should he try and take charge? There should already be somebody in charge – the duty officer. If Sam now tried to take charge, he might confuse things. But clearly, there was nobody in charge.

'Some of you get breathing sets. And extinguishers.' Sam steadied himself, to speak slowly and clearly. He must not criticise too much, or he might precipitate a panic. People would lose confidence in what they were being told to do. 'Come on, let's get started on this. The sooner the better. Come on, we've wasted enough time, as it is. Come *on*, chop chop!'

As Sam walked towards the watertight door leading forward, he could hear the eerie warbling noise of the general alarm. At *last*. Somebody would have to have an investigation into why the officer of the day had done absolutely nothing so far.

The door was shut. Sam pulled on the clip. The door swung slowly open.

After one look, Sam slammed the door shut again with all his strength. The fire was within feet of the other side. He had heard it, and smelled it, and there was a body lying in the passageway.

He now realised this was a most dangerous fire, where nobody had expected it, where it was particularly difficult to fight – down in the complex of living spaces forward, where the ship's company lived and slept. It was a warren of interlinked messes and bunk-spaces, well-stocked with foam-filled mattresses. What was more, every bunk had its individual punkah louvre, so that the occupant could regulate his own air supply. These would feed oxygen to the fire, wherever it was.

Opening that door, even for a few seconds, had released fumes into the control room. Sam felt the smoke catching at his throat.

'Come *on*, damn you! What the hell's keeping you? There's

182

somebody just the other side of the door, if you don't bloody well hurry up, he's going to die! Somebody stop the ventilation fans, at *once*.'

He was conscious of the cessation of noise, as the fans stopped, but the smoke was getting thicker, and more acrid, and it seemed the air temperature was actually rising, as though the control room was already getting hotter.

Sam took down a face-mask and plugged it into the emergency breathing system which ran right through the boat. It was connected through reducing valves to the ship's high-pressure air storage bottles. The air smelled as though it had just come from a stable, and the mask as though someone had recently been sick in it. But it was better than breathing smoke.

Through the eye-pieces he could see other masked figures, swaying towards him. He crooked a finger, and took one of the self-contained breathing sets. He slipped the straps over his shoulders. The gauge showed the bottles full. At least, that was *something* that had been done right.

Sam changed masks, and felt around the edges of the new one, to check that it fitted neatly. He breathed in deeply: the breathing-set air was slightly musty, but with a faintly sweetish smell, which made the saliva flow in his mouth. He wanted to spit, but had to swallow. He crooked a finger again, and took the foam extinguisher someone offered him.

They were all still hesitating. Sam took off his face-mask, to bellow at the figures in front of him. '*Torch* for Christ's sake! For God's sake one of you get me a torch so I can see something! Don't just stand around like a lot of . . .' He could not think of a suitable epithet. 'Have none of you guys ever done a fire-fighting course, for God's *sake*! Two of you come with me and back me up. *Move, move!* It's not going to get any better by standing and goofing at it!'

He felt somebody knotting a life-line round his waist. Thank God, *somebody* had remembered their training. That was the problem with these fire-fighting courses. They all did them, and passed them, and got bits of paper to say they had passed

183

them, and then they thought they knew it all. But the moment they had to confront a real fire and felt the first whiff of real heat, they all began to behave like a lot of zombies. *Zombies*, that was the word he had been searching for earlier.

There was no torch, but he could wait no longer. He opened the door again. It was noticeably hotter, there was no doubt about that now, and darker. There was only the emergency lighting now, glowing in the passage-way, as though from a very long way off.

Sam could not see the body on the deck, but stubbed it with his toe. He bent down, put his arms round the shoulders, and lifted. Hands from behind helped him. He felt the body being dragged away from him. There was no way of knowing whether or not it was still alive. He had hardly put another foot forward when he tripped on something else. Bending down, he felt another face. Ye Gods, they must have been trying to escape, or maybe even fight the fire, and had been overcome. This fire must have crept up on everybody. Nobody seemed to have noticed anything.

This body felt much heavier. Perhaps the other one had been still alive and this one was dead.

Somebody nudged Sam in the back and passed him a torch. Although he could feel by its weight that it must be a large and powerful torch, he could only just see its light. He held the torch up to his eyes until he knew that it was only inches away from his face. But even then, he could only barely see its beam. This smoke must be the thickest in the world. He flashed the torch downwards several times, to indicate the body on the deck. He sensed rather than saw the other figure nod. At least somebody had their heads screwed on the right way.

There was now not the slightest vestige of light in the passage. He was advancing into total blackness, a blackness so all-enveloping, so complete, that anybody who had never experienced it would never comprehend it. Sam switched off his torch. It was of no use. He might as well save the batteries.

The extinguisher in Sam's left hand felt as though it weighed a ton. At least that meant that it must be full. It would be

184

entirely in character with what had just been happening if he found that he had been carrying an empty extinguisher to the fire. He put it down on the deck, whilst he felt with his hand along the bulkhead. His hand strayed into nothingness. There was an opening here, into one of the bunk spaces, possibly. Or was it the entrance to the galley? He tried to visualise the submarine's layout just here, but he could not remember. So much for all those Rounds, every evening at sea. He must have walked up and down this passage a thousand times at the very least. Now, he could not even remember what this particular stretch where he was standing looked like.

The heat was now very much greater. Suddenly he could feel it through his trouser cloth on his knees, on his bare hands, and through the material of his face mask. There was a glow, low down and in front of him. It was moving slowly, like molten metal, flowing over a ledge. As he watched, parts of it began to drop, like pieces of a heavy curtain falling to the ground. This must be the very core and heart of the fire.

The surrounding air was getting much hotter by the second. He had to step back. In an onset of panic he looked for the extinguisher. It had gone. It was lost, somewhere in the blackness. He bent down to search for it and hit his head on its rim. He picked it up and banged it to activate it. By instinct, or training, or happy chance, he knew how to operate it correctly, even in this blackness. He felt the heavy canister vibrate, come reassuringly alive in his hands. It was working. The heat was now so intense he could hardly bear to look in its direction, but he sprayed the foam towards it.

At first, he seemed only to be aggravating the fire. The molten sheet glowed more brightly, so that he could actually see flecks and spots, like eyes or mouths, in its surface. The blackness in front of him changed momentarily to grey. He thought he could hear the sounds of hissing and cooling. The extinguisher in his hands was lighter, and had stopped vibrating. It was empty, and dead.

At the same time, he became aware of the urgent tugging on the life-line around his waist. How long that had been going on, he had no idea. He stepped back, as though pulled by the line. He put one hand behind his back to grasp the line and began to walk backwards towards the water-tight door, but still looking in the direction of the fire, as though he dare not take his eyes off it, even in that blackness.

Sam felt others pushing past him towards the fire. At the watertight compartment door, hands grasped him by the elbows and, to his surprise and annoyance, hauled him backwards through the door. Somebody untied the life-line from his waist. It seemed that his part in fighting the fire was now considered to be over.

The control room was still dark, with only emergency lighting, but where it had been almost empty it was now in a flurry of confused movement, full of people moving about, men in helmets and men using the emergency breathing system and men wearing self-contained breathing sets, and men unreeling hoses and carrying up extinguishers, and more men just standing, apparently waiting for somebody to tell them what to do. There was a deafening noise, with several voices apparently yelling against each other. Somebody was shouting stridently into a telephone. Somebody else was shouting up the tower, to somebody else up there.

Sam could see nobody he knew or even vaguely recognised. Of course, these were the Starboard Crew, with others from shore. Nobody asked Sam what he had seen or what he had done. In fact, nobody took the least notice of him. He pushed through this crowd of strangers to the chart table. The weight of the self-contained breathing apparatus had become intolerable. He slipped out of it, and somebody took it from him at once, jerking it away, just as though they felt it did not belong to him and he had no right to have it. He was content to let it go. Presumably somebody else had the situation in hand now.

Sam looked at the water-tight door, which was now shut again. He knew that, if that door opened now, he would not be able to bring himself to go through it again, and do what he had just done again. He knew now how powerful and dangerous that fire was. It was only ignorance that had made him brave the first time. Anybody could be brave just once. But the true bravery was to go back and do it a second time and that, he knew, he could not bring himself to do.

He leaned over the chart table, breathing deeply, in and out. There was the smell of smoke in the air, and an even stronger smell of the fire, rising from his own uniform. He saw Janet's appalled face, smelling that in her house. He rubbed his hand over his face. Even his fingers smelled of the fire. His throat was uncommonly dry, and he longed for a drink of some sort.

'*Sam!*' It was Ralph, from the Starboard Crew. 'What on earth are *you* doing here?'

The strain, the heat, the disturbed night, the lingering smell of the fire, and the memory of it, all combined to snap Sam's temper. 'Helping to put out your fire for you, that's what I've bloody well been doing, if you really want to know.'

'But . . .'

'I don't *normally* come down to the boat and mess about with breathing apparatus and fire extinguishers in the middle of the night when I'm off-crew. Nor do I, for *choice*, put my uniform on over my pyjamas and drive into the base in the early hours of the morning when I could still be at home in bed with my wife on my first night in after a patrol . . .'

'I beg your pardon . . .'

'For your *information*, Ralph, I've just spent the last I don't know how long in *there*. . .' Sam jerked his head towards the forward bulkhead. '. . . In heat and total blackness and general unpleasantness, trying to put out a fire that some careless bastard started in there somewhere. And precious little thanks I get for it. How's it going, anyway?'

'Nearly there. It's under control. Thanks to you, I suppose. Look, I'm really sorry, Sam. But it just seems there's something very strange here.' Ralph was quite clearly puzzled and taken aback. 'How did you know? Who told you there was a fire on board?'

'Told me?' Sam frowned. 'Phone call. Somebody rang me at my house. Told me to get down here right away. So I did.'

'Who was it, do you know?'

'No. I assumed it was your duty officer. Didn't recognise the voice. But I don't know your crew very well anyway, and anyway it might have been somebody just joined. I didn't wait to argue the toss with him, and ask him if he really meant a fire or something else. And it didn't occur to me to wonder why he phoned me and not you, either.'

'I'm sorry, Sam, I didn't mean that . . But that fire could hardly have even started when you say somebody rang you . . .'

'I didn't just *say* somebody rang me. Somebody *did* ring me.'

'All right, all right, Sam. How long does it take you to drive in, normally?'

'*Come* on, Ralph, you know where I live. Quarter of an hour. Twenty minutes. But maybe less, there was nobody on the road.'

'But how long did it actually take you to get on board, from the time of the telephone call?'

Sam recalled the delays and arguments with the MoD PloD. 'Oh, over half an hour, I should say. Who is your duty officer, anyway? I never saw hide nor hair of him when we needed him most. When he should have been organising things.'

'That was him in the passageway. Derek, our Sonar Officer.'

He was a neighbour of theirs at home, living in the next road but one.

'How is he?'

'He's dead.'

'My God . . .'

'Asphyxiated. Looks as if that smoke got him before he could do anything.'

'But there was somebody else there, too . . .'

'Yes. One of the duty watch.'

'What happened to him? Don't tell me he's . . .'

'He's dead, too.'

'Oh my *God*.' That accounted for the duty watch running around in circles like a whole load of demented chickens with no heads. Poor buggers, they had no idea what was happening and there had been nobody to take charge and tell them what to do. It had all just begun to happen when Sam himself arrived on the scene.

'One thing's pretty well certain, Sam. You couldn't have had a telephone call from here. You must have dreamed it. That's the only possible explanation. Just as well you did, though.'

CHAPTER 9

CAPTAIN S/M LEANED FORWARD and put his elbows on his desk. He placed his hands together, with his fingertips touching. It was the gesture of a bureaucrat, but Sam was fascinated by it. He had a sudden unexpected memory from childhood, of his father doing it as a kind of party trick: here's the church, here's the steeple, here's the parson, here the people.

But Captain S/M was still speaking.

'. . . This, of course, puts a slightly different aspect on matters. At least, I hope it does.'

'I don't quite see what you mean, sir?'

Captain S/M frowned, with obvious displeasure at having to elaborate on a point which he clearly thought needed no further explanation. 'I mean . . . That I no longer see any reason for you to leave the Polaris programme.' It was awkwardly expressed, but Captain S/M waited for some encouragement or at least some reaction from Sam, and then went on. 'Surely the events of last night have put a completely different complexion on things?'

'I don't see why, sir.' Sam decided that, after the way he had been treated in his last interview with S/M, it was no part of his business to make things easier for the man.

Captain S/M cleared his throat. 'I mean, that you undoubtedly helped to avert a much more serious incident in that submarine. From what I hear, that had all the makings of a very serious fire, which was got under control, thanks very largely to you, and your prompt action. I think it would be a pity now if you left. We would all regret it. I think you would regret it.'

'I don't think the two things are related in any way, sir.' Sam did understand, very well, what Captain S/M was driving at, but he perversely refused to give him any assistance. 'Putting out a fire, or helping to put out a fire, just because you happened to be there on the spot, and one's feelings about nuclear weapons in a much broader context, well, sir, I don't think they are connected in any way, in my opinion, sir. They are nothing to do with each other, sir. One is an action done because you are trained to do it. The other is a matter of conscience. If I had *refused* to put out the fire, say, because of my views about nuclear weapons, then the two *would* have been connected, sir.'

Sam knew that he was now straying dangerously close to the edge of disrespect, if not impertinence. But he felt the usual constraints of rank and respect loosening. This was, after all, his life they were talking about. He was entitled to speak his mind. If they could talk to him in the way they did, then why should he not reply in kind? It was disgraceful that he should be interviewed and questioned and harried in this way. Other people had left the Polaris programme with none of this demeaning cross-questioning. It was not as though they even valued his services particularly highly, whatever pious platitudes S/M might be mouthing now. No great shakes as a submariner – that was the key phrase to remember.

Captain S/M was a disconcerting man to be interviewed by. There were always these lengthening silences, whilst one wondered who was to speak next. But Sam took advantage of this silence to put the question uppermost in his mind.

'Does this interview . . . Is this instead of the interview . . . You said you wanted to see me in a week's time, sir. Is that still so, sir?'

'Not if you are still of the same mind. I see no point.'

'I am, sir.'

'Let me say something to you. I don't like threatening my officers . . .'

Which meant, Sam thought, you are just about to make a threat.

'. . . But I feel there is something you ought to be quite clear about in your mind before you go any further with this. We live in a competitive world. We live in a competitive Navy. The Navy has to compete for money and ships. We in the Navy have to compete to survive. I'll be honest with you. I doubt if your career will prosper if you insist on leaving the Polaris programme in the way you intend to. I certainly would not be able to recommend you whole-heartedly for any appointment in general service . . .'

'I don't see why not, sir. You said yourself that I had done well. There are other things in the Navy besides Polaris . . .'

'There are, true. But, let's not be mealy-mouthed about it, you will carry a stigma . . .'

'I don't see why, sir . . .'

Once again, Sam found himself adrift in a lengthening silence. At last, Captain S/M pulled his hands apart, and stood up.

'Let us leave it at that. I accept that you genuinely want to leave the Polaris programme. Please write me a formal letter through your own Captain and I will start the ball rolling.'

'Thank you, sir.'

Once again, in an eerie repetition of the last interview with S/M, Mouser followed Sam outside into the sunshine.

'I'm afraid we can't recommend you for anything for that fire, Sam.'

'I wasn't expecting anything.'

'Normally you certainly could, and we would certainly put you up for something. But you did everything wrong.'

'Did I?'

'You were the senior person on the scene. You were the fire-master . . .'

'But I didn't know that.'

192

'Precisely. You didn't tell anybody you were taking charge or what you were doing. You didn't brief anybody or ask anybody where the fire was or what was happening. You didn't establish any procedures. You broke every rule in the book.'

'Did I?' Establish any procedures? What the hell did *that* mean? Surely the important thing was to get the bloody fire out first and then worry about *procedures* later.

'Yes you did. But astonishingly you went right to the heart of the fire and nailed it. You didn't put it out completely. But you knocked it back for just long enough. Quite remarkable.'

'Thank you.' Thanks for nothing, Sam thought. 'When I got there, nobody was doing anything, as far as I could see. What was it, anyway?'

'Oh, bedding, I'm told. It's those bloody lethal mattresses, filled with that foam. Somebody's cigarette, possibly. They're still sorting it out. There'll be a board of enquiry. Which you will have to attend. Sam . . .'

'Yes?'

'I know you feel pretty bitter and twisted at the way you think you're being treated . . .'

'You could put it like that.' Sam decided that there was no point even in trying any longer to be polite to this man.

'. . . But you have to understand that Father is acting under quite a lot of political pressure. Trained and experienced officers opting out of Polaris on moral grounds is not what Their Lordships want to hear, just at the moment, just when we're upgrading the deterrent and we're all looking forward to the possibility of a new generation of more modern and bigger submarines. It's not the sort of publicity we want, at what is now a very sensitive stage, politically.'

'Oh I quite understand *that*. That's been made abundantly clear, that I'm being *inconvenient* . . . But *surely* . . . *really* . . . I can't believe that what one obscure officer does or doesn't do is going to have an earth-shaking effect in Whitehall. I just don't bloody well believe it.'

'It's the little things like that . . . But no. No. Perhaps you're right.' Mouser did have the grace to look a little sheepish. But

193

not for long. 'But I still think you could be a bit more tactful towards Captain S/M. Be a bit more accommodating. Try and see his point of view as well as your own.'

The words left Sam speechless, incredulous. Try and see Captain S/M's point of view! It was incredible. What about his own point of view? Nobody at all was making any effort to see that.

When he got into his car, Sam had no doubt about where he was going. Proper protocol was breaking down. The rules of correct behaviour were being weakened. In uniform or not, he was going to call at the peace camp on his way home.

He drove past the camp, parked beside the road further down, where he had parked in the past. There was already a large Mercedes parked there.

There were, as he had already noticed, many more caravans. Perhaps the campers were like swallows, migrating north to colder climes in the summer. The whole camp was much greener. The trees were in full summer leaf. The grass was greener and higher and thicker. There was a small flower border, growing on one side of the communal eating caravan. Perhaps Mary Carmichael was responsible for that. In the hot sunshine, the site looked peaceful and rural, like a travellers' encampment in some old Victorian engraving.

There were plenty of people moving about, but Sam could not see anybody he remembered. Perhaps the protesters also had Port and Starboard Crews. Nobody took any notice of him or his uniform, but as Sam walked towards the large caravan, El Tel appeared.

'Oh hello, squire. It's Admiral Horatio Nelson, isn't it? Is this a social call?'

'Yes. Good morning.'

'Don't tell me. You've been away. And I know what you've been doing, too.'

'I've been on another deterrent patrol, yes.'

'I can see that by your face. That just-crawled-out-from-under-a-stone look.'

El Tel had with him a young man in a grey suit, holding a

briefcase. He looked like an accountant, or a lawyer, but certainly not a peace protester.

'I'll let you know as soon as I get the papers from London. Shouldn't be very long.' The man spoke with the faintest Scottish inflexion in his voice. He shook hands with El Tel, walked down to the Mercedes, got in and drove away. El Tel followed Sam's stare.

'Our solicitor. One of the best in Scotland.'

'What on earth do you want one of the best solicitors in Scotland for?'

'We're preparing a case against the Prime Minister. Conspiracy to commit genocide through possession of nuclear weapons.'

'Good God! You haven't got a hope.'

'Maybe.' El Tel bit his lip, clearly annoyed. 'We'll see. There's just been a similar case against the Prime Minister in the High Court in London. Same charge. Conspiracy to commit genocide.'

'What happened?'

'It failed. All right, it failed, and it was expected to fail.'

'How do you know?'

'The case was due to come on first at ten o'clock or whenever and they had two or three cases slated for the same time. That happens in magistrates' courts but not usually in the High Court. It meant they didn't expect us to detain Their Lordships for very long. Nor did we. Only for about ten minutes before they threw it out. But it got much further and did much better than we ever expected. We got a barrister to take the brief and we got expert witnesses from all sorts of sources. And there were certain aspects of it which give us a little hope. So we're going to try it again in the Scottish courts.'

Sam had always thought of the behaviour of the peace protesters as basically play-acting. But this court case was evidence of a much deeper conviction. It had failed, but the fact that it had been brought at all showed a long-term commitment and a confidence in their cause. Suddenly, Sam had a glimpse of a truth he had not suspected before. Most of these people were deadly serious. There was a frivolous element, of course. Certainly, there were those who joined for the excitement and the companionship, from a sense of woolly idealism, and for the whiff of danger of brushes with the law. But for some of them to take on the government and the legal establishment in this way, even in a lost cause, demonstrated a faith which was not just touching but reassuring. It was refreshing to know that there were people ready to act in this manner. Curiously, and unexpectedly, Sam felt that the knowledge that there were such people gave him some encouragement and support in his own predicament.

Mary Carmichael had just appeared at the door of the yellow Gerard Manley Hopkins van. She had done her red hair differently, and most attractively; instead of being drawn back tightly, it was now fluffed out, to outline her face like a halo.

'Like your hair. You're looking very well.'

'I like your uniform. It's lovely.'

El Tel guffawed. 'Wouldn't you believe it, all the nice girls love a sailor.'

'Would you like some coffee?'

'Yes, please.' It was, in fact, just coming up to stand-easy time in the forenoon. His throat was still slightly sore and ticklish from the lingering effects of the fumes and smoke of early that morning. In all the turmoil and comings and goings in the control room, it had soon become clear that Sam was no longer needed there, and in fact he was in the way. Nobody had asked him any more about what he had done or seen, or consulted him or took the slightest notice of him.

He had gone straight home without saying anything to anybody and, seeing Janet still asleep, taken off his uniform and gone straight to bed, his pyjamas still smelling of the fire. Janet had noticed it when she woke up. He was sound asleep when the telephone rang and he had had to drag himself into the base, because Captain S/M wanted to see him. Now, he felt unnaturally bright and clear-headed. But that would probably only last until this afternoon.

The main caravan seemed not to have changed at all, except

that there was a jamjar full of flowers on the window-sill. Maybe Mary Carmichael arranged that, too. But Sam had still not seen a familiar face, apart from El Tel and Mary Carmichael.

'Where's what's-her-name, that large girl?'

'Who, Gillie? Great big slut. I dunno know where she is. Haven't seen her around for ages.'

'What about Desmond, the climber?'

'Oh he's still around. He comes in and out.'

'How did he get on with his last court case and all that? Did he get off?'

'Can't remember, to be honest. Fined or bound over, I shouldn't wonder. There are so many court cases, you lose track.'

Sam thought it extraordinary, now he came to consider it, that he should be swapping gossip about mutual acquaintances in this way.

'Here's your coffee.'

Sam took it, and sipped it, and put it down. He could not repress a long cavernous yawn, that left his face tingling. His eyes were itching now, with tiredness. 'I'm sorry. I was up very early this morning.'

'Oh? Why so?'

Before he was properly aware of what he was doing, he was telling them about the fire. The story came bursting from him. He discovered he had been longing to tell it. He told them of the mysterious telephone call, the drive to the base in the diamond-bright early morning, the puzzling lack of urgency or activity anywhere, the blackness below in the submarine, the first confusion, the uncertainty about the fire, the discovery of the dead bodies, the sight of the fire, the heat, the frantic search for the lost extinguisher, the satisfaction of actually playing the extinguisher foam on to the fire, the control room full of people, and the journey home again. He wanted to tell them of his interview with Captain S/M and almost did, but restrained himself.

El Tel and Mary Carmichael made an excellent audience,

197

appreciative and sympathetic. Both of them sat and listened with rapt attention until he had finished.

El Tel let out a long whistle. 'Yeeee. They certainly make you earn your money. Now, I really enjoyed that. They should give you a medal, mate.'

'No, that's exactly what they're not going to do.'

'It's a very funny thing, mate, but the more you tell me about those submarines of yours, the more interested I get in them.'

'Yes, I knew you were interested. I could tell that by your reading material.'

'If it weren't for the nuclear weapons, I could be a fan.'

'Ah yes. If it weren't for the nuclear weapons.'

Mary Carmichael leaned forward and sniffed at Sam's jacket. 'This is no' the jacket you were wearing, is it?'

'Oh no, I had to change before coming into the base.' In fact, he had put on his best No. 1 uniform for Captain S/M.

'How many uniforms you got then?'

'Oh, three. One best, one working, one steaming.'

'Steaming?'

'The one I wear down the boat at sea, when I have to wear uniform, that is. We call what we wear at sea 'steaming rig'. Although we're not as informal now as we used to be. You used to see some glorious steaming rigs in the old days. Woolly caps and Davy Crockett hats. They really did look like a lot of pirates in those days. Now, it's really only the galley staff. They wear cowboy boots and scarves.'

For the first time that Sam had ever noticed, El Tel looked taken aback. 'Whatever for?'

'Just for fun. Relax the tension a bit.'

'Is there a lot of tension?'

'Fair amount, yes. It's an unnatural sort of existence, being locked away like that for weeks on end.'

'Me heart bleeds for you, mate. You chose it. All you've got to do is say you won't go on with it.'

'Ah yes, but it's not quite as cut and dried as that.'

Once again, before he was properly aware of what he was doing, Sam had begun to tell them about the events of the last patrol, and his changed feelings towards nuclear weapons. His first sensation of guilt at revealing such things about the Navy and about himself, of guilt at being there in the camp at all, soon evaporated in the warmth of the sheer pleasure and relief of being able to unburden himself to those who would understand, who would not retaliate with pressure for him to change his mind, would not disapprove, and purse their lips, and hardly wait for him to finish speaking before countering with their reasons as to why he was wrong.

It did not take long to tell. He was amazed by his own new-found fluency. It was as though his history had matured, ripened, found better words in which to express itself. Until then, his new convictions about nuclear weapons had been indistinct, as though just appearing on the horizon like the loom of a distant lighthouse beam. Now, they were in full view and in broad daylight. He was more certain than ever he was in the right. He found himself relaxing, as though amongst friends and allies, after a long time in a hostile questioning world.

But El Tel, though he listened with unbroken concentration, did not react as Sam had quite expected. 'What do the rest think?'

'The rest?'

'Yes, the *rest*, mate. The rest of the base. Yer mates. Yer fellow nuclear rocketeers. Do they think you're a traitor?'

'No, not at all.'

'Well, *I* bloody well would!'

'Would you?'

'Yes I bloody well would.'

'I don't agree with that, Terry . . .' Mary Carmichael was indignant. 'He's braver than the rest, to say what he did. Much braver than anybody else. I think it's marvellous. To come right out and say it like that.'

'Oh I see that, all right. That's almost a commonplace. To come out and bravely go where no man had gone before, go against the pack, to rebel against one's *peer* group, that's *very* brave. Look here, mate . . .' El Tel looked directly at Sam.

'You're not like us. You're not like *any* of us. If someone came to me and said what you've just said normally I would say, come and join the club, mate, there's a bunk next door, see you on the next march. But not you. You took the Queen's shilling.'

'So what?'

'So *what!* I can't believe I'm hearing this. So it makes all the difference in the world. All the difference there is! You take the Queen's money all these years, you come here and lecture us about nuclear weapons the last time you were up here, and now you come bouncing in, the light shining from your eyes, and expect us to say Yes Bwana No Bwana three bags full Bwana, come and join tribe Bwana. 'Cause that's what you expected, isn't it? Us to swoon away and say, Good Golly, we've got one of the Bombers' crew on our side at last, one of Her Majesty's Naval Officers, he's seen the light, Glory glory.'

Sam felt his face burning bright red, and he avoided Mary Carmichael's eye. This was more shaming, by far, than anything that had happened on board. El Tel was exaggerating cruelly, but there was just an element of hurtful truth in what he was saying. If he were truthful with himself, Sam had to admit that he had indeed half-expected El Tel to welcome him with something approaching rapture, as though Sam's conversion to the anti-nuclear cause were the opportunity, the case history, the propaganda ammunition El Tel had been hoping and praying for all these years. But, on the contrary, El Tel was regarding him as though he were a renegade, as though El Tel, and not for the first time, was looking at Sam's behaviour from the point of view of the Submarine Service.

'You know, I think you're more, what's the word, hidebound than the Navy is. It's *me* who's the real protester.'

'Maybe. But that's your problem, squire.' El Tel stood up and slapped his hands against his thighs. 'Well, can't stay here any longer. Got to go and see a man about a Hiroshima Vigil.'

He looked downwards and sideways at Sam, hoping for a response. Sam knew El Tel was being deliberately provocative, but could not resist the bait. 'What's that?'

200

'Thought you'd never ask. We're going to hold a twenty-four-hour vigil outside the main gate of your base on the anniversary next month, to remember the hundred and fifty thousand dead and injured at Hiroshima, and all the thousands who died later as a direct result of radiation. They're still dying, in fact. We've even got some Japanese coming up specially.' El Tel smirked. 'Maybe you'd like to come and hold a candle with us? With your new views? All genuine converts welcome. After all, it *was* the biggest single act of genocide in our history . . .'

'*Balls* . . . The atomic bombs at Hiroshima and Nagasaki were net life savers . . .'

El Tel's snort of derision stung Sam on the raw.

'Now *you* listen for a change. There were going to be at least a million Allied casualties in capturing the Japanese home islands, and that's a very conservative estimate. That's not counting the Japanese themselves who were getting ready to die to the last man and woman, and I *mean* the last man and woman, and child . . .'

'You've been believing your own propaganda . . .'

'No, *you* listen . . . On top of that, there were over a quarter of a million Allied prisoners of war and internees in all those camps from Java to Japan and right up to Manchuria. If you just listen, you might learn something. The Japanese were getting ready to massacre all of them, the *moment* the first Allied troops set foot anywhere on metropolitan Japan. They had all the plans ready. The prisoners knew about them. They had plans to try and resist. The moment the Allies invaded Japan there would have been an absolute *bloodbath* . . .'

Sam could see El Tel was impressed in spite of himself, and felt he had regained some of his lost position. 'The Japanese were beat, they'd lost the war, but that didn't mean they were about to surrender. No fear of that. No *normal* weapon could make them do that. But the atomic bomb . . . that had a touch of the supernatural about it. It was a weapon from the gods. They wouldn't lose any face surrendering because of that. So they did. Otherwise, believe me, we could well have been

201

fighting them still. So don't give me any more of that silly crap about genocide . . . It was a life *saver*, and don't you forget it.'

'All right, squire. Have it your own way. But all this sounds a bit funny when I remember what you were sounding off about earlier, just now. All about your convictions and how you suddenly felt a repugnance towards nuclear weapons and decided you just couldn't take part and all that crap, to use your phrase, any more. Where does this leave you? Where do you stand, exactly? When do nuclear weapons stop being life savers, as you say they were at Hiroshima, and when do they start becoming morally repugnant and weapons of mass murder as you say your rockets are now? Eh? Eh, eh, eh?'

Sam could not at once frame a reply. He could not think of anything to say. The victory was El Tel's again. 'I didn't say they were weapons of mass murder.'

'No? Well, you could have fooled me.'

It was a comprehensive victory, and El Tel knew it, and left.

'Would you like some more coffee?'

Sam had quite forgotten Mary Carmichael was there.

'No, no thanks. I must get home. I'm supposed to be on leave.'

'Don't mind about Terry.'

'Oh, I don't.'

'Oh, I think you do mind him. Everybody does. But if I can just say something to you?'

'Yes. Why not? Everybody else does.'

'Now don't be like that. My advice to you is, just be yourself. If you don't want to go on with something, don't. It's your life.'

'Huh, I wish it were so simple . . .'

'You have to live with yourself. You're obviously upset, deep down, I can see that. I don't like to see you like that. You're good looking, in your uniform. You're brave. You're honest. And I think you fancy me, a wee bit. Are ye married?'

Her cheeks were flushed and her eyes sparkling. She looked what they called the picture of health, in her jeans and her check blouse. Once again, Sam could not avoid the thought of how pleasing it would be to see her naked.

'Yes, and I think you've asked me that before. Yes, I am married.'

'Good. You should be, a man like you. You know, I like you better now, much better. As Terry would say, you came on pretty strong last time you were here.'

'Did I? As I remember, I was dog tired and hardly said a word.'

'Och no, that was the time before. I'm talking about the time you came here *twice* in one day.'

'Oh yes. All that kissing and wrestling.'

'Aye, all that kissing and wrestling. I'm glad you remember. But I do, I like you better now.'

'You mean, you like men better when they've been defeated a bit?'

Mary Carmichael considered for a moment. 'I didnae think of it in that way, but I suppose that's right.'

'Well then, it's odd that you stick with someone like El Tel. He's never been defeated in his life. At least, he acts that way.'

'Aye, nor he has, but as I think I told you once, I need him more than he needs me.'

'I'm almost jealous of him. To have you, and all that confidence. Must be a rare thing.'

'Och, don't you be jealous of him. As I told you, be yourself. Do what *you* want. It's the only way, in the end. It's your life. It's *you* that has to live with yerself.'

He studied her, standing in the sunlight, in front of the main caravan. It seemed strange to hear such advice, from such a girl, in such a place. 'That sounds like standard advice, you read in all the agony columns. Do you really mean it?'

'Aye. I do that.'

'Well, thank you for that.'

'You can come again, if you want to. But remember, I told you once, we're no good for you here.'

'I'll remember that.'

As Sam walked back to his car, Desmond the Climber came out from behind some trees, almost as though he had actually

203

been waiting there. He still had a gap in his front teeth and was still wearing the same braces.

'Hello Guv!' Desmond's surprise at meeting Sam was obviously genuine. 'How're things going with you?'

'All right. I was going to ask you the same thing.'

'Thanks for putting in a word for me. If you did.'

'I was going to ask you that. How did your court case go?'

Desmond pulled a resigned face. 'Fined and cautioned. It's all part of the job, Guv. Occupational expense. Like the prostitutes.'

Sam laughed in spite of himself. 'I suppose that's one way of looking at it.'

'It's the only way of looking at it, Guv. You been to see El Tel?'

'I have, yes. But I didn't come here to see him. I just found myself curious about you lot, and how you were getting on. So I called on my way home.'

'Well, we're always here if you need us, Guv.'

'Yes, I see that! In a funny sort of way, it's reassuring to know it's you out there, roaming round the fence. It wouldn't be the same if it were anybody else.'

Sam felt oddly cheered as he drove away. It was curious how his spirits seemed to rise whenever he visited the camp.

The main topic of conversation at lunch was, of course, The Fire and Sam's part in putting it out. As expected, it was Johnny who was most interested. He seemed fascinated by his father's description of the darkness and the uncertainty. In his young imagination, every submarine was a place of magic and mystery and, now, of menace. 'But it wasn't *really* dangerous, was it, Daddy?' he asked, again and again.

By the end of the meal, Sam could hardly keep his eyes open. He recognised the symptoms, that he was approaching the edges of exhaustion and should sleep.

Nevertheless, he spent some time walking round the house and garden after lunch, on what Janet called his 'Captain's Rounds', to look for the small jobs that Janet always left for him to do when he came home: two tiles were loose on the roof, some of the window frames badly needed painting, there was a pane of glass missing in the small window in the garage door and, of course, the lawn needed mowing again.

It seemed an unusually hot afternoon. Sam got a deck-chair out of the garage and set it up on the lawn at the back of the house. He sat down, and within a few minutes was in a sleep as sound as death itself.

He woke to Janet's voice, calling from a window. 'It's teatime, darling, and there's somebody for you on the telephone.'

He took the receiver from her with a vague sense of foreboding. 'It's some Glasgow paper, darling. Want to talk to you about the fire.'

'Hello, Commander?' The reporter's voice had only a slight Scots accent. 'I've just been talking to the press officer down the submarine base . . .'

'How did you get my number?'

'Directory Enquiries, of course.'

'Ah. Well, I have to get permission, you know, before I can talk to the press about Service matters.' Really, the Press officers in the base ought to be able to handle all this sort of thing. What the *hell* were they paid for, but to field this sort of thing, to stop people being woken up in their homes in the middle of the afternoon . . .

'That's all right. They mentioned your name and I just wanted to get things right. It's quite a good story, this, you see.'

Sam felt that there was nothing wrong in at least discussing the story, if it gave the base and the submarine a bit of good publicity.

'I gather you played a major part in putting the fire out, although you were actually off-crew at the time?'

Whoever he was, he was remarkably well-informed. It could not be general knowledge that Sam was off-crew.

'Yes, I did go down there, and I did assist in extinguishing the fire. But there was a duty watch on board.'

'But it was still burning when you got there? Is that right?'

'Yes, it was still burning when I got there.' There seemed no harm in confirming that: it was only the truth, after all.

'So you were the first to get to it, even though there was a duty watch there?'

'Yes.' Again, it was true.

'I don't suppose you'd like to enlarge on the story a bit for us, would you? Give us a bit more detail of what if felt like and all that? We're going to run a piece on it anyway . . .'

'Yes?' Sam refused to be drawn by the staged silence.

'. . . And of course we'd like to get it right, if we possibly can.'

'Well, it was quite scary while it lasted . . .' It did seem ungenerous not to tell the man anything when he was so obviously interested. 'And it was all dark, pitch black, and difficult to find out just what was going on.'

'But you managed to find the fire and put it out?'

'Well, no, I'm not sure I actually put it out. I think I checked it long enough for others to come up and finish it off.'

'Are you all right? Personally? No injuries?'

'None at all. I'm perfectly all right. Just a bit tired.'

'I can imagine. And how did you feel when you . . .'

'Now, I'm afraid I really can't say any more, I can't give you any details. There'll be a board of enquiry . . .'

'Oh, will there?' The casual cajoling voice at the other end was at once alert again. Sam realised his slip. 'When will that be?'

'I'm afraid I don't know. But it's standard practice to have an enquiry, after a fire like this . . .'

'You say a fire like this. Was it a particularly bad fire?'

'Well, two people were killed . . .'

'So we understand. Did you know them?'

'Yes I did. Look, I'm sorry, I'm afraid I really can't discuss it over the telephone. I'm sure the base press officers have given you the story as far as we are allowed to tell it at the moment.'

'Of course. Thank you so much for your time, Commander . . .'

'Pleasure.'

That, Sam thought, had really been quite painless. It was a pity the Navy always made such a mystery and a fuss about talking to the press. Maybe that was why they were traditionally so very bad at it. The Silent Service, so called, threw a long shadow.

'. . . One final thing, Commander, I understand you yourself are thinking of leaving the Polaris submarines, for moral reasons, because you don't agree any longer with the use of nuclear weapons? Is that right?'

The shock of the words was almost physical. Sam felt the hair prickle on the back of his neck and the sweat start on his forehead. He could see now how appallingly indiscreet he had been in telling El Tel of his changed views. Because this was El Tel's handiwork, without a doubt. El Tel had his contacts with the local press. He had given them some good copy over the years. He had given them this story. He was the only one who could have done, and would have done. He might have scorned Sam's change of heart openly, called him a renegade and a traitor, deriding any contribution Sam's defection – if that was what it was – might make to the protesters' case. But El Tel was quite capable of realising what a splendid story it would make, what public ammunition it would give his cause: a submarine officer, a Polaris officer, a *hero* in fact, turning against nuclear weapons – it was a marvellous publicity *coup* for the protesters.

'How did you know that?'

'We have our sources of information . . .'

'Yes but . . .'

'I'm sure you wouldn't expect me to tell you. Is it true?'

'But surely you couldn't put that in this story?'

'No. What we'll do is we'll run *two* stories. First you and the fire, to set it up, so that people will know who you are. Then, we'll follow up with you wanting to leave Polaris submarines . . .'

'Good God.' What a bloody cynical way of going about it.

'. . . That is, if you do want to leave. Is it true?'

207

All Sam's resentment and irritation at being questioned, and badgered, and harassed, and argued with and about, boiled to a head. 'Yes, it is true.'

'Why is that, sir? Why do you want to leave Polaris submarines? I understand you've served in them for some years . . .'

'Yes I have. And I can't tell you why I want to leave. I haven't even put in my letter of application yet.'

'Oh, do you have to write a letter giving your reasons?'

'I can't say any more. Thank you very much for calling.'

Sam put the receiver down firmly, conscious that he had already said far too much.

Janet was still waiting. She had heard the whole conversation, or at least, Sam's end of it. 'Darling, what was all that about?'

'Some bloody reporter. Wanted to know about the fire. He'd also . . .' Sam stopped abruptly. He could not tell Janet how the reporter had come to know that he wanted to leave the Polaris programme.

'What was all that about you leaving?'

'I don't know. He'd got hold of some rumour.'

'That's a pity. Nobody's going to like that. Still, he can hardly write that in the newspaper. What business is it of anybody else what you do?'

'That's bloody ironic you should say that. It seems to be everybody's business what I do with my life.'

'Oh, darling, don't be daft.'

It was in the paper the next day. It was not the headline lead story, but it was on the front page.

Johnny, who was clearly thrilled by the publicity given to his father, read it out. ' "Fatal Fire On Board Polaris Sub. Off-duty officer hero." Off-duty officer hero. Oh, Daddy.' Johnny's eyes were shining. 'I'm going to cut this out and show it to the boys at school!'

'Here, before you do that, let me have a look. As I'm the hero.'

It was very accurate on the whole. There had been a fire

208

which had been put out, with some difficulty. But two men had died, and it gave their names and addresses. Otherwise damage had been minimal and mostly caused by smoke. Sam recognised here and there the dead hand and leaden phrases of the base press officers, but the facts were certainly there. He thought that perhaps the account made too much of the fact that he had come down whilst off-duty and tackled the fire although there was a duty watch on board. The Starboard Crew would not like that very much. And the report seemed to hint at some sinister significance in the fact that there would be a board of enquiry when, as Sam had told the man, it was normal procedure.

Sam's own quotes, such as they had been, were accurately reported. It had been 'quite scary' and 'all dark' and it had been difficult to find out what was happening – the Starboard Crew would certainly not like *that*. The paper commented on Sam's modesty in not claiming to have put out the fire completely. If anything, it made him appear more of a hero and more reluctant to talk about it than was strictly true. In fact, the whole report was slanted and exaggerated in a way Sam could not precisely describe. There was nothing actually untrue in the report. But it was simply not quite the way Sam remembered things happening. Now he came to read them again, somehow his own remarks did seem a little wet, and they would certainly lead to some leg-pulling. Sam remembered a remark by a visiting admiral, who once said that he did not complain that the press misquoted him; the trouble was that, on the contrary, they reported him with embarrassing accuracy, and what had seemed so witty and urbane when it was said looked so limp on paper.

Sam wondered whether to tell anybody about the threat of the follow-up piece. Maybe the newspaper had exaggerated his part in the fire so as to build up his image and importance, to fatten him for the kill. But who could he tell, and what could they do, even if they knew? They would say, wait and see, face it when it comes, it might never happen. Sam hoped that it never would, and spent a nervous day convincing himself that the newspaper would surely have much more important stories to report.

But it was there in the newspaper the next day. It was on the front page again, under the headline 'Polaris Sub Hero Quits'. Sam read it, with a sick feeling, swallowing the saliva flooding into his mouth. Once again, like the report the day before, it was accurate enough, but quite untrue. He had admitted that it was true he wanted to leave. But the paper gave the impression that he had already left. It mentioned his letter, calling it 'a letter of resignation', in such a way as to suggest he had actually written it, when he had specifically told the man he had not. Worse still, the newspaper included a quote from the peace camp. It was obviously El Tel speaking, although he was not named. ' "We welcome new recruits wherever they come from," said a peace camp spokesman yesterday', it read.

But most dismaying of all for Sam was Johnny's reaction. The boy read it again and again, as he had done the day before, but his face was white.

'Daddy, I won't cut this out. Will they say you're a coward? They won't say that, will they?'

'No, no, of course not. What rubbish.'

But Sam now saw, for the first time, that his sons would have to face their schoolmates, who could be the cruellest animals on earth. He was a hero to his sons, he knew. They were both, but particularly Johnny, intensely proud of their father, as a submariner. Now, they might have to face the accusation that their father was a coward. That was an aspect of this whole affair which had not occurred to him before.

The telephone was ringing again. Janet had the receiver in her hand.

'It's someone from the base. They want you to go in and see them. Whoever it is sounds very curt. Oh, Sam, darling, what's going to happen to us?'

CHAPTER 10

FOR THE THIRD TIME, Sam stood outside the main base offices in the hot sunshine with Mouser, after another interview with Captain S/M. Sam had a momentary thought of the ridiculous catch-line 'We'll have to stop meeting like this'.

'. . . The best thing you can do now, Sam, seriously, to mend the situation, is not to write your letter, or withdraw it if you already have. Have you? The paper gave the impression you already have.'

'Well they were wrong. I haven't.' Sam knew that his tone was unusually, almost unacceptably, abrupt. But he felt that the last shreds of his respect for these people were literally shredding away under the impact of these interviews which he was beginning to regard as assaults upon himself, upon his own integrity. This last interview had been the roughest of the lot. Captain S/M had pulled no punches. Naval officers were supposed to preserve a proper respect towards each other, whatever the circumstances. But S/M had been perilously near the edge of unseemly behaviour. He had seemed to realise it himself but the knowledge had merely urged him on.

'Well, don't write it is my advice. Stay with it and try and pick up the pieces as best you can.'

'I'm getting very tired of all this advice, from all and sundry. It was not my fault the papers got hold of all this.'

'How did they get hold of it?'

'I don't know. But I always thought that was one of the reasons we had these press officers round the place, to save us

211

from this sort of thing. They seem about as much use as a hole in the head, when it comes down to it.'

Mouser shrugged. Sam understood the gesture. It merely meant that the press officers, like all MoD bureaucrats, like all bureaucrats, were principally concerned with safe-guarding their own positions, ensuring no blame attached to them personally, making sure they themselves were 'fire-proof'. Anything else came a very long way second with bureaucrats.

'Well, however they got hold of it, I can tell you it's exactly the sort of thing the Boss does *not* need right now.'

Sorry to make life so difficult for him, Sam muttered, under his breath.

'I can only say again, Sam, and it's good advice, believe me, the best thing you can do is to forget all about this idea of yours and try and get back inside the fold as quickly as you can and pretend it never happened. As I said, try and pick up the pieces. And by the way, again, I hear you've been back at that camp?'

'There's no regulation against it.'

'No. No regulation, exactly, but it's still not advisable to do it. And especially not to give them encouragement or support, or even hint that you find their pressence reassuring.'

'Reassuring? That's an odd word to use, surely.'

'Not really.' Sam fancied Mouser looked disconcerted, like a man who had inadvertently said too much. 'Anyway, bear what I've said in mind.'

On his way to his car, Sam thought over their conversation. It was not surprising he had been seen at the camp. After all, he had stood outside it for some time, in broad daylight, in uniform, talking to Desmond.

The memory of Desmond made Sam stop, stock still, in his stride. There had been some echo, some familiar resonance, about the word 'reassuring'. He had said something of the sort to Desmond. Maybe it was not chance, after all, that had made Desmond appear just then. He could have been waiting. Desmond could, in fact, be an informer, infiltrated into the protesters. Now that Sam came to think of it, it was very likely that the peace protesters had been penetrated by the Special Branch. And Desmond the informer, if he was an informer, must work fast; he had apparently reported already a conversation Sam had had with him only forty-eight hours before.

Once again, Sam had no doubts where he was going to go when he reached the end of the base approach road. He knocked on the door of the Gerard Manley Hopkins van, and then pushed it open with his foot. El Tel was lying on one of the bunks, hands clasped behind his neck, looking at him.

'Good morning, squire, good of you to knock . . .'

'Good morning, nothing. Thanks for nothing . . .'

'Keep your hair on . . .'

'You gave me the impression you weren't interested in my views about nuclear weapons, because I'd taken the Queen's *shilling*, or whatever.'

'Hold on, hold on. What I say to you, and what I actually think, are not necessarily the same, mate. You must be bloody naïve to think that. I thought it was a good story. The papers thought it was a good story. We all thought it was a good story. Have the telly people or anybody else chased it up?'

'No, thank God.'

'That's a pity.' El Tel looked genuinely sorry. 'Thought they'd have followed something like this up. Perhaps I should give 'em a ring, jog their memories a bit.'

'Doesn't it ever occur to you that what you did was a kind of treachery? Didn't it ever occur to you, the effect of a newspaper article like that on me and my family . . .'

'Now *you* look here, mate.' El Tel sat bolt upright on his bunk. 'You've got quite the wrong idea about us. You think this is a whole load of play-acting, don't you? All the marches and the banners and the colours and the publicity in the papers, you think it's all a big game, don't you? It's high time you realised we're serious. We're deadly serious, mate, just as serious as your lot are with your rockets, your *cost-effective* rockets. If I think our cause is going to be advanced just a little bit by giving a story about you to the papers then I'm going to

213

do it and I'm not sorry about it and I'll do it again, like a shot. Does that tell you what you wanted to know?'

Sam turned to go, but then remembered Desmond. 'Is Desmond here today?'

El Tel shrugged. 'Probably. He's around somewhere. He usually is.'

'Do you . . . It's difficult to know how to say this . . . Do you ever suspect him?'

'Of what?'

'Do you ever suspect him of being an informer?'

'Desmond a stoolie? He could be, now you mention it.'

'Doesn't that worry you, that everything you do may be reported to the police?'

El Tel shrugged again. 'Not a lot. It wouldn't be to the police, not the local police anyway. More likely the Special Branch. There's a lot of funny things go on, squire, which you as a loyal citizen and a servant of the Crown, although yer having yer problems just now, you just wouldn't believe.'

El Tel stretched himself out on the bunk again, lazily, the very embodiment of confidence and lack of concern at what Sam had told him. 'It does confirm one or two things I've noticed, now you mention it. But it don't worry me. We act within the law, mostly. If the Old Bill want to tie up manpower spying on us, that's up to them. It's a compliment in a funny way. *They* must take us seriously, which is more than your lot do. I'll keep an eye on Desmond. Try him out with a few things. Thanks for the tip.'

Sam left the site without seeing Mary Carmichael, and with, once again, that feeling of disappointment after a conversation with El Tel. He really had expected El Tel to be much more openly concerned over the suspicion that there was a traitor in his camp. But, once again, El Tel seemed invulnerable.

There was a strange car parked across their drive way, in such a position Sam could not get past it. He could guess the car's ownership from the arrogant way it was parked.

The Captain was in their kitchen, leaning his bottom against the table, talking to Janet. The two of them were drinking coffee.

'Morning, Sam.'

'Morning, sir.'

'I was just driving south to start my leave, I thought I'd call on my way and see you both. I thought maybe I could persuade the lovely Janet to persuade you to give up this idea of leaving us.'

Sam scowled, at him and at Janet. He had known the Captain was going on leave today and, now he thought of it, he should have checked with him before he left. So, in a way, the Captain was right to call.

'Don't look so gloomy, Sam.'

'I'm not gloomy, sir.'

'You always did tend to suffer from the glooms, Sam. But then you generally come bouncing back after a bit. You want to watch it, though. One day you might not be quite so resilient and you might not come bouncing back quickly enough. Isn't that right, Janet?' The Captain turned to Janet for support. 'Don't you find him hard to live with occasionally?'

'Now, you don't expect me to answer that, do you?'

'How did it go with S/M, Sam?' The Captain had effortlessly changed the subject. 'I'm sorry I wasn't there this time to give you moral support. I was getting my gear together to go on leave.'

Some moral support you give me, Sam thought.

'It was the roughest yet, sir.'

'Oh dear. Well, you have to see it from his point of view. He's under a bit of political pressure right now. We're just approaching a stage where a whole new generation of submarines is up for grabs. It's a tricky time for everybody.'

'Yes, sir.' Once again, everybody was looking at it from *their* point of view and telling him he should do the same. Sam decided that there was no point in arguing. Just keep one's head down, agree, in a sullen, non-argumentative sort of way, and hope they would all get tired of it and go away. His decision

215

to leave Polaris was flavour of the month now. Next month it would be something else.

'It was a pity about the newspaper, Sam.'

'Yes, sir.'

'There's something about the newspapers that always gets the Navy on the raw. I don't know why.'

'Yes, sir.' Sam was going to leave it there, but he suddenly tired of his own inaction and submission. Why *should* he just stand and take it? 'Well, of course, sir, nobody seemed to have any objections to the piece in the paper about me the day before, did they, sir? You could argue that we should take the rough with the smooth?'

'Yes, you could argue that. But they always remember the rough and not the smooth. I got the impression that this was the old one-two punch, that somehow the first piece was just setting you and the base and the Navy up for the second. Did you get that idea?'

'It's possible, sir.' There was no doubt, the Captain was no fool.

The Captain put his coffee cup down. 'Well, I did come here hoping to have a chat with you both about your future, Sam. But I've come to the conclusion that this isn't a good time, so I'll love you and leave you. Maybe we can have a chat together when I get back. I do want to help, you know, Sam. I'm truly sorry if there has ever been any misunderstanding between us.'

'Yes, sir. Thank you, sir.' The Captain was rarely so conciliatory. Perhaps, Sam thought, the Captain had at last recognised that what Sam was saying was of real importance to everybody, himself included.

Sam accompanied the Captain outside to his car. He wanted, in any case, to drive his own in when the Captain had gone.

'You know, for someone like you, Sam, you're causing an awful lot of uproar.'

What, Sam wondered, does he mean by 'someone like you'; no great shakes as a submariner, no doubt. It was difficult to know what to reply to that, so Sam said nothing.

The Captain climbed into his car. 'You've got my telephone number? Call me *after* it's come on to blow.'

'Aye aye, sir. Have a good leave, sir.'

'Oh, I shall.'

No doubt, Sam thought.

Janet was just finishing washing up the coffee cups. 'He's a nice man, basically, under all that blah.'

Sam did not rise to her invitation to discuss their visitor, and what lay behind his visit. There would be another and better time for that. But the Captain's presence and the reason for it remained unspoken but not forgotten throughout the rest of the day, while Sam took the boys swimming, and Alice to Morag's, and mowed the lawn, and cut and inserted and puttied a new pane of glass in the garage door, and collected Alice from Morag's, and bought an evening paper on the way, and watched television news, half-expecting to see either El Tel or himself on it, and had supper with Janet and the children, and read Alice a story, and told Johnny again that nobody would ever say anything to him at school about the newspaper cutting.

But 'the Polaris matter', as Sam had come to think of it, could not be avoided indefinitely; like Amfortas' wound, it would be unhealed so long at it was unspoken.

It was Janet, as usual, who grasped the matter firmly, just before they went to bed.

'Darling, we must talk about this. In a way, it was very good of your Captain to turn up this morning like that. He's doing his best. We all are.'

'All right.'

'Darling, don't be so grumpy. I just want to do the best for us, and for you.'

'Oh don't be so damned condescending!'

'I'm *not*. I'm not being condescending! It's not fair of you to say that. So long as you're treating this as a matter of honour . . .'

'Honour. Nobody talks about honour anymore, not these days. What I particularly object to in all this, is that everybody is always putting words in my mouth and thoughts in my head I never had. Everybody's always threatening me, always telling me what I should and shouldn't do with my life. Nobody ever gives a damn about what *I* think. It's as though the Navy has always done what it wanted with me and ignored me and insulted me . . .'

'Oh, darling, they haven't . . .'

'. . . And *now*, just because I question something important for the first time in my life, they try and tell me what I should and shouldn't do with my life. They might have been able to get away with that with naval officers in the past. But not *now*. Things are different now, very different. Perhaps in your fathers' day . . .'

'Ah, I thought we'd come to that.'

'In your father's day, they could still talk about honour and duty and all that crap. The Navy's just a job now just like any other . . .'

'Darling you don't really believe that . . .'

'Oh *do* stop interrupting. The Navy's just a job now and it's the Navy's own fault that it is just a job. Because that's what the Navy's been trying to achieve over these last years. They've brought it upon themselves. Now they shouldn't complain when we take our line from them and behave as they seem to want us to behave.'

'You mentioned my father. It's true he never had to make up his mind about nuclear weapons, and I never heard him express any opinion on them. But I do know that he would have gone wherever the Navy said and done whatever the exigencies of the Service demanded. And anyway, what you're saying now would have been much more convincing if you had said it at the beginning. You've been serving in these submarines for years now.'

'That's true. But I don't feel any less genuine because this is so recent.'

'Darling, your grammar is a bit mixed up.'

'I don't care. The meaning is there. I just want to be able to live my own life and make my own decisions.'

'But darling, when you joined the Navy you gave up the freedom to do as you wished. That's part of it, part of the job as you call it, and a most important part of it.'

Sam was silent. What Janet was saying was absolutely true. But it did not meet his case. It seemed they were talking about different things.

When he got into bed, Sam noticed that there was only a sheet on it. That was very rare indeed in Scotland, even at the height of summer. He lay back, tensing himself for a sleepless night, for one of those interminable dark passages of time when his thoughts raced round and round, tormenting him. But, strangely, he felt only calm. He went to sleep with Janet's arms around him.

Sam awoke with a headache and the vaguest memory of his last dream. He could remember nothing of it except its overwhelming menace. In it he had glimpsed the shape of something that threatened himself and his family. He rubbed his hand over his face. The skin on his forehead was rough, as though with grains of sand, as though indeed sweat had dried on it. Looking into the bathroom mirror, he tried to recall his dream. It was gone, but it had left behind, like the tissue of a hideous scar, the trace of a prophecy which had terrified him.

'Did I shout out in the night?'

'No. I didn't hear anything.' As usual, Janet's voice was grumpy in the morning. 'Why do you ask?'

'I don't know. I just had an idea I might have. Is it tomorrow the boys are going to their summer camp?'

'Day after.'

As the days passed, the leave fell into its usual comfortable pattern, burnished by the unusually good weather, which continued. The boys went for a week to the school camp, Johnny leaving unwillingly, almost as though he expected his father to be gone when he came back. Alice went to stay for a week in Norfolk with Janet's eldest sister, who also had a daughter of the same age. At home, Sam pottered about the place, painting the house, clearing up the mess of old paint tins, tools, assorted bits of wood, and lengths of hose from long-defunct vacuum cleaners in the garage. He enjoyed sorting out the flotsam, and identifying it, and stacking it and tidying it up.

One morning, Sam had an unexpected letter from Danny Bennett. It was, he reflected, the first he had had ever had from him. '. . . Just thought I would drop you a line'. Danny had the most elegant copper-plate handwriting. Perhaps they had taught him that as an artificer. The Navy did do the most surprising things.

> 'I hope you are enjoying your leave. Harriet and I are enjoying the south. You know how she hates Scotland. I must say living is a lot easier down here. Get away from that bloody rain for a change!'

Sam looked through the kitchen window at the back garden. It had not in fact rained for weeks. The whole place was beginning to look dried up.

> 'I have some news. I am leaving the boat. Rather earlier than I expected, but just as welcome, because I am going to a job on FOSM's staff at Northwood. I have just heard. Imagine me, part of the Fosmery! But it will suit Harriet and me down to the ground. It's just what I hoped for . . .'

Danny Bennett, fallen jammy side up again.

> 'My relief is Michael Bacon, who knows as much about Bombers as I do, so there is no need for a turn-over patrol.
>
> 'I have not heard how you are getting on. But, Sam, I do hope everything does work out all right for you in the end. I feel a little guilty about it all. I am sure some of the others do, too. You helped us all a great deal and certainly interceded for us with the Captain. An advocate with the Father, as the prayer book, and you, would say. I feel we haven't supported you enough. Anyway, there it is. If there is anything I can do, you only have to let me know. Hope to see you again, sometime, in Blockhouse perhaps. Love to Janet. Yours aye, Danny.

'PS. That old banger of mine has finally packed up! It's gone to that great scrapyard in the sky. Or rather, to the one on the Winchester road. Remember that strange chap changing the wheel for us that day? Cheers. D.'

So Danny Bennett was leaving, and with a good job to go to. He deserved it. He had worked hard. He was a loyal soul. But Sam laid Danny's letter down on the kitchen table with a sense of profound melancholy and loss. Here was another friend gone. He might never see Danny again. It was a fact of life in the Navy. Unlike the Army, with their regimental life and their stable long-term friendships, the Navy offered a fragmented nomadic existence; one could serve with a man, know him well as a friend, and then never see him again.

'Come on, darling.' Janet had come bustling into the kithen. 'Do cheer up. After all, this is our big evening.'

'What do you mean?'

'Why, dinner with Captain S/M and Margot, of course! What did you think I meant?'

'Oh my *God*. I'd completely forgotten. Oh my *God*, so it is.'

The thought of the dinner with Captain S/M had lain like a great shadow across the whole leave. And now it was actually here, today, this very evening.

Sam had always thought it an odd convention in the Navy, this forced, duty hospitality, extended by seniors to juniors, as a necessary part of their jobs. Sam had heard of admirals whose dinner parties were a delight, whose guests were sad to leave, whose company was genuinely enjoyable, but he himself had never had the pleasure of being entertained by one. His own memories of senior officers' hospitality, from breakfast with the Captain as a cadet under training, to dinner with Captain S/M as a flotilla officer, were of awkwardness, of carefully guarded tongues, meticulously avoided subjects of conversation, jokes too heartily laughed at, and silences which seemed to last for as long as a Chinese water torture. They had all been occasions to be approached with the greatest circumspection and apprehension in advance, endured while they lasted, and escaped from as quickly as decently possible.

As usual, Janet seemed to take an age to get ready. Sam had been ready for some time, in his best dark grey 'drinking' lounge suit and his submariners' tie, while Janet was still sitting naked in front of her dressing-table mirror, painting her nails.

'Darling, don't *prowl* around the place like that. I won't be long.'

'Good God, I sometimes think we could get the whole squadron of boats to sea in the time it takes you to get ready to go out for the evening.'

'I won't be long.'

As usual, Janet was worth waiting for. She had had her hair done in town that morning and she was wearing her long earrings and her black dress, which Sam always thought was her most elegant, with her 'naval wife's uniform' brooch, a naval crown in seed pearls and diamond sparks, pinned to it. Sam had given it to her when they were engaged. She was carrying the fur stole Sam had given her when Simon was born.

'You do look delicious.'

'Thank you. It's a lovely evening, let's walk. It's only about ten minutes.'

Sam looked at his watch. It was a good idea, but they were already running slightly late, thanks to Janet.

'It means we can both have a drink.' Janet suddenly turned away, as though confronted by a terrible sight. 'I'll never forget that bobby with that dreadful thing to blow into. In our own drive. I shudder still when I think of it.'

'It makes you wonder, is that the reason why we have police forces, to do that sort of thing to people in their own homes? Actually, when I think about it, it would be much more awkward for us if you lost your licence, from the family and home point of view, than if I lost mine. I really only have to go into work. Okay, let's walk. We'll have to step out, though.'

They began to walk, hand in hand, up the hill towards the main road at the top of their own road. Captain S/M had his own house down in the south, Sam had heard. But while he was here, he and Mrs Captain S/M lived in a large house, much nearer the centre of the town than Sam and Janet's bungalow, which they rented from the Ministry of Defence. There were a number of such houses, all built before the First World War by prosperous Glasgow merchants for themselves, their families and their servants. Sam knew where the house was because he had once called there to sign the visitors' book on the table in the hall. It probably had some name, like Clyde View, or Lyndhurst, but the Squadron always called it 'The Manse'. It was, Sam guessed, a good quarter of an hour's walk away. They would have to step out briskly.

'It does seem funny without the children at home. I miss them, I don't think they've ever all been away together before. I do miss them.'

'Never mind, all back on Saturday, and it'll be bedlam again. At least it means we don't have to worry about babysitters or anything tonight.'

Janet carried her stole over her shoulder. She might need it for the coolness of the night when they walked back. But now, the evening air was still very warm. It really was astonishing summer weather for Scotland. There was not a breath of wind off the river. The leaves on all the trees were motionless. There were people out in almost every front garden. One man had the bonnet of his car open. Another was repairing the brickwork in his low front garden wall. Someone else was mowing his lawn. Several were sitting in deck-chairs, watching passers-by. One or two nodded, although Sam and Janet knew none of them. Two boys on bicycles with high handle-bars pedalled furiously by, shouting at each other. The shapes of cars flicked steadily across the junction at the top of the road.

'It's almost as if this town was specially laid out in the beginning. Not our bit, but the bit in the centre and the roads leading out from it.'

'Actually I think it was. By some distinguished Scottish architect, or philanthropist, or something.'

223

'Why do you think we've been invited tonight?'

'Well, I did go and sign their book, after all. And Margot is a pretty determined lady, by all accounts. She obviously takes it all very seriously and she's now working steadily through the Navy List up here. I'm told they're not over-generous with the booze, though.'

'Well I don't suppose they can afford it, if they do a lot of entertaining. Darling, don't walk so *fast*.'

Sam realised that he had unconsciously been quickening his pace.

'I've only got my high heels on, you know. They're not hiking boots. And I'm enjoying the walk.'

'So am I.'

But Sam knew, as soon as they arrived at The Manse, that they were late. He could see it in the face of the steward who took Janet's stole, and in Captain S/M's face when he came out to greet them. There was a fine line of unpunctuality which etiquette allowed guests like themselves. It was only a matter of five minutes or ten, but it was enough, and Sam knew that they had trespassed across it. He was glad and relieved that Janet did not appear to notice. At least, her evening had not been spoiled at the start. But his own mood changed abruptly to one of irritation.

S/M was affable enough, rubbing his hands together unctuously, like a landlord anticipating unusually good business. 'Just beginning to give you two up. Come in, come in and meet everybody.'

'Everybody' was much as Sam had expected. The Squadron Electrical Officer was there, with his wife, and there was a little bald Scotsman with his even smaller wife with some name like McTavish, which Sam did not quite catch; he was somebody very high up in a trade union, possibly the regional secretary for the west of Scotland. Sam had heard that recently senior technical officers in the base were spending some 80 per cent of their time dealing with labour relations, so clearly McTavish, if that was his name, was a political fence-mending invitation.

Also there was S/M's daughter Jane, a pretty girl with

shoulder-length blonde hair and large round red-rimmed spectacles. She had her current boyfriend with her, a red-haired lad with a faint Irish accent, called Kelly. He had a noticeably belligerent manner; when he had identified which of those present were in the Navy, he seemed to bristle towards them, as though daring them to justify their existences. Sam wondered how young Kelly got on with Margot and S/M himself.

Margot was unmistakably Jane, twenty-five years on, even to the blonde hair and spectacles. She greeted Sam like an experienced hostess, glancing over his shoulder while shaking hands, as though checking up on something going wrong behind him.

'Drink, sir?' The Captain's steward was at Sam's elbow.

'Yes, I'd like a glass of white wine, please.'

The steward's face clouded with uncertainty. 'I'm not sure we've got a . . .'

'Okay, G and T would be fine then. With ice and slice.'

'Sir?'

'Ice and lemon, please.'

'Oh yes.'

While waiting for his drink to arrive, Sam began to talk, *faute de mieux*, to Mrs Squadron Electrical Officer. He remembered meeting her before, at some function in the base at Christmas. She was wearing an evening dress of some kind, with pale sleeves, but she wore it without style, as though it were a pair of dungarees. With her noticeable West Country accent and her round nut-brown face, she was everyone's idea of a cheerful Cub mistress. Her chin came to a point, and every now and then she greeted a remark she thought was supposed to be funny with an elfin shriek.

'Your drink, sir.'

Perhaps as punishment for being late, Sam was allowed almost no time to drink his gin and tonic. He had hardly taken two sips when he saw Margot begin to make motioning signals towards the dining-room. People were setting their empty glasses down on the sideboard and on the small sidetables. Sam

225

was forced to finish his drink in two mighty swallows, so that the bubbles went up his nose and stung. He reached the dining-room coughing and almost in tears.

They were ten for dinner. S/M and Margot sat at the ends of the table, facing each other. S/M had Mrs McTavish on his right and Mrs Squadron Electrical Officer on his left. Margot had Mr McTavish on her right and Squadron L.O. on her left. Thus, clearly, the McTavishes were guests of honour. Sam sat midway down one side, with Mrs McTavish on his left and Jane on his right. Janet was on the other side, not quite opposite Sam, with Kelly on her right and Mr McTavish on her left.

The first course was cold consommé, very suitable for the weather, and it was delicious. Sam began to make conversation with Jane on his right. She was, she said, just starting her 'year off' between leaving school and going to university. She had just heard she had three quite good A-levels, so she and her parents were pleased. She hoped to do her Oxbridge exam and go to Oxford and read history in the autumn of next year. Meanwhile, she could do what she liked, or almost what she liked. She seemed to have a clear idea of what that would be. 'Kelly and I are just going to take off. We will probably go to Khathmandu. Overland.'

Sam looked at S/M at the head of the table, talking animatedly at Mrs McTavish, and wondered how he would react to the prospect of his only daughter going to Khath-mandu with Kelly. Overland.

Jane, like most senior naval officers' daughters, was used to dinner parties, to entertaining and being entertained. But Mrs McTavish, on his other side, Sam found almost impossible to talk to. It seemed she had no conversation of her own. She responded to all Sam's ventures, about the weather and where she lived and what was her family, by muttering something like 'Is *that* ye say?', at the same time ducking her head and, with a grimace, drawing her chin close to her neck. The repeated cacklings of 'Is *that* ye say, is *that* ye say?' and the ducking and grimacing and bobbing of her head reminded Sam irresistibly of some demented parrot or farmyard fowl. At the same time, she seemed in a highly nervous state, apparently terrified of committing some solecism, such as using the wrong utensil. She sipped constantly and rapidly at her wine, which a conscientious steward continued to replenish, until Sam eventually realised, with a sense of foreboding, that Mrs McTavish was becoming tipsy.

The second course was a whole salmon, cooked in a sauce of cream and wine. It too was delicious. Margot had an announcement to make about it.

'This salmon was caught by Admiral Smith, Jane's godfather, up in Helmsdale. He delivered it here on his way south this week. Scottish salmon!'

Everybody, except Mrs McTavish, made the appropriate sounds of approval and their appreciation of the privilege of having access to such a fish.

It was while he was eating and enjoying his portion of exquisite salmon that Sam became aware that S/M was talking about him and to him, by way of Mrs McTavish.

'It was Sam there, on your right, who put out that fire in the submarine the other day. Maybe you read about it?'

As he prepared to make some deprecatingly modest disclaimer, Sam was conscious that S/M's remark had come during a lull in general conversation and everybody else was listening.

Mrs McTavish had turned full face on towards Sam as though she had noticed he was there for the very first time.

'Och, I ken who ye are the noo . . . Ye're the wee *scab* as ma husband would say who wants to leave Polaris!'

Sam put his knife and fork down. He felt his face reddening. It was as though a red curtain of fury had descended upon him as his patience with this woman, with all of them, finally snapped.

'How dare you say that to me? How *dare* you? Who *do* you think you are to say such things? You know absolutely nothing about the circumstances . . .'

Anything more Sam might have said was drowned by the

227

shriek from Mrs McTavish. Her face seemed to have lost all shape and expression and become flesh, contorted to emit this one bloodcurdling scream. She stood up, putting one hand down on her plate so that it tipped towards her, throwing its remaining contents down the front of her dress. Then she turned and ran from the dining-room.

Everybody else sat frozen still in their places, as though in an actual enactment of everyone's worst nightmares of social gaffes. Then Margot wiped her lips, put her napkin down on the table and went out. She was followed by Mr McTavish, who added to the surrealist atmosphere with a remark made over his shoulder to Sam as he passed him.

'I'll speak to Mr *MacGregor* aboot this the morn's morn, dinna fash yerself.'

They all sat on at the table, listening to the sounds of Mrs McTavish moaning and sobbing in the hall outside.

How long they might have sat there, stunned, Sam did not know. Surprisingly, it was Jane who spoke first.

'I read that, too. I think it was one of the bravest things I've ever heard of, for someone in your position to speak out like that.'

'Hear *hear*.' Kelly was banging the table with approval. 'Nuclear weapons are obscene, anyway. If more people thought like you and were as brave as you, we might get somewhere at last and get rid of these things.'

Sam did not welcome their support. Looking at S/M's face at the end of the table, he knew that if anything more was needed to complete that evening's disaster, so far as he and Captain S/M were concerned, it was Kelly's approval and the defiant look Jane was giving her father. It seemed that he had inadvertently jabbed at a long-standing sore in Captain S/M's family.

Mrs McTavish did not return. Neither did Mr McTavish. But the rest recovered their composure very well, in the circumstances, and the evening continued, with a pudding, of Scottish raspberries and cream, coffee, and desultory chat in the living-room afterwards. Some semblance of normality had been re-established. But, at the very soonest moment it was seemly to do so, the guests took their leave.

Going home, Sam did not have to quicken the pace. Instead he had to walk hard to keep up with Janet. It was still a very warm evening. The street lights were shining through the leaves, throwing moving patterns of light and shade on the pavements. It should have been an enjoyable walk back, to round off the evening.

Janet said nothing until they were nearly at their house.

'Well. I've known some disastrous evenings but I think that must come near the top of the list. Or bottom, rather.'

'I'm sorry.'

'I think you are sorry. So you should be. Darling, I was absolutely horrified by the way you turned on that poor woman . . .'

'Poor *woman*! How *dare* she talk to me like that. A wee *scab*. How *dare* she. Bloody little Scottish *bitch*, she was a pain in the arse anyway, you didn't have to sit next to her as I did . . .'

'But couldn't you see she was a little drunk and didn't really know what she was saying? She was out of her depth there, couldn't you see that?'

'Well, I suppose I could . . .'

'Darling, I don't know where this Polaris business of yours is leading us, but I wish you'd stop it. It's taking us down a long dark tunnel and I don't like the look of it. I talked to Margot while we were powdering our noses. Tried to repair the situation a little. Darling, they're out to get you, you know. They're out to ruin you over this business, unless you give way . . .'

'I don't know why they're taking this so hard . . .'

'For God's *sake*, Sam, does it matter why? The fact is they're going to do it, that's all that matters.'

After such an evening, there was only one possible joy, one consolation. But when Janet felt his fingertips upon her, she firmly turned over and showed her back to him.

'Oh, is this the old Lysistrata caper then?'

'Oh, don't be ridiculous!'

But later in the night, when Sam awoke from another dream, his pyjamas and his body and the sheet under him wet with sweat, it was Janet who tried to console, to make amends. And it was Sam, in tears, who refused.

CHAPTER 11

'PLEASE, CAN WE TALK about it?'

Sam sat at the kitchen table, with a cup of coffee. He had a headache, as he normally did after one of his dreams. The events of the night before were a dim memory whose full horrors had yet to be realised.

'Please darling, we *must*. The children are coming home this weekend. We must talk now.'

'All right.'

'Darling, you look terrible, sitting there.'

'All right, I look terrible. Come on, you wanted to talk about something.'

'This Polaris business, you know very well. It's not too late to drop it. Margot was making signs of that loud and clear last night. And I think *he* was going to have a quiet word with you, too, later on. Only he never got a chance. I think if you did one more patrol, till the hue and cry had died down a bit . . .'

'I'd rather die than go back in that again. I would be betraying something I believe in very much . . .'

'Oh *why* does this business make you talk in such a pompous way? I've never heard you talk like this before . . .'

'Probably because I've never felt like this before.'

Sam was suddenly struck by the significance of what Janet had said earlier. Here was his wife, talking about him, discussing his naval future, even suggesting deals, with Captain S/M's wife.

'And what's this about you talking about me with Margot, while you were both powdering your noses?'

'Darling, I know from my father's time the Navy prefer things to be done politely and quietly. Why shouldn't I have a word with Margot if it'll help?'

'Things are different now from your father's day, I told you that.'

'I don't think things are different, not basically. It's *you* that's changed.'

'Yes, I think that's true. I can't describe it, really, I've tried, and I'm not going to try again.'

'Is it those . . . those women who have affected you in some way?' Janet spoke as though it was costing her something to force out the words.

'No. I just have this absolute repugnance against going on doing what I was doing before. It's almost as if I'm ashamed of myself now. I'm absolutely determined I'm not going on with it.'

'Yes, I think I can see that. One impression I did get from Margot last night was that they now think they mishandled the whole thing. They never realised you were so determined. Neither did I. But that doesn't mean *they* aren't determined, too.'

'Don't think I don't know it! I'd say my chances of promotion now are zilch, whatever happens. I should think last night blew it completely, as far as I'm concerned. If there ever was any chance left, it's gone now.'

'But darling, what are you going to do? Will you soldier on, as my father used to say, until you retire as a two-and-a-half at forty-five?'

'No, definitely not. I'd leave. Do something else.'

'But what about us? It's going to change our whole lives. Me, Simon, Johnny, Alice, all of us.'

'Nuclear weapons do have a trick of changing people's whole lives.'

'Oh don't be such a selfish *prig!* Think only of yourself all the time.'

232

Janet set her mouth in a such a way that Sam knew she was going to change the subject. 'Now don't forget you're taking me to Glasgow to catch the train this morning. I'm going to be away two nights, staying with Sarah. Alice and I will come back on the train on Saturday afternoon. I've written the time down on the pad there on the sideboard. So you can come and meet us. The boys'll be home that evening. So we shall all be together again. I must say it does seem a long time since they all went away.'

This, Sam knew, was where Janet was in her element. Talk about nuclear weapons and an uncertain future worried and frightened her. Family evolutions were her forte. Going down south, staying with her sister, picking up Alice and bringing her home, getting ready for the boys coming home, these were the familiar patterns of Janet's existence. She excelled at organising them.

'I can't think why you don't drive down there.'

'Now you know very well I hate driving long journeys. And you know Alice suffers from car-sickness on long trips. Besides, what would you do if I took the car? You'd be stuck here with no transport, wouldn't you? Then you'd be even more gloomy than you normally are when you're left on your own.'

'I'm not gloomy when I'm left on my own.'

'There's food in the fridge and in the deep freeze. There's cold meat and salad for lunch today, and I've written down some things you can cook. You can always go out and get yourself some fish and chips.'

Sam quite enjoyed cooking for himself, for a time, anyway. His cuisine was of the basic 'Choc Ice and Chips' variety, but the boys had always appreciated it and complimented Sam on his cooking in the past, when their mother was away and Sam was left in charge.

Janet did not refer to the 'Polaris business' again until she was on her train.

'Please don't wait, Sam. I hate these goodbyes. Now don't

get too gloomy. I don't like leaving you when you're all upset like this.'

'I'm not upset.'

'I know how gloomy you get if you're allowed to. Now behave yourself. There's food in the fridge and in the deep freeze.'

'I'll be perfectly all right.'

'I'll be back on Saturday.'

'I'll meet you.'

'Oh, I *do* hope you'll have all this sorted out by the time I get back.'

'Sure to.'

Driving back from the station, Sam reflected on Janet's passing remark about 'those women'. Had 'those women' affected him? That, now he thought about it, was an odd question. His visits to the peace camp had been infrequent and, in his view, innocent. Nevertheless, he had not told Janet of them all. He had not been strictly honest with her. He wondered how much she did know. It was possible that somehow, in some way, somebody, perhaps the malign influence of El Tel, might have got information back to Janet. Thinking over it now, Janet's question left an uncomfortable feeling behind it.

When Sam opened the front door, he was struck at once by the stuffy, airless gloominess of their tiny hall. He had never noticed it quite so sharply before. It was gloomy, with nobody there at home. He could not remember a time when he had come home without Janet being there to meet him. Now that he looked at it, theirs was basically a ghastly, gloomy, jerry-built little bungalow. He wondered how Janet had put up with it for so long. Today the sun was shining and it was hot. But what must this place be like in the winter, when it was cold, and the wind blew off the river, when it was dark for most of the day, and he was away at sea for weeks on end, and Janet had to sit by the fire by herself every evening? It hardly bore thinking about.

There was cold meat and salad in the fridge, as Janet had

234

said. She had gone to the trouble to get his favourite ham, with the yellow particles of crumbs round the edge. There was a half-bottle of white wine there, too. He poured some out. It was pleasant to see the mist forming on the outside of the glass. Unfortunately, the sight of it immediately reminded him of the wine, and the events, of the night before.

Sam opened the windows to let some of the stuffiness out. But that only let in the noise of the neighbourhood and dust and insects. Soon, there was a bumble-bee blundering about, bashing its head against a window pane. It was a very large insect and Sam could hear the thumps as it cannoned into the glass. Perversely, it was trying to escape through the window pane that would not open, ignoring the wide open window next to it. It seemed there was a Sod's Law, even for bumble-bees. He got up and tried to fan the bee sideways but it persisted in evading his efforts. Finally, more by accident than intent, it unexpectedly side-slipped into clear space and was gone.

Eating his lunch, Sam thought again about El Tel. There was no question the man had a kind of influence, which was not at all for good. Ever since that first day, with Danny's puncture, El Tel seemed to have had some effect on Sam's life. Ever since then it had been all down hill, as the sailors would say. It was as though he had infected Sam in some way, with an infectious idea, perhaps, which had grown like some great malignant tumour, afflicting his whole being and way of life. Meanwhile, El Tel himself had flourished like the proverbial green bay tree, appearing to be able to manipulate people and events just as he wanted. He seemed to have some weird power over people, making them do what he wished, whilst he himself remained invulnerable, inviolate, untouchable and untouched. Yet, he was basically only a garage hand.

Sam decided he must see El Tel and face him before he finally made up his own mind. If that meant he was being manipulated by him, so be it. It would be for the very last time.

There was no sign of El Tel, but Mary Carmichael was there, pegging up washing on her line. She looked the picture of health and domesticity.

'Och, I was just thinking about you.'

'Well, *that's* a compliment. You're looking very pretty.'

'Well, thank *you*.'

'Where's El Tel? He about?'

'No, he's in Glasgow, seeing to his Hiroshima Vigil. They're going to have a March of the Dead, from Glasgow to here, and a service of remembrance, and a barbecue, and a vigil outside the gates of the base there . . .'

'The social event of the year, in fact.'

'Aye, it could be that.'

She seemed more amused by it all, than concerned. It was annoying, nevertheless, and a somewhat deflating anticlimax, that El Tel was absent. He was one of those opponents who was never there when there was a chance of a confrontation. When you were ready and keyed up to take him on, he just slipped away.

'I'll just finish this and then I'll make you some coffee. Would you like that?'

'Yes please.' Sam looked around the camp. There seemed to be nobody else there, nobody except himself and Mary Carmichael. 'Where is everybody today?'

Mary Carmichael shrugged. 'I think they're all helping Terry with the march. Something like that.'

'Is Desmond here? Desmond the climber.'

'No, haven't seen him for days. I think he's gone.'

'Doesn't that worry you, people just disappearing?'

'Och no. People come and go here all the time. Like you do. We've got some Japanese coming soon.'

'What, for the Hiroshima thing?'

'Right.'

'But don't you . . .' He searched for the right way of putting it. Talking to her was like approaching a wild animal. One had to be careful, or she would take flight. 'Don't you ever want something more permanent?'

'I've got something permanent.'

There was no answer to that.

The main caravan was more spartanly furnished than Sam

remembered it. The good carpet he had once noticed was gone. The floor was bare except for some newspapers strewn here and there. The whole caravan looked as though the best things had been stripped out of it.

'It looks different.'

'It's Gillie. She came back after a bit, but now she's left and she's taken all her furniture with her this time. She was quite rich, you know. Went to Roedean or somewhere, I heard. I think she even had a title, I'm no' sure. Or a bit of a title, anyway.'

'Why did she leave?'

'She set her cap at Terry.'

'Good God!'

'That's what Terry thought. So she left.'

Sam remembered Gillie, the huge, ungainly, unsightly bulk of her. So she had hoped to ensnare El Tel with her charms. Mission impossible.

It was odd, Sam thought, how quickly he had fallen into an easy, comfortable relationship with Mary Carmichael. It was just as though they were old friends, gossiping together about other long-standing mutual friends. It seemed as though Mary Carmichael was the only really natural person he had met in a long time. Maybe she gave him something, reassurance perhaps, that he had not even known he needed so desperately.

Mary Carmichael set the coffee down on the table. Sam tasted it. It was very good, as usual.

'You always make super coffee. It's one thing I particularly remember about this place.'

'Is there anything else you remember?'

'What do you mean?'

'Well, me for instance.'

'Of course I remember you. I remember you the first time I ever came here, and El Tel mended that puncture. I remember thinking how pretty you were.'

'That's nice. I like to hear that.'

'I like to say it.'

She took a tin of biscuits down from a shelf. They were ginger nuts. Sam took one.

237

'I was going to ask you something . . . Are you with us now? Do you agree with what we stand for?'

Sam was taken aback by such a blunt change of direction. 'In a way, yes.'

'Why don't you join us? You'll be free then.'

'There's no such thing. Besides, didn't you yourself once tell me that you're no good to me here?'

'Ah, that was before I liked you.'

'I have a wife and a family. I couldn't just up and leave. Off with the raggle-taggle gypsies, oh. I forget how it goes. She left her lord, she left her hall, and was off with the raggle-taggle gypsies, oh.'

'So that's what you think of us? Raggle-taggle gypsies.'

'Not really. But in a funny sort of way it says what I mean. About somebody leaving all their responsibilities behind, to go chasing off after something that doesn't exist. I love the Navy. It's just the Polaris business that sickens me. I don't want to go on with that. The more I think of it, the more it sickens me. But the rest of it all, I love. I always have done. Ever since I was a small boy and went to Navy Days. I believe in it.'

Sam was surprised by Mary Carmichael's laughter. 'What's so funny?'

'It's Terry. *He* says he doesn't think you believe in anything. Except yourself. He says one day you're going to have to face yourself.'

'He should talk.'

But Sam found himself obscurely pleased and gratified that El Tel should have thought about him in such terms.

'You say you love the Navy but you don't like the Polaris. But doesn't it all go together? Don't they get after you about that, and call you a fraud, and ask you why did you suddenly change your mind, and you can't be serious, and all that?'

'Oh yes, they said all that, and much more.'

'And it didnae worry you?'

'Oh yes, it worried me all right.'

'But no' all *that* much.'

'No.'

She leaned back and stretched, so that he could see her nipples clearly through her shirt. It was, he suspected, a deliberate gesture.

'Like your figure.'

'What are you going to do about it?'

'Is that a challenge?'

'If you like. I think you deserve something nice to happen to you.'

'Do I?'

'You should have seen yourself when you got here today. All the troubles of the world on top of you. It's the way you've been treated, I guess.'

That was true enough, in fact it was the first true and sensible thing Sam had heard for a long time. It was the first time for ages that somebody actually seemed to be looking at *his* point of view.

'It's the middle of the afternoon.'

'So. It's the best time for it.' She looked directly at him. 'No, not here. In the other caravan.'

He followed her towards the yellow Gerard Manley Hopkins van. Although the space inside it had the strongest remembrances of El Tel and of his own past rebuffs from her, Sam felt no sense of present triumph, just as he felt no sense of betrayal towards Janet. All that seemed long ago, and inappropriate now. She opened the door, and was already pulling her shirt up over her head. He followed her naked back inside.

'Wasn't it Robbie Burns who said the softest beds were the bellies of the lassies. Your own poet.'

'You'll soon find that out for yourself, won't you? Now, don't be in too much of a hurry.'

The roundness and shapeliness of her body were what sailors dreamed of, even to the red marks on the flesh of her waist, where some elastic had pinched her. This was what men imagined, day-dreaming on their bunks, weeks and miles from home. Sam had always thought of her as a country girl, a rustic almost, and unsophisticated. But he found her surprisingly expert, being as subtle and supple as a courtesan. He was

239

astounded by her boldness. She knew how to give the most pleasure, and to take it. He realised that hers was a gift of friendship, an act of consolation, rather than love. But that could be more appropriate now. Love might follow.

There was no room for him to lie side by side with her on the bunk, though he wanted to. He stood up.

'You're puffing.'

'I'm shivering.' He looked down at her. 'What shall I say?'

'Don't say anything. If you're wondering about it, I meant to do this with you as soon as I saw you this afternoon.'

So, Sam now had to concede to himself, had he. If he were honest with himself, the thought of sleeping with Mary Carmichael had never been far from his mind. If the man himself were not here, then the next best revenge, surely would be to seduce his woman. It was an unworthy, a despicable motive, but she had at least been willing. The wench had been more than willing. And it had not just been revenge. That was too stark an explanation.

She stretched out on the bunk.

'I must say that looks very sexy.'

'It's meant to. But you've had your ration. A good ration, too.'

He bent down, and she put her arms round him as he kissed her.

'What are you going to do now?'

'I'm just going to lie here for a bit. Then I'll get up and get the tea. Maybe they'll all be back by then. Now, you go home. Away ye go to your wee wifie.'

'She's away.'

'Ah hah, now I understand a bit. No matter. Go carefully. As Terry is always saying, don't forget they're always out to get you.'

Sam had a sudden memory of one of Chief Bluntstone's cartoons, put up on the control room noticeboard towards the end of a patrol, two or three patrols ago, of the Chief himself sitting in a corner of the senior rates' mess, shivering and wild-eyed, with the caption 'Just because I'm paranoid doesn't mean they're not out to get me'.

'I'll remember.'

Sam came away from the camp, encouraged and optimistic. He had to admit, it had this mysterious effect upon him, ever since the first time he had gone there. The feeling persisted. He woke the next morning, free of headaches and the aftermath memories of dreams. It was cooler, with a wind off the river. There had been a shower of rain during the night. It seemed the weather was about to break at last.

On such a day, it was time to write his letter of application. He had put it off as long as he could. Although his determination to leave the Polaris programme was as great as ever, he had hesitated to make the final, irrevocable move.

There was no writing paper in the desk. They had run out and Janet had obviously forgotten to put it on her shopping list. The only pad there belonged to Alice. It was white paper, with a black Scottie terrier with a giant red ribbon tied round its neck embossed at the head of each sheet. Alice had been given it in her Christmas stocking. Sam could remember seeing it.

This would only be a rough draft. He would copy it out on to proper official stationery later. So, on this absurd notepaper, Sam wrote 'Sir, I have the honour to request permission to . . .'

Permission to what? Permission to change my life completely, sir. How does one put into words such a fundamental upheaval in one's working and family life? After several attempts, Sam had discovered for himself the dilemma he had watched others experiencing: that it was almost impossible to write an official letter, giving one's reasons in writing, without appearing either hilariously pompous or patently shifty.

Sam made himself some scrambled eggs for lunch, followed by ice-cream from the deep freeze. Afterwards, he made better progress with the letter, and had worked out a final rough draft which said what he wanted to say in a believable way, when the telephone rang.

He and Janet had a pact not to ring when they were apart on

241

these occasions, except when something was wrong, or for a change of plan. He had wanted to telephone her the previous evening, just to hear her voice, but had refrained. This trip away was supposed to be a small break for her, to get away from housework and cooking and shopping for a very short time. But maybe she had decided to catch a different train.

But it was not Janet. Sam could not understand the caller's name, but he did catch the word 'Security'.

'Could you come down to the base now, please, sir? We want your opinion about a Tape.'

A Tape? 'You do realise I'm on leave now? The Starboard Crew have got the weight now. I'm Port Crew.'

'Yes, sir. But I understand Commander S/M says you're the best person to comment on this for us.'

Mouser? What on earth did he have to do with it?

'All right, I suppose I could. When do you want me to come?'

'Now, sir. Right now, sir.'

'All right.'

The MoD PloD on the gate were almost welcoming, and there was plenty of space in the car-park. Of course, it was getting latish on a Friday afternoon and people were starting to go on weekend. It was a case of POETS: Piss Off Early Tomorrow's Saturday.

Sam had assumed he would have to go to the submarine offices, but at the entrance he met Mouser, who clearly knew the purpose of Sam's visit.

'Oh no, not here, Sam. Up at the sickbay.'

'The *sickbay?* What . . . What's going on?' There was something in Mouser's expression which, for the first time, caused Sam alarm. Mouser plainly knew something.

'D'you know what this is all about?'

'Yes, but . . . Anyway, I should get up to the sickbay, and they'll tell you all about it.'

It was not actually the main sickbay, but a small office next door to it. In fact, it was more of a storeroom than an office. Sam had never been in it before, had never even known of its

242

existence. There were cabinets along the walls, with cardboard boxes full of medical stores piled up on top of them. There was no window but there was a table, with two chairs, facing each other, one at each end. It seemed an odd place for any sort of interview.

A man got up from the chair at the far end. He had a ginger moustache and wore a sports coat, with a buff-coloured waistcoat which somehow matched his moustache. He smelled strongly of tobacco.

'Ah, hullo. Glad you could come. Good of you.'

Sam shook hands with him. The man sat down again. He had not said who he was, or where he came from. There was a tape-recorder on the table. Sam looked at it. What did they want him to hear, Soviet submarine sound signatures? Bird song at eventide? Surely not pop music?

'Ready?'

The man switched on the tape-recorder.

'*Like your figure.*'

'*What are you going to do about it?*'

'*Is that a challenge?*'

'*If you like. I think you deserve something nice to happen to you.*'

The voices were flawlessly reproduced, without any background hiss or distortion, almost in stereophonic sound, almost as though he and Mary Carmichael were both standing in the room. Sam listened, transfixed with shock, as though bound to the spot where he stood. The silences were more suggestive than the speech. But meanwhile, the man with the moustache kept up his own running commentary. 'Cheeky little *bint*! . . .' 'Well, she would say that, wouldn't she?' At Sam's reference to Robert Burns, the man nodded approvingly. 'Very good, very good. Very erudite.'

' . . . *Don't say anything. If you're wondering about it, I meant to do this with you as soon as I saw you this afternoon.*'

The man with the moustache blew out his breath disgustedly. 'There's a brazen little bitch for you. I always say it's the women lead the men on, you know.'

243

Sam tried to speak, but for a moment found that he had difficulty forming words.

'Who are you?'

'I don't think it'd help if I did tell you. Putting it briefly, I represent a department which specialises in surveillance.'

'And you've been carrying out surveillance on me?'

'My, don't kid yourself!' The man with the moustache looked amazed by such a suggestion. 'What gives you the idea you're that important! You just happened to be there when they were testing out the gear. If you'd done it at a Christian hour of the night, nobody would ever have known. But if you insist on doing it in the middle of the day, well, I *ask* you! Our lads don't like working overtime, you know.'

'I beg your pardon?' Sam had the nightmare feeling that what this man was saying was of desperate importance to himself, but he still could not make any sense of it. 'What exactly are you talking about? Overtime?'

'They don't like setting up new gear after normal working hours, you know.'

'You mean this surveillance gear?'

'S'right.'

'Where was it?'

'Can't tell you that.'

'Well, it must have been quite close.'

'Not necessarily. Using lasers, we could hear you two fornicating at half a mile. Just across the main road would have been quite enough. Give you a tip . . .' The man with the moustache leaned forward confidentially. He had a kind of ghastly bonhomie. 'You know that stuff they use in sieges, to hear what the hostage-takers are saying, and all that?'

'Yes?'

'Same thing. Same gear. Basically.'

'But why?'

The man with the moustache shrugged. 'Somebody rumbled our man inside the camp. Or he gave himself away. Doesn't matter which. Funny, the campers didn't mind him. They

244

thought it was hilarious, having a stoolie. But *we* minded. So we had to do something else. And we came up with you. Must say, you were much better than 'Listen with Mother'. Should be a classic. Ours would be a dull life, if it weren't for the occasional comedian like you, you know.'

It was ironic, Sam thought, that he himself had betrayed Desmond the Climber, hoping to discomfit El Tel. He had hoped to gain a malicious pleasure from the sight. *There* was a petard that had truly hoisted its designer.

'This is blackmail. That tape is blackmail.'

'Oh I think that's far too strong a word.'

'Well, what word would you use?'

'*I* don't have to use any word. Just as I wouldn't use the tape, if it were left to me. You attach too much importance to yourself and your little troubles, if I may say so. We're not threatening you . . .'

'Not *much* . . .'

'. . . But we're not playing games here, either.'

There, Sam thought, he caught yet another echo of El Tel. Had he not once said something similar, that he and his fellow protesters were not playing games. It was only Sam, it seemed, who was somehow left, haplessly playing games, in the middle.

'Do you want to hear it again?'

'No thank you.'

'Don't blame you.'

'What are you going to do with it now?'

'Nothing. I was just told to play it to you, and I've done it. I know nothing about you. But I rather gathered that listening to that tape might have some bearing on what you're going to do next. There's somebody waiting to see you next door. Good luck. Keep smiling.'

It was Mouser, sitting on one of the desks in the sickbay, waiting, with his hands clasping the edge of the desk on either side of him. Sam realised that they had chosen the one man to hear his recantation, his confession almost, whom they knew would hurt him the most. The sickbay seemed an odd choice of venue, too. But, on reflection, if you were going to cut out a man's heart, what better place than the surgical surroundings of the sickbay?

'Well?'

'Well.' Sam gestured helplessly. 'Nothing much to say now, is there?'

'You'll stay.' It was not a question, but a statement.

'I have to now, don't I? It's funny, I've spent most of today composing my letter, my reasons in writing. And now it's all over. Got to tear it up.'

Mouser shook his head. 'You know, you're taking this much too much to heart, Sam. Your letter, whether you write it or not, and your case generally, are only small things. Insignificant. But the Powers That Be have to take notice of them. Take care of them, if they possibly can. You'll have to do one more patrol.'

'Must I?'

'Oh yes. Till all the brouhaha dies down a bit. Who knows, you might even change your mind. To know us is to love us. A *minimum* of one more patrol.'

'*More* than one patrol?' They wanted to make the recantation complete, the surrender abject.

'Maybe.'

In his mind's eye, Sam saw the endless days stretching out, like the columns of the rocket tubes in the missile compartment.

'All right.'

'Sure?'

'Yes. Quite sure. Yes.'

'Good. Well you can get back to your leave again, then.'

'Yes, of course I can.'

Sam drove back and put the car in the garage. The kitchen was airless. There was going to be a thunderstorm, but it was still some way out to sea. The whole bungalow was stuffier and gloomier than ever. He took off his jacket and tie, and changed into his slippers. He might as well be comfortable while he was about it. Janet's pad was still on the table with her suggestions for meals. He would not need those again. He tore off the top

246

page and began to write. Although he filled two pages, they were only small ones. It did not seem much to say, after so many years of married life.

He went out to the garage again, and turned over the junk in the nearest box until he found the hose from Janet's old vacuum cleaner. It was actually longer than he remembered it and should do. As he was measuring the length of hose up to the car exhaust pipe, he sensed rather than heard someone behind him.

'Moles, is it?'

It was their next door neighbour, who worked shifts in the hospital. Sam had always, on no evidence at all, thought of their neighbour as being half-cracked. But now, it seemed, he might have been right after all.

'I beg your pardon? Moles?'

'You got trouble with moles then?'

'No?'

'Oh.' The man sounded disappointed. 'I thought that was what you were doing. That's the best way.'

'The best way of doing what?'

'Getting rid of them. You put a hose on your car exhaust, stuff the other end down the mole-hole and run the engine. The gases finish them off.'

'Oh, do they? No, we don't have any trouble with moles.'

'Oh, well, I just thought I'd call. I knew your wife was away and you're normally out during the day and I heard somebody here . . .'

'That's very good of you. That's very good of you indeed.'

'Och, that's all right.'

Sam watched his neighbour shuffle round and into his own garden, and went back to his work. The hose was long enough to reach the back window. It had a sort of metal snout on it, like a duck-billed platypus' bill, which he jammed in place by winding the window up tightly on it. He secured the other end over the exhaust pipe with wire. It was not a tight fit, but he was confident it would not come adrift and so it would do.

He shut both garage doors tightly, got into the driver's seat, and started the engine. He lay back, staring at the garage wall. It was a good job he had mended that broken pane in the door. The vibration of the engine was so slight, he reached back to check that something was actually coming in through the pipe. He felt its heat on his fingers. The engine was certainly running.

They said that one's whole life flashed before one at times like this. In fact he could only remember the last few weeks. You're no great shakes as a submariner, Sam. I feel we should have backed you up a bit more than we did, Sam. Don't take it to *heart* so much, Sam. You chickened out, Sam. But was I disloyal? What should I have done? What else could I have done? Why not treat it as a professional challenge, which is what it is? After all, they're only *kit*. You took the Queen's Shilling. All you have to do is be yourself. Don't forget they're out to get you. Just because I'm paranoid doesn't mean they're not out to get me. Is it dangerous, Daddy. Polaris Sub Hero Quits. There's a lot of funny things go on, squire, which you as a loyal citizen and a servant of the Crown, although yer having yer problems just now, you just wouldn't believe. It's the way you've been treated. They would have to find another school for Johnny. Somewhere he had read once about being half in love with easeful death and ceasing upon the midnight with no pain. Very good very good, that man in the moustache would say, very erudite. Carbon monoxide and carbon dioxide were supposed to be odourless and tasteless. This would be a tasteless death, in the very worst of taste, in fact. He could sense something knocking but whether it was inside himself or in the garage he could not say. It was like seeing that fire down the boat again, a hint of bright light in the blackness. This must be very like one of Able Seaman Draper's dark dreams, only Draper had never been able to describe them as clearly as this.